HULK™

BY PETER DAVID
BASED ON THE MOTION PICTURE SCREENPLAY
WRITTEN BY JAMES SCHAMUS

BALLANTINE BOOKS • NEW YORK

Hulk is a work of fiction. Names, places, and incidents either are products of the author's imagination or are used fictitiously.

A Del Rey® Book
Published by The Random House Ballantine Publishing Group

© 2003 Universal Studios Publishing Rights, a division of Universal Studios Licensing LLLP. The movie "THE HULK" © 2003 Universal Studios. "THE INCREDIBLE HULK" and all related comic book characters: TM & © 2003 Marvel Characters, Inc. All Rights Reserved.

www.delreydigital.com

ISBN 0-345-45967-9

Manufactured in the United States of America

First Edition: May 2003

OPM 10 9 8 7 6 5 4 3 2 1

*"Oh soul, be changed to little water drops
and fall into the ocean, never be found."*
—Marlowe, *Doctor Faustus*

PART ONE: ID

suspicion

David Banner had just made his son, Bruce, angry, and discovered that he rather liked it.

David had an attitude of quiet-yet-desperate genius about him, with eyes that glittered with intelligence and a foxlike face that suggested not only cunning but also an insatiable desire to learn the truth about things. His hair was thick and brown and he wore it combed back. He was dressed in the suit he'd worn to work that day. It wasn't unusual, however, for him to spend time with baby Bruce from the moment he came home until his wife, Edith, told him that dinner was served.

David sat on the floor, keeping a wary eye on the kitchen. He heard Edith within, banging around pots and pans and doing whatever the hell it was she did that made most of their dinners taste so vile. But his focus at that moment wasn't on how her beef Stroganoff was going to turn out, but instead on the activities of his infant son.

There was Bruce, six months old, crawling along nicely. He had been developing swiftly in terms of his assorted motor skills, even though the boy himself had been small at birth and probably wasn't going to grow up to be any sort of Goliath. He was also, however, overly dependent on the pacifier, sucking on it with vacuumlike force whenever he had the opportunity. David was glad about that, because he could make use of it.

He watched warily as little Bruce crawled across the shag carpeting of the modest living room. The room had been baby-proofed, with rubber bumpers put on the sharp edges of the coffee table and little inserts slid into the electrical outlets so that tiny fingers couldn't work objects into them and sustain a shock. At that moment, Bruce was crawling toward the overstuffed recliner, the one with a large piece of electrical tape on one arm to prevent some errant stuffing from poking any farther out. Making little ah-ah noises like a tiny train engine, Bruce crawled all the way over to the chair. He was wearing a sleeveless red-and-white-striped outfit with leggings so he didn't get rug burns on his knees. She was thorough, Edith was. It was something that David would have loved about her very much, presuming he had, in fact, loved her, rather than hating her now with a burning passion because she had forced him to provide her with this . . . this crawling, mewling monstrosity for her amusement. . . .

Still . . .

Still, Bruce provided opportunities. Unwanted opportunities, to be sure, but opportunities presented themselves when they saw fit, and as a man of science, David Banner had to accept them and roll with them.

David Banner watched raptly as Bruce hauled himself up to stand, balancing as carefully as he could on his skinny little legs. The sucking on his pacifier continued so loudly that Banner was certain they could hear it all the way down at the military base where he worked. It was a nice theory, actually, how far the sound of Bruce's sucking would travel, although he wasn't going to have the opportunity to test it.

There were, however, other theories to test.

Looking once more to make sure his wife was otherwise engaged, David Banner moved quickly over to baby Bruce and yanked the pacifier out of his mouth. The shock of the pacifier's departure totally bewildered Bruce, so much so that he lost his balance and tumbled backward, landing hard on his back and striking his head on the floor for good measure. The carpet cushioned some of the impact, but it was painful and startling nonetheless.

Bruce Banner's face twisted in infant fury and reddened. He was getting ready to uncork a major bawl, and his father kept glancing at the kitchen, muttering to his son, "C'mon, c'mon," wanting to have as much time as possible to observe the child's reaction.

And then it came, the veins bugging out at his temples, his eyes closing. An ear-splitting howl blasted out of the child's throat like a cyclone through a wind tunnel. The first cry was relatively soft, but he had two good lungsful of air for the second, and that was when he really kicked it into high gear.

Banner watched him raptly, looking for some small sign.

"What happened?" came Edith's voice from the kitchen.

"Nothing! He fell! It's nothing!" David called back, having no desire at all for his wife to come in, because he didn't want her to see what he was seeing. Little Bruce's arms were beginning to distend at the elbows, to grow and expand and twist into positions that could only be described as deformed. And it wasn't just his arms that were deforming. It was his entire body. David could see it under the little outfit, see the bumps and ripples bubbling on Bruce's skin. And his face, *God, look at his face*. With the upper brow starting to slide forward, Bruce looked like a Neanderthal. David felt as if he were watching millions of years of evolution being rolled back.

That was when he heard an alarmed shriek from Edith. He hadn't heard her enter because he'd been so enraptured with what was occurring with Bruce. Quickly he shoved the pacifier into Bruce's mouth even as he turned toward Edith and tried to reassure her.

"I said he's fine!"

"Fine!" Edith Banner practically howled. She was a pretty enough woman, with curly brown hair and, normally, a quiet authority about her. Not at this moment, though. At this moment there was nothing at all quiet about her. "His arm's broken! His head's swelling! He has lumps the size of golf balls!"

"Edith, darling, you're exaggerating. Kids fall down . . ."

"David, did you look at him?"

He cast a quick, nervous glance at his son, who was still lying on his back, and then he visibly relaxed and grinned. "Why, yes, I have. Have you?"

She pushed past David, and stopped and stared. There, lying on the floor, was Bruce, contentedly sucking on the pacifier, which his father believed gave the baby's life all its meaning. His arms were normal, his head was fine. There were no signs of lumps on him, golf ball–sized or otherwise.

Edith was completely perplexed. "But I . . . I could have sworn . . ."

David spread wide his hands and shrugged. "What can I tell you, except that, you know, I told you."

She knelt down, inspected Bruce's arms. David

watched her passively, as did their son. Then she shook her head and said firmly, "I'm taking him to Dr. Ungaro."

"He doesn't need to go to his pediatrician!" David told her in annoyance.

"I think he does. I know what I saw, David. I've got to make sure he's okay. What kind of mother would I be otherwise?"

David Banner repressed a snarl, and instead substituted a very forced grin. "I suppose you're right, dear," he said with strained courtesy, but the thought of the boy's doctor being brought in at this developmentally vital point in Bruce's life was upsetting.

As it turned out, he needn't have worried. It was all Banner could do to suppress a chuckle as the pediatrician studied the boy from top to bottom, turned to his parents with the air of the accomplished pedant, and announced, "It's hard to say. Somehow, when he feels too much frustration, his cell tissues . . . well, there's some kind of hardening. I don't think it's much to worry about. A kind of tendinitis, I think."

All the way on the drive back home, his mother held Bruce tightly and made clucking noises about tendinitis and what it meant for the child's long-term health. She was skeptical of the diagnosis, but didn't know what else to think. As for David Banner, he kept speaking to her reassuringly about how he'd read a paper once about "infant tendinitis" as a syndrome that usually passed after the first year. All the time he did so, he kept trying not to laugh at both the doctor's idiocy and his wife's gullibility.

That night, after Edith had gone to bed and drifted into an uneasy, worried sleep, David Banner went down to his private study. It wasn't very large, but that didn't bother him. David didn't concern himself with such useless trappings as possessions or the size of one's home. All he cared about was the research. And he wanted to update his journals and log entries while the results of his experiment on Bruce were still fresh in his mind.

He pulled his journals out from a locked drawer and began flipping through them, looking for the appropriate one in which to make an entry. As he did so, he stumbled across notations that he had made several years ago, back when . . . *it* . . . had all started. He paused and started reading the entries, reliving the sense of frustration he'd felt when his theories and plans were given short shrift.

When he'd first arrived at Desert Base in Nevada, he'd had high hopes for himself, for his research, for everything. He'd been ambitious, *so* ambitious, convinced that soldiers would sing his praises for the advances he was going to bring to them and to the world.

And then he'd hit a brick wall: a high and mighty colonel named Thaddeus Ross, who'd acquired the nickname "Thunderbolt" for his tendency to launch his anger, straight and true, at whoever had offended him and effectively incinerate the poor fool on the spot. Word was that he was in the fast lane to make general. And Banner couldn't help but think, then and now, that if the future included General Thunderbolt Ross, then the military establishment was pretty much going to be spiraling straight down the tubes.

He found one notation written in a quavering script. He remembered making the entry; he'd been so furious that his hand had been shaking. He was still able to make it out, though:

Meeting went as poorly as it possibly could have. Tried to convince Ross there is simply no way practically to shield against every weaponized agent. Instead I can make superimmune systems by strengthening the human cellular response. Ross didn't get it. Didn't even try. Said that manipulating the immune system is <u>dangerous and stupid.</u> Said that both he and the president's science adviser have made it clear I can't use human subjects. How am I supposed to proceed? How can I prove to them that I'm right, prove the effectiveness of my work, if they won't give me the tools to do it?

He stared at the entry for a long time. He tried to cast his memory back to what his state of mind had been when he'd written it. Had he known, even then, what he was going to do? Or had he been trying to build up the nerve to face the inevitable?

The phone rang, the noise cutting through the still air so loudly that it caused him to jump. He grabbed up the phone and said, "Banner."

"Banner," came the sharp, challenging voice of Ross. "Sorry to call you at home. Is this a bad time?"

Any time I talk to you is a bad time. He felt a distant pounding behind his eyes, and rubbed them.

"No, Colonel, not at all. What can I do for you?"

"I've got a report here regarding your data from the animal studies. There appear to be discrepancies in your results."

The pounding increased. It looked to be the start of a long, long night.

love

It was difficult to differentiate Christmas from any other time of the year out in the desert, but the Banners did their level best, as did everyone else in the neighborhood. That wasn't particularly surprising since there was a great deal of common ground for all the residents. Everyone either worked at Desert Base or else was a family member of someone who worked there. The town didn't even have a specific name as such. It had just sprung up in proximity to the base out of necessity.

The small, artificial Christmas tree, the same one the Banners pulled out every year, glittered in the corner. Bruce, now three years old, was gallivanting around the room astride a hobbyhorse while Edith took films of his pure childish joy with a Super 8 camera.

David, for his part, was feeling more relaxed than he had in a long time. It had been ages since Ross had expressed any suspicions about, or even overt interest in, his work. His newly relaxed attitude had spread to how he treated his wife and son, and they had been grateful for the change. He watched Bruce jump around a bit more, and then reached into his briefcase and extracted two small, floppy cloth dolls. It was hard to tell what the bizarre-looking animals were supposed to be, specifically. They had long ears and whiskers, but the feet were closer to cat paws than they were to rabbit feet. They were somewhat mutated-looking, really, which was probably what drew Banner to them when he'd spotted them in the Base Exchange, looking rather shabby and forgotten on an upper shelf and marked down to fifty cents each.

"Bruce," he called, and the boy turned and looked. His face immediately lit up with an ear-to-ear smile, and he dropped the hobbyhorse as if it had leprosy and bolted toward the two dolls. He jumped up and down, David holding them just out of the boy's reach in amusement. He finally relented and gave them to him when Edith good-naturedly chided him about "tormenting the boy."

And then he and his son played with the stuffed toys.

Just . . . played.

He didn't conduct any experiments on him. He didn't seek out any mutagenic properties. He didn't try to find ways to excuse himself so he could make notations in his journals. He. Just. Played.

For one evening, David Banner had a taste of the nice, ordinary life he could have had and which, he knew on a fundamental level, would never be his. And because of that, as the boy laughed with that pure, unbridled, unrestrained laughter that only children can command, David Banner discovered there were tears running down his cheeks. Tears in mourning for that which he would never have, and that which he could never be.

"It's my fault . . . it's all my fault," he whispered.

It was a horrifying discovery for David Banner to make, that he loved his son. That was a development that simply didn't fit into the overall plan. And he resolved that that night, that very night, he had to reestablish the status quo.

Edith had been invited over to a friend's house to make a fuss over their new baby. In point of fact, both Edith and David had been invited, but he had begged off, citing a sudden headache, and insisted that Edith go on without him. As soon as she was gone, with Bruce settled down for the night, David went into his study and pulled out a syringe and a test tube.

"Need blood samples," he muttered. "It's the only thing that will do. Have to study the mutagenic properties. Absolutely the only thing that will do."

He padded upstairs and opened the door to Bruce's bedroom. There was the boy, in his pajamas, smiling and bouncing the two floppy dolls around without a care in the world.

David smiled and said, "Bruce, I need you to do something. Give me your arm."

The boy obediently extended his right arm. He had no reason to doubt, no reason to have any suspicions. He blinked in surprise when his father gripped his wrist firmly . . . and gasped when a hypodermic was driven into his arm, whereupon he let out a shriek like the damned consigned to the abyss.

"David! What the hell are you doing?"

He yanked the syringe clear, spattering drops of blood, and Bruce was howling in hurt and fury as Edith stood in the doorway. Perhaps she'd forgotten something, perhaps she'd gotten bored quickly, perhaps she'd been seized with some massive fatigue. It was impossible to say, and in the final analysis, it didn't matter. Like a thief in the night he froze there, and between Edith's yelling and the boy's howling, he had no idea where to look first.

And then Edith went dead white and pointed, her finger trembling. David turned to see what she was looking at.

It had been several years since the famed "tendinitis" incident, and Edith had more or less managed to file away the distant and unwanted memory; perhaps, she had even chalked it up to an hallucination. But what she was seeing now was far, far worse than the previous episode.

As Bruce shrieked in protest, his feet began to swell, his arms distorted, and the entire right side of his head bulged out. Then they receded but other things bubbled and rippled, his skin undulating as if a swarm of bugs were making their way beneath the surface and spreading throughout his body. Bruce seemed oblivious to it, so caught up was he in the hysterics of his tantrum.

Edith Banner let out one loud, horrified yell, and fainted dead away.

The heavy thud of her body hitting the ground caught young Bruce completely by surprise, enough to cause him to stop crying. The bubbling of his body promptly stopped and his crying was replaced by wide-eyed whimpering as he saw his mother lying insensate upon the floor.

David looked from his son to his wife and back again, and saw a perfect opportunity. He pointed a quavering finger at his son and snarled, "You did this, Bruce! You *hurt your mommy*!"

"N-no," Bruce stammered out, his lower lip trembling, his eyes like saucers and his skin the color of curdled milk.

"Yes!" shot back David, advancing on the child, stepping over the prostrate body of the boy's mother. "Because you yelled! Because you cried! Because you weren't a big boy!

"See? See what happens when you get upset? Bad things happen! *Very bad things happen when you get upset! Bad things happen to your mommy, and to you! And if you let yourself get upset, even more bad things will happen! Do you understand? Even more bad things!*"

"I'm sorry . . . I'm sorry!" And Bruce's chest started to convulse as his breathing speeded up. He looked on the verge of apoplexy.

David stabbed his finger in the boy's face. "*You're doing it again!* You're getting upset! You're going to start crying or yelling or shouting! Don't do it, or more bad things will happen! Maybe your mommy will even die, and it will be all your fault! *Do you want that? DO YOU?*" And when the boy frantically shook his head, his father continued, "When you start getting angry, you just smash the anger! Do you hear? Smash the anger! *Don't let it take you!* Smash it! Understand? Are you going to let the anger get you? Are you?"

Bruce shook his head even faster, so violently that it looked as if it was going to topple off his neck. He wiped the tears from his face with the backs of his hands.

Very softly, David knelt down and held the boy's face between his rough hands. "Good. Very . . . very good boy. Now lie down, go to sleep."

"But Mommy . . ."

"I'll take care of Mommy. I'll make sure she's okay." He lifted Edith to a sitting position and, a moment later, shifted her weight so he was cradling her in his arms. "Daddy will take care of everything. You go to bed . . . and remember what we discussed."

Without another word, young Bruce scrambled into bed. David had already secreted the tube of blood in his pocket, and he clicked off the light. It left Bruce in darkness, except for his night-light on the opposite wall, which was a small, green bulb. David exited the room, carrying Edith, while Bruce stared raptly at the green glow and burned his father's words into the deepest recesses of his memory.

When Edith came to, she was lying on her bed, and David was staring down at her.

"What happened?" she whispered. "What in the world happened? Did you . . . did you see Bruce? And . . . you were taking blood from him . . ."

She tried to sit up, but his strong hand kept her in place. "David." She endeavored to shove away his arm. "*David!* Tell me now! Tell me, or I'll take him away. I swear I'll—"

"If you do, you doom him."

She stared at him uncomprehendingly. "What—?"

He licked his suddenly dry lips, and said, "I'm the only chance he has of being normal. But I have to continue my research. And you"—he pointed at her fiercely—"you have to shut up. You have to keep it to yourself, or they'll take him away from us, lock him in a room, and dissect him. Me, too, for that matter. If you say you love him . . ."

"Of course I love him," Edith said desperately. "He's my son!"

"He's more mine than yours. That much is certain." He drew in a deep breath and let it out, rising from the edge of the bed and wiping away a coat of sweat from his forehead. "Edith, I had . . . have . . . theories. Things I wanted to work on involving mutations . . . mutagens. Tinkering on a genetic level that would allow the body to heal itself . . ."

"I don't understand," she said. "What does that have to do with anything . . . ?"

He turned to face her and, his words laden with the heaviness that can only come from a great unburdening, he told her, "They wouldn't let me use human subjects."

She stared for a long moment, her growing disbelief obvious. "You . . ." She couldn't speak above a whisper. "You . . . experimented on Bruce?"

He rolled his eyes. "No, of course not."

"Then . . . what . . . ?" And then she got it, her hand fluttering to her mouth. "On yourself. Oh, my God, David. You . . . you did something to yourself."

"Yes."

"Before we conceived Bruce. Conducted experiments on yourself."

"Yes."

"Oh, my God," and she looked in the general direction of Bruce's bedroom. "He . . . you passed it on to him."

"Yes," he said once more.

Edith turned to him, grabbing at his arms. "Get it out of him! Whatever's been done to him, cure him! You've got to!"

"And I intend to," David lied to her.

"Is it possible?"

"Yes," he lied once more. And now it was his turn to take her by the arms and draw her close. "But it stays between us. Otherwise . . ."

"They'll take him away. I know. And you're right. And I'll trust you, David, to do right by Bruce, because I know you love him. It explains so much . . . so much . . ." And then she looked up at him, her eyes flashing fire. "If you fail him, David—or if you hurt him in any way—I swear to God, I'll kill you."

"I understand," he said, and he truly did. The problem was she didn't. But she would.

Eventually she would, if it was the last thing she did.

instinct

David Banner was just checking the readings on the latest cyclotron experiment when he saw General Thunderbolt Ross barreling toward him. Banner took a deep breath to calm himself and forced a smile, even though his immediate instinct was to head the other way.

Instead, he said, with a joviality he didn't feel, "Why, hello, General. The new rank sits well on you, I have to say."

"In my office, Banner," Ross said without preamble.

Banner rose from his workstation, and pointed at the cyclotron. "This might not be a good time, General. We're right in the middle of accelerating the atomic nuclei of gamma part—"

"Do I appear to care, Banner?" He took a step closer, his mustache bristling. He was a barrel-chested man with graying hair cut to regulation army shortness, and the brusque manner of one who has nothing but distaste for civilians, since they didn't take well to orders. "It will keep. Now get over to my office, on the double."

"Very well," said Banner coolly after a moment's consideration. "Lead the way."

"Get out of the way."

Bruce Banner was playing in the street with his friend

Davy when suddenly a bigger boy, whom Bruce had seen around from time to time, blocked their path. His name was Jack, as Bruce recalled, and although to an adult he would have looked like a child, to a child he looked like a giant.

Bruce knew that he was no danger to the boy. Jack was far wider than Bruce, and taller, and Bruce was a skinny and unthreatening four-year-old even under the best of circumstances. He did precisely as he was ordered.

The bigger boy smiled lopsidedly, and said, "Thanks, runt," and suddenly Bruce knew that something bad was going to happen, because he always had a sense of these things. Sure enough, Jack had a large stick in his hand, a twisted branch he'd snapped off a tree somewhere. He swung it and struck Bruce on the side of the face, leaving a line of blood where it had hit.

Davy let out a yelp of anger on his friend's behalf, but Jack ignored him, shoving him aside, and aimed the stick again at Bruce. He swung for the same spot, and hit Bruce again. Bruce staggered from the impact, but didn't fall.

Nor did he cry. His face remained utterly impassive, even though one side of it was running with blood.

"C'mon! Aren't you gonna try to hit back?" Jack challenged.

Bruce made no move.

Jack threw the stick down and poised there, fists cocked, and bellowed, "See? Got no stick! C'mon! *C'mon!*"

Bruce began to tremble, and at first Davy thought he was trying to avoid sobbing, but that wasn't the case. Instead he was shaking with suppressed anger. No cry escaped his lips. He just stared and stared, and finally Jack lowered his fists in disgust. "Baby! Chicken baby!" he snarled and turned away.

And still Bruce just stood there . . . and said nothing.

David Banner stood in front of Ross, trembling with such fury that he couldn't manage any words. Ross was leaning against his desk, holding up lab reports. "The samples we found in your lab, they were human blood," Ross said with the satisfaction of someone who has just had a suspicion, long denied, finally confirmed. "You've ignored protocol."

"You had no right snooping around in my lab. That's my business," said David.

"Wrong, Banner," said Ross. "It's government business, and you're off the project."

And David Banner screamed with rage. He cursed at Ross, he bellowed about the army's ingratitude and short-sightedness. He questioned Ross's parentage and, for good measure, almost took a swing at him before good sense made him realize that Ross could probably kill him.

"Shut down whatever you're working on, Banner," Ross said icily, never once coming close to losing his temper despite Banner's extended rant. "You're off the project and off this base."

Realizing there was nothing to be said but something to be done, David Banner exited the office and headed off to carry out General Ross's last order to him.

"You want it shut down," he snarled, "you got it shut down." And as he stormed away, the same angry, un-reasoning, infuriated thought kept going through his mind:

It was all Bruce's fault.

If Bruce hadn't been born, he wouldn't have been using

the boy's blood in experiments and, consequently, been found out. If Bruce hadn't been born, he wouldn't have had Edith yammering at him about finding a cure for his condition. If Bruce hadn't been born, David could have experimented at his own pace, on his own schedule, and in his own way. But the arrival of Bruce, and the freak way in which the mutagens in his blood had reacted, had thrown everything off.

David Banner had been working nonstop for week upon week, and it had taken its toll on his already fragile psyche.

He headed down to the cyclotron to do what needed to be done there. After that, he'd head home and attend to the monster who had ruined his life.

"Bruce, you're hurt," said an alarmed Edith Banner.

She'd been sitting and having a quiet afternoon coffee with her friend Kathleen from next door when Bruce was hauled into the kitchen by Kathleen's son, Davy. Davy's words spilled out: "Jack hit him with a stick, but Bruce wouldn't even hit him back. He just stood there shaking, and—"

And then she saw it. Just for a moment, she saw Bruce beginning to tremble just from the recounting of the incident, and there was a telltale bubbling of his skin. Kathleen and Davy were too distracted by the blood on his face to notice the odd distortions of his arm, and then, just like that, they were gone. Bruce let a relieved breath hiss through his front teeth—an overstressed engine letting off steam—and his mother sighed in silent relief as well.

"It's okay," Bruce said, as much to himself as to his mother.

It was the work of but a few minutes to get Bruce's face cleaned off and a bandage applied. Fortunately the cut wasn't especially large, nor did it require stitches; it had simply bled a good deal. In no time at all, Bruce and Davy were running back outside. Kathleen, shaking her head, settled back across the table from a wan but smiling Edith.

"Strange; he hardly made a peep. Any other kid would've wailed his head off," Kathleen observed.

Not wishing to dwell on it excessively, Edith simply shrugged and said, "That's Bruce. He's just like that. He's just so . . . bottled up."

Professor O. T. Wren, a lean man with an occasionally distracted air but incisive mind, had been working with David Banner on and off for the last year. He found Banner to be an aggressive researcher, but somewhat unpredictable. Professor Wren had heard through the grapevine that Banner had had some sort of altercation with General Ross, and strongly suspected it had not gone well for Banner. Deciding that an avuncular approach to the problem might be in order, he sauntered down to Banner's workstation near the cyclotron to talk with him.

When he arrived, all of Banner's material was gone: all the work papers, everything, cleaned out. He stood there scratching his head, puzzled, and then he realized something else.

The cyclotron was shut down.

Completely shut down.

And the second this horrified realization hit him, the alarm bells around the huge particle accelerator began to sound in a unified blast of noise.

"Oh, my God," said Professor Wren, and ran to sound a general alarm throughout the base.

And as he did that, David Banner drove at high speed across the desert, heading home to settle accounts with that little monster of his, once and for all.

sabotage

The one thing that gave Thunderbolt Ross's day any meaning was running toward him.

"Daddy!" Betty cried out. She toddled toward him, all of two and a half years old, in a yellow sundress and her hair in pigtails. Ross stepped down out of the jeep that he had driven back to his home, a modest white A-frame with a neatly trimmed lawn. He went down on one knee, scooped Betty up, and held her high in the air, swinging her around in a circle. Betty let out a delighted squeal and shouted, "Again!"

"No 'again,' little girl. Last time I did, I wound up wearing your lunch on my uniform jacket."

"Not lunch. Ice cream," she said proudly. "We went for ice cream, and then I got sick on you."

"How charming you remember that," he told her, but he didn't sound charmed about it. He set her down, and she promptly wrapped herself around one of his legs. "So what did you do today?" he asked.

"Played," she informed him. "Mommy had a headache. She lied down."

"Ah," was all Ross said, and his gaze flickered toward the house. He knew all about his wife's headaches. Betty understood that every so often her mother needed time to rest. Betty didn't understand about something called brain cancer. She didn't need to. All too soon, she'd have to deal with it, but not yet. Not yet.

Then Ross heard the phone ringing inside his house, but as he started toward it, there was an abrupt, frantic honking from a car horn behind him. He turned and saw a small convoy of cars and jeeps. In the lead was one of his aides with Professor Wren, one of the scientists from back at the base, in the backseat. In the passenger seat was Colonel Billings, Ross's second in command.

"Billings, what's wrong?" Ross said immediately.

Billings wasted no time. "Sir, I've had to order an evacuation of the base."

"*What?* Why?"

"It's the cyclotron, sir," Professor Wren stepped forward, looking extremely flustered. "It's been shut down."

Ross felt as if he'd missed something. "Shut down?"

"Yes, sir."

"And why is that a problem?"

"I didn't understand either at first, sir," Billings started to say, "but . . ."

Turning toward Wren, Ross said briskly, "Professor, I keep the military aspects of the base running. I know jack-all about the science half. So why don't you tell me why turning something off is worth evacuating the base."

"General," Wren said, talking calmly with great effort, "the cyclotron has been running for over a decade. It's not like . . . like a light switch or a Buick that just gets turned on and off when it's needed. This is a seventy-million-dollar Tandem Accelerator Superconducting Cyclotron. It's . . ."

"It's really large; I've seen it. Big, cylindrical, blue . . ."

"Yes, all true," said Wren, "and shutting one down

properly is a very lengthy and involved procedure. We never do a cold shutdown of a cyclotron. Ever. Understand, General: The cyclotron holds about 2,000 liters of liquid helium, maintained at a temperature of minus 270 degrees Celsius. Shutting it off cold, as was just done, means that the core temperature will eventually rise to room temperature. The liquid helium will then convert to 2,000 liters of helium gas, enough to fill approximately 1 million balloons. It's like . . . like putting water into a pot, screwing a lid on tightly, and then putting the pot on a burner. Sooner or later—probably sooner—there's going to be an explosion."

"My God," said Ross, beginning to grasp the immensity of the situation. "How big an explosion? What type? Nuclear?"

"From the cyclotron itself? Probably not."

"Probably?"

"I'm not an expert on cyclotron explosions, General!" Wren said in obvious exasperation. "I'm not sure what we'll get! And need I remind you there are other potentially explosive materials in the lab as well. When the cyclotron goes . . ."

"I understand the problem, Professor," said Ross, and he turned to Billings. "Is the base clear? Are we far enough away where we are right now? How long have we got?"

"Evacuation was almost accomplished before I came out here, General," Billings told him. "According to the professor, the farther away the better . . . and we're not sure how much time we have."

"I make it twelve to fifteen minutes from now," Wren said helpfully.

"Wonderful. Who in blue blazes did this?"

And then he knew, and before anyone could respond, he answered himself. "Banner. David Banner."

"He was the last one logged into that station, sir," said Wren.

"Billings! Get my wife taken out of there, and bring her and Betty to safekeeping. I'm commandeering one of the jeeps and going after Banner."

Betty apparently heard that, because she dashed over to her father and cried out, "Daddy! I want to come with you!"

"You can't, sweetheart."

"Please! *Please!*"

The child was bordering on hysterics, and Ross didn't have any time to stand around and discuss it. "Fine!" he said, and practically tossed her into the back of the jeep. He pointed to one jeep filled with MPs and shouted, "You! With me! Billings, can you and Wren get another jeep to get my wife out of here?"

"One's on the way, sir. ETA, one minute."

"Excellent!"

Ross gunned the jeep forward, with Betty holding on in the back and calling out "Daddy! This is fun!" as the jeep sped away toward the Banner house.

Ross hurtled down the road, chewing himself out for not having anticipated this. He should have had MPs escort Banner down to his workstation, should have made certain the fool didn't try something exactly like this. Ross knew that nothing would come from berating himself, but nonetheless he was furious because, in his confidence and arrogance, he had allowed it to happen.

He checked in the rearview mirror; the MPs were right behind him. Just ahead of him, down the road, was Banner's house. He saw Banner's car parked outside at an odd angle, and there was shouting coming from within. And suddenly someone cried out as Ross pulled the jeep up to curbside.

From the backseat, Betty observed it all without comprehending any of it. Then she peered toward the top window of the house and saw a little boy there. She started to bring up her hand and wave very tentatively.

And then, suddenly, from far, far in the distance behind her, the air was split by an ear-shattering explosion, and the sky filled with light, and that was when the screaming truly began.

awakening

The screams came this night as they came many a night. The gray-haired woman sprinted down the hallway with a speed that belied her years and threw open a door. She flipped on a light and teenage Bruce Krenzler sat up, staring around blankly. His hair in disarray, his pajama shirt soaked through with sweat, Bruce Krenzler clearly had no idea why the woman who he called Mom had suddenly taken it upon herself to burst into his room.

The light from the hallway revealed the room of a typical teenager, with posters festooning the walls. Except instead of posters of rock bands and the like, they were posters that featured the entire play *Hamlet* in tiny print and a photo of Albert Einstein sticking out his tongue. The furniture was simple and unadorned and surprisingly neat—except for the bed, where the sheets were twisted into knots.

"Another nightmare, Bruce," said Mrs. Krenzler. It was part explanation and part question.

Slowly he nodded, comprehending, but he clearly wasn't going to be of much help when it came to specifics. "I don't know; I don't remember," he admitted.

His adoptive mother smiled patiently. "Well, that's probably better then, isn't it," she said cheerfully.

Bruce, squinting against the light from the hallway, said, "Probably. Yeah." Whereupon he rolled over and fell back into a deep—and, mercifully, dreamless this time—sleep.

Betty Ross woke up screaming.

She sat up in bed, her chest heaving, gasping for air like a nearly drowned swimmer. Her long, dark hair hung in her face and she reflexively pushed it back. The images were fading quickly, but it didn't matter; she knew what they were. She'd had the dream so many times that they were second nature to her.

She'd once tried telling her father about them, but he'd simply said dismissively, "It's just dreams, Betty. They don't mean anything. There's too many real things happening in the world to worry about things that are unreal."

And, as was usually the case with her father, that was that.

He hadn't always been that way. When Mom had been around . . .

She knocked that train of thought right off its rails. What point was there in dwelling on it? It would just end up making her miserable, and if her father provided her little consolation when it came to dreams, he was of even less use when it came to talking about Mom.

Her nose wrinkled as she smelled eggs being cooked up downstairs. That was unexpected. Dad wasn't usually one for making breakfast. Usually he'd just be off to work, leaving Betty on her own to get to school. At most, she'd see him heading out the door and barely have a chance to wave to him.

She glanced out the window, saw it was going to be a

nice, sunny Maryland day, and then trotted down the stairs while tossing on her robe.

"Dad?" she called.

"Down here," he said somewhat unnecessarily.

She walked into the kitchen and skidded to a halt, caught off guard.

There was a well-groomed young man wearing an ROTC army uniform, and he was the one cooking break-fast. Thunderbolt Ross sat at the table, sipping coffee, and he gestured for her to come in. The young man turned and grinned at her. He had black hair, slicked back, and a pencil-thin mustache that he probably thought made him look older.

Caught off guard, Betty was still wearing the very short nightgown she'd slept in and her hair was in disarray. Her robe had been hanging open and she pulled it more tightly around herself with one hand while making vague and futile efforts with the other to pull her hair into line. "Uh, hi. Did I just wake up in an alternate universe where you have a son?"

The young man at the skillet laughed. "She's funny. You didn't tell me she was funny." He looked back at Betty. "How do you like it?"

"*It?*" she said, unsure of what he was referring to, but a bit suspicious of the possibilities.

"Your eggs." He nodded toward the stove top.

"Oh! Uh, scrambled, I guess. Dad . . . ?"

Ross, who was busily studying the newspaper, nodded absently. "Yes, you like them scrambled."

"No, I know that. I mean . . ." And she sharply inclined her head toward the young man.

"I think she means 'Who the heck is this dashingly handsome fellow cooking up eggs?' "

Despite the awkwardness of the situation, Betty laughed lightly at that. "Well, I don't know about the 'dashingly handsome' part, but . . ."

"This is Glen Talbot," Thunderbolt Ross said. "Out here visiting his uncle, Colonel Talbot."

"Ah. Okay, so, welcome to Fort Meade, Maryland," Betty said, being as affable as she could considering it was first thing in the morning. "Significant for—well—not much, really."

"Well, I hear you won't have to worry about that much longer," Glen said, deftly mixing the eggs in the skillet.

She looked in confusion at him. "Why not?"

Ross set down his newspaper. "Yes, ah . . . I was going to tell you this, Betty."

"Oh!" Talbot looked a bit chagrined. "I'm sorry. Did I spoil the surprise?"

"Surprise?" Her befuddlement grew.

Ross cleared his throat and said, "We've been reassigned, Betty."

"Awwww, no." Betty sagged into a chair at the table, dropping her head into one hand. "Not *again*. I was just starting to get used to *this* place."

"I know it's difficult," Talbot said sympathetically as he flipped the eggs onto her plate. The aroma wafted up from them, and she had to admit they didn't smell bad at all. She poked at them experimentally and took a bite. Didn't taste bad, either.

"Actually, it shouldn't be so unpleasant this time, Betty," Ross told his daughter. "In fact, it may be like old times."

She started to get excited. "Italy? Back to Italy?" She'd loved the time they'd spent there, two years ago, and had hated that it had only lasted a couple of months.

"No, not Italy. Desert Base."

Slowly Betty lowered her fork, letting it clink down onto the plate. "You're . . . not *serious*."

"Very serious."

"Do we have to?"

Talbot looked curiously from Betty to her father. "Is there a problem with Desert Base? I hear Nevada's pretty nice, actually."

"We have some . . . unpleasant memories of it, that's all," said Ross.

"Yeah, if you consider we almost got killed when it blew up and, by the way, my mom dying there a week later 'unpleasant.' "

She was unable to keep the sarcasm out of her voice, which was unfortunate because she knew that attitude put her father on edge. But he maintained his cool, which was to be expected since they had a guest.

"Sorry," mumbled Talbot. "I had no idea."

Her heart softened a bit. "It's okay. You couldn't have known. But at least, knowing the army, it'll be temporary . . ."

"Permanent, actually," Ross said. "At least as permanent as such things are."

Betty couldn't believe it. Of all the glorious places they'd been to, that damned desert was where they were being stuck for good? "I thought the place was leveled!"

"It was rebuilt. I'll be taking command of it."

"Oh, God," she moaned, convinced that there wasn't a teenager in the world who was having a worse day than she was.

Bruce Krenzler, hard at work in the lab at school, had his attention drawn away from the slides he'd been studying under the microscope by a specimen of a very different sort. Specifically, a lovely girl who had just entered the room and was looking shyly in his direction. Bruce became so flustered that he almost knocked over some test tubes, but caught them at the last moment and prevented a spill.

Her name was Alice, and he had noticed her any number of times. She had never given him so much as the time of day . . . and that was literally true, because he'd asked her what time it was once or twice between classes, and she'd just breezed right past him. But now she was sauntering right over to him as if they were the best pals in the world.

"Hi, Bruce. Whatcha doing?"

"It's cool. Uh, you can check out the DNA, you know, the proteins," said Bruce.

"Can I see?" asked Alice, sounding genuinely interested.

"Sure," he replied.

Alice leaned in closely over the microscope and he became aware of the heady smell of her perfume. "You know," she said, "I really get turned on by brainy guys."

Bruce stepped back, scarcely able to believe where the conversation was going. For years he had been gawky and awkward and utterly tongue-tied when it came to the opposite sex, and now this lovely young girl had actually noticed him and was being nice to him, and maybe they could go out some time and who knew what the possibilities might be, and this was just the most incredible thing that had ever happened to him . . .

At which point, while stepping backward, he tripped and fell over a stool. He went down bruisingly with it, tangled in the crashing metal, and as he lay there in a heap, he heard a chorus of laughter. He twisted around to see a group of other students watching, and realized with rapidly burning anger that it had all been a setup, that Alice had been coming on to him for the amusement of some of her friends.

"Poor Bruce," said Alice, and she was laughing the hardest of all. "You're such a nerd."

Bruce's face filled with anger, then his whole body started convulsing. He grabbed the side of the table, lifting himself up, and, flailing, scattered everything, including a lit Bunsen burner. The burner struck the spilled liquid from one of the test tubes, which just happened to be alcohol, and immediately ignited it. A fire roared to life in a heartbeat, and the others ran screaming from the room.

Bruce staggered to his feet, staring at the fire, and the burning was reflected in his eyes as his body started to convulse again. He fought to contain it

. . . smash it, bad things will happen, smash it . . .

just as he always did, for reasons long forgotten but deeply ingrained. But the images of the laughing kids kept coming at him, and for once, just once, he wanted to cut loose . . .

. . . and suddenly an automatic fire alarm started to clang. The overhead sprinkler system snapped on line, and cool water soaked Bruce to the skin, calming him. He stood there, letting it come, letting it extinguish the fire in front of him—and the fire within—at least temporarily.

desire

Betty strode along the main Tarmac of Desert Base. A typical blast of heat rolling off the desert hit her in the face, but she had readapted to it by this point. Her father came right after her, shouting, "Hold it right there, young lady! We weren't finished talking!"

She moved with the coltish grace that had become hers as she hit her late teens. She was clad in tight-fitting jeans and a Metallica T-shirt that her father absolutely despised, which was why she wore it at least twice a week. Some passing soldiers glanced at them, and Betty snapped off, "Eyes front, soldiers!" They promptly found something else to be interested in as Thunderbolt Ross came up behind her.

"I said we weren't finished talking!" he snapped at her.

She turned and looked him angrily in the face, making her the only person in the area who was capable of doing so. "When did we *start* talking? When do we ever start? You talk, I listen. That's about as far as it goes!"

"That's as far as it needs to go," Ross told her. "Is it true? What Glen told me? That you broke it off with him?"

She drew herself up. "Yes, that's right."

"Why the blue blazes would you do that?"

"Because I only went out with him to make you happy, Dad, believe it or not. And he was talking about marriage. About building a life together."

Ross's eyes widened. "And what's wrong with that? He's an up-and-coming lieutenant! I brought him out here because he's going places and—"

"And because you wanted to hook him up with me. I'm not stupid, Dad. You've had your eye on him ever since Maryland."

"And what if I did?" demanded Ross. "I'm just watching out for your best interests."

"It's my best interests if this was 1962! You want me to get married and be a good little army wife, throwing nice demure parties when hubby brings home officers, raising as many children as my husband chooses to produce, and otherwise keeping my big mouth shut!"

"It was good enough for your mother!"

Her face went ashen, and she could see that the moment the words had escaped his lips he regretted having said them. Before he could recant them, she said coldly, "I'm not Mom. I'm sorry I wasn't able to live up to her example. Maybe I should have just died and then you'd be happy."

"Betty!" He looked taken aback. "Now you're just saying things to try to hurt me, is that it?"

Indeed, that was true, and she was as sorry for it as much as he'd been moments earlier. But she wasn't about to back down, not now. She looked at the tops of her sneakered feet and said, "You just don't understand, that's all."

"Then explain it to me," he said. "We're both intelligent people. You should be able to explain why you tossed aside a man like Glen Talbot, why you—"

She sighed in exasperation. "Dad, Glen isn't what you think he is."

"Oh? And what do I think he is?"

"You. You think he's a young version of you. But he's not, I'm telling you. I got a chance to know him . . . really know him. He's always making plans. . . ."

"And what's wrong with that?" demanded Ross. "We need more strategists in—"

But she shook her head. "Not strategies, Dad, and maybe 'plans' isn't even the right word. 'Schemes' is probably more accurate. He's got a lot more up his sleeve than his arm, Dad. I mean, we've had our disagreements, heaven knows." He rolled his eyes at the understatement, but she continued, "But there's one thing I've never doubted, and that's your love for this country. You place it and its citizens and your responsibility for protecting them above everything. Even me."

"That's not true, Betty."

"Yes, it is," she said, and forced a smile, "and that's not automatically a bad thing. And maybe someday, when I'm older, I won't take it so personally. The point is," she continued before he could interrupt, "Glen's an opportunist. An opportunist and a power seeker. I just . . . I just know it. Watch your back with him when I'm not around."

"Oh, really. And where might you be going?"

She took a deep breath, preparing for the plunge. "I've been accepted to Berkeley."

"What?" He gaped at her. "That's absurd! What do you need with college? For that matter, you're only a high school sophomore!"

"Dad, did you *ever* look at *any* of my transcripts? All I've taken are accelerated courses and extra credit on top of that, and aced them all. While you were busy getting Desert Base organized, I was blowing through high school. You were just too busy to notice. I nailed my SATs and got accepted for early admission."

"You couldn't have applied," Ross said defiantly. "You have to have a parent sign the application form—"

"You did. I slipped it in when you were at home doing some paperwork. You're so conditioned to signing next to wherever someone sticks a Post-it note, it was no problem."

"Oh," he said, and then rallied. "And what about application fees? Where did you get the money?"

"From Glen in exchange for sexual favors."

"Betty!"

She couldn't help but laugh at the abrupt purpling of his face. "I borrowed it from my friend Kelly, Dad. I promised her she'd get paid back as soon as you got past your hissy fit over my being accepted."

"I'm a general in the United States Army, Elizabeth," he said stiffly. "I'm not prone to 'hissy fits.' "

"Dad . . ." She moved toward him, but didn't touch him, for he stood so stiffly, radiating anger, that she was afraid to. "Dad, I want to be a scientist. Not an army wife. Not even an officer. I want to work for a private lab somewhere and do research and live my own life. Not your life, or the life that the son you never had might have lived. I've been offered a scholarship; my way will be paid. They're that impressed with me." She paused, and then added in a small voice, "Why can't *you* be?"

A long moment passed between them, and she could almost sense him pulling away from her.

"Do what you want," he said finally, and turned and walked away without saying anything further.

It was the last thing he said to her for more than half a decade.

Bruce Krenzler lay on the floor of his room, stacks of books spread around him, reading. He looked up as his mother entered and dropped down on the floor beside him.

"Hey, Mom," he said.

Monica Krenzler surveyed the apparent disorganization of the room. It was a stark contrast to Bruce's usual tidiness. "Bruce," she said, sighing. "Already off to college." She ruffled his hair and said, "I'm going to miss you terribly. But someday you will be a remarkable scientist."

And Bruce, seeing an opportunity, asked, "Like my father?"

Slowly she removed her hand from his hair, and to Bruce it seemed as if the temperature in the room had dropped. "Do you remember him?" asked his adoptive mother, and there was a certain amount of caution in her voice.

"No, but you said once that he was a scientist," said Bruce.

"Did I?" She seemed surprised that she had done so, and searched her memory. Then, very casually, she said, "I must have been guessing, seeing how brilliant you are." She studied him thoughtfully, and then she leaned toward him. "Someday you will discover there is something inside you so . . . so special, some kind of greatness, I am sure. Someday you will share it with the whole world."

He hugged her tightly, and thus was unable to see the narrowing of her eyes, and the curious combination of sadness mixed with quiet and distant contemplation, as if she were perceiving Bruce not as a loving son departing home but as a project that was entering a new stage.

PART TWO: EGO

PART THREE

repression

The cabin had seemed the ideal place for a getaway.

Betty had talked about it any number of times. Her father had built it with his own hands, and it held many fond memories for her of when she was a little girl playing hide-and-seek under the porch. The Ross family had known their happiest times here.

But after Betty's mother passed away, Thunderbolt lost his taste for the cabin. Betty had always surmised that it no longer held any joy for him, because all he did was associate the place with his late wife. It was understandable. Her mother had decorated every inch of the cabin, and although that sort of presence was a comfort for Betty, her father obviously found it disconcerting, even sad. At one point he had simply told Betty that she should consider it hers from now on, for he had no more use for it and it was a shame to let it go to waste. She had taken him at his word, and now she had brought Bruce here to spend the weekend.

Now in her late twenties, Betty had grown into a beautiful young woman who was—painful for her father to admit—the image of her late mother. When she spoke it was with quiet confidence, and when she moved it was with a dancer's grace, even though she had never actually taken lessons. And the most charming thing about her was that she had no idea just how stunning she really was.

All she knew was that she wanted the weekend to be perfect. The only problem was she'd been working like a maniac at the lab to try to clear the time for their weekend expedition, which for most people wouldn't have been a problem, but Betty tended to work hours that bordered dangerously on 24-7. She felt exhausted. Her hair, she believed, was matted and disgusting, and ordinary cosmetics couldn't begin to cover the wan look of her face.

Both of them were dressed in outdoorsy camping clothing, plaid shirts, and pants with lots of utility pockets. Bruce and Betty posed in front of a camera that was perched on a tripod, and Betty—feeling anything but photogenic—gamely smiled into the camera in a way that she was sure was evocative of someone on death row maintaining a stiff upper lip. As the flash went off in her face, she could feel how awkward and disgusting she must look, and suddenly she was more self-conscious about it than ever before.

Bruce, displaying his customary obliviousness to anything that wasn't practically shouted in his face, didn't pick up on Betty's discomfort at all. The light of the flash hadn't begun to dim in her retinas before Bruce was already on his feet, approaching the timer.

"Let's try another," he said.

"No," protested Betty. "I look tired." She ran her fingers aimlessly through her hair, as if she could restore it to some degree of attractiveness through sheer willpower.

Bruce didn't notice. He was far too engaged with the mysteries of the timing mechanism to care about something as mundane as his girlfriend's feelings. Small wonder, she mused, considering how little his own feelings meant to him. So at least he was consistent in that respect. Then, as if he had taken long seconds to recall what she had just said, he replied, "You are tired, but you look great."

She smiled sadly. There was no doubt that he was sincere. But usually when a guy compliments a girl, Betty thought, she could sense any range of emotions or wants filtering through the carefully chosen words. Whereas Bruce was just . . . Bruce. She wondered, not for the first time, if he was gay. He reset the camera and then went to sit beside her. He put his arms around her and the camera took the picture. He looked at her and brushed her hair back. "Hey, what's the matter?"

Betty had no intention of telling him, but she blurted it out before she could stop herself. "It's the dreams. They're terrible. I keep having them."

"Then do like me: Don't sleep," said Bruce. There was an air of forced joviality in his tone, but it didn't fool Betty for a moment.

She placed a hand atop his. "Not an option . . . and it shouldn't be for you either," she said in a serious tone.

It wasn't difficult for Bruce to turn somber. It was his natural state of being; anything else he did was an affectation assumed for Betty's benefit. His face clouded, he drew her closer in a protective manner. "Tell me about your dream."

She liked the weight of his arm around her, and snuggled in even closer to him. She felt like she fit there, one piece of a jigsaw puzzle finding its mate. In doing so, she relaxed enough to talk about her dreams for the first time in ages. "It starts as a memory. I think it's my first memory. An image I have from when I was maybe two years old. There's this . . . this little girl . . ."

"You?"

She nodded, half-smiling. "You don't miss a trick, do you? Yes, it's me. I'm in an ice-cream parlor. And I'm being tossed into the air, caught, tossed again."

"Who's doing it?"

"My father. He's in full uniform. He looks so—" She paused, trying to figure out the best way to phrase it. "He's looking the way I always saw him when I was a child. Big, proud, invincible. More than human."

"I'd be careful about things that are more than human, if I were you." He paused thoughtfully. "So you're bouncing up and down, and your father's involved. Sounds vaguely Freudian."

"Oh, you!" She elbowed him in the chest and was rewarded with a startled grunt. "One more comment out of you like that . . ."

"I'm sorry," he said, rubbing his chest where she'd struck him. "Okay, so . . . your father . . . invincible, et cetera. Then what?"

"Well, then this jeep pulls up, and soldiers are calling my father over. And things start getting jumbled together—you know, the way they do in dreams. Like, one moment I'm still in the ice-cream parlor, and suddenly I'm in a desert, and then there's a house with a little boy looking out a window, and then I'm back in the parlor. Except it all makes sense when it's happening." She could almost see the images now, as if watching a film unspooling. "He's putting me down. I'm crying. Then there's this . . . this rumbling sound, like a storm coming in, but it's not a storm. There's this cloud . . . with a green tint. It's almost like it's alive. . . ."

"You think it's a memory," Banner asked, "or is it just a dream?"

She shook her head. "I think it's something that must have happened out at Desert Base with my father, when I was growing up," said Betty.

"Desert Base. That's the one filled with aliens and UFOs, right?"

She knew perfectly well that he knew the difference, but she laughed anyway, appreciating his endeavor to lighten the mood a touch. "That's Area 51, silly," said Betty. "Desert Base is even more secret. Anyhow . . ." Her thoughts drifted back to the narrative, and now that she was talking about it, she could see it even more vividly. "The dream keeps going. Suddenly I'm alone. I'm crying and crying, and then a hand covers my face."

"Your father's?"

She shook her head, and couldn't quite look him in the eye as she said softly, "Yours."

He withdrew from her then, just as she suspected he might. Still seated, she turned to face him, expecting him to look appalled or horrified or hurt or . . . or *something*. Instead his expression, as always, was totally, infuriatingly impassive.

"But that's terrible," said Banner. At most he sounded ruffled, as if the idea was ludicrous. "You know I would never hurt you."

"You already have," said Betty, affectionately but pained.

"How?"

"You're breaking my heart."

She watched his eyes carefully as she said it. Once again she sought . . . astonishment? Surprise? Hurt? Anger?

Nothing. Just that same, infuriating calm, as if the very notion of acting in any manner that suggested depths of emotion was anathema to him. "I don't understand why you would say that." He made the comment with the same puzzled air that might pervade him if an experiment didn't quite go right.

"Do you love me, Bruce?"

"Of course. You know I do."

"You see! Right there!"

Finally an emotion: bewilderment. "Right where?"

"Right there, right now. The way you said that. 'You know I do.' Bruce, the woman you love has doubts about how you feel about her, and you respond with such detachment that you might as well be saying that it looks like it might rain."

"I'm not detached," he assured her.

"Aren't you? Bruce," and she squeezed his hand even harder, "we've talked about things, made plans, but I've never gotten a feeling from you that you have anything truly emotional invested in our relationship."

"I thought you knew me better than that."

"Oh, I know you . . . better, I think, than you know yourself . . ."

"No."

Betty was startled at the firmness, almost the ferocity of the denial, as if something had slipped ever so slightly. As if a curtain had been pulled aside just a few inches to reveal something unexpected and surprising . . . surprising to Betty, if not to Bruce.

And then, just like that, it was gone. A veil was once again drawn over Bruce's eyes, and he was saying with far more restraint, "No. You're wrong about that, Betty. You have to take my word for that: You're very wrong. I know myself, far better than anyone else could."

"But you see, that's what a relationship is all about. Letting the other person know you as well as you know yourself."

"Then I guess we don't have a relationship."

She was utterly taken aback by the words. Even Bruce seemed mildly surprised at his own pronouncement, but he made no effort to retract or elaborate on what he had just said. Instead his Adam's apple bobbed up and down, as if he had just swallowed something very large.

"Is . . . that how you want it, Bruce?"

"No," he said very softly. "But apparently . . . that's how it is."

"But why? Why can't you let me in?" she asked with growing urgency, desperate to comprehend why this relationship, which she felt was possibly the greatest thing that had ever happened to her, seemed to be slipping away between her fingers.

"It's not a matter of letting you in." He rose from the couch, his hands thrust deep into his pockets. "That's not it at all."

"Then what is it?" she demanded. "You owe me that much, at least. If it's not about letting me in . . ."

"It's not. It's about letting me out." He said it with the air of a doctor diagnosing a fatal disease.

"I don't understand," she told him.

Bruce had walked toward the door, and now he stood there with his hand resting on the knob. "Neither do I," he said, as much to himself as to her, and then he let himself out the front door of the cabin, shutting the door gently behind him.

By the time he returned some hours later, Betty had

cried and dried her tears and reapplied her makeup. They stayed the night at the cabin, she in the bedroom, he on the couch. It wasn't how she had planned for the weekend to go, and late that night the tears came once again and Betty sobbed miserably into a pillow. She didn't know if Bruce heard her, nor did she care. She wondered if, in that regard, she was getting to be more like him.

one year later . . .

Benny Goodman was a harmless enough fellow.

In his early sixties, with a perpetual smile, a thick beard, and a good sense of humor, which was necessary for someone who'd grown up enduring jokes about the Benny Goodman orchestra, Benny prided himself on not having an enemy in the world. So it was that when he heard a knock on his front door late one evening, he opened it without a second thought.

There was a man standing there who was about Benny's height and weight, and sported a beard not dissimilar to Benny's. Three ratty-looking dogs were grouped around him; well-trained, they stayed precisely in their places.

"Benny Goodman?" asked the man. His voice was low and gravelly.

"Yes."

"Benny Goodman, who works as a janitor down at Lawrence Berkeley labs?"

Benny was beginning to get a faint buzz of warning. "Is there a problem down at the lab?" he asked.

"No, no. It's just . . . my dogs are hungry."

Benny stared at them. They growled. "I've . . . nothing to feed them," he said.

"Not a problem. We'll improvise," said the old man, and he snapped his fingers. The dogs were upon Benny in a heartbeat, one of them—a pit bull—clamping his teeth around Benny's throat before he could get so much as a scream out. The old man stepped through the door as the animals bore Benny to the floor, and as the janitor writhed in his death throes, the old man said, "By the way . . . love your orchestra," as he closed the door behind him.

Not for the first time, Bruce Krenzler had the oddest feeling that he was staring into the mirror at someone else's face. Or perhaps it was something other than that. Yes. Yes, it felt as if he were studying his own face, but eyes other than his were gazing back at him with intensity and curiosity and . . . hatred.

Why hatred?

Why not?

The query and the reply ran through his head, one stumbling over the other, and the impact of their collision nearly jolted him from his reverie. His mind split ever so slightly, and he saw himself from beyond the restrictions of his mortal shell, as if he were having an out-of-body experience. How ludicrous it would have seemed to someone on the outside looking in. Here he was, standing bare chested, a towel wrapped around his middle, staring into a mirror as if his own reflection were simply the most irresistible thing he'd ever laid eyes on. He would have come across to an observer as a world-class egomaniac. Or a narcissist. *Or an actor*, he added mentally, and tried to laugh at his little unvoiced jest. Oddly, he found he couldn't.

His straight black hair was still slicked down from his

having showered minutes before, but his skin had dried. He studied his face more closely. His ears stuck out a bit on either side. He thought he looked like a reasonably intelligent individual, and then wondered whether that again wasn't the consideration of someone who was too self-obsessed for his own good.

Bruce looked a bit older than he felt. He was reasonably muscled. He didn't get the chance to exercise all that often, because he was so busy in the lab. He used to have much more of a tan, but lately he'd been eating, sleeping, and breathing in the laboratory, and some days it seemed the only reason he came home was because Betty practically forced him to.

Something flickered in his eyes when he thought of Betty. Again, he wasn't sure what it was, and that bothered him a lot. He thought of the time when they'd been on their way up to the cabin, and Betty had gazed at him lovingly and spoke of how the eyes were the window to the soul. Bruce had laughed and said in an offhand manner, "Yes, but whose soul?" When Betty had asked him what that was supposed to mean, he didn't have an explanation. He still didn't.

"My God, Bruce," he said out loud. Although the shade was drawn in his bathroom, the light of dawn was visible through it. "Could you possibly waste time any more comprehensively than you already have?"

He then wondered for some odd reason if he was going to respond to himself. *They always say talking to yourself is no big deal; it's when you start replying that you've got a problem.*

He didn't reply, which provided at least some temporary degree of relief.

Deciding that he'd been screwing around for far too

long already, Bruce quickly lathered up his face and began to draw his razor across it. He did so with the same careful, methodical strokes he always used when attending to—well, just about anything, really. Betty had once said that with the slightest push, he could easily trip over into the realm of obsessive-compulsive disorder. "I could never have OCD," Bruce had assured her. "I'm too anal retentive." That made Betty laugh, and the matter had been dropped. Not forgotten by Bruce, or Betty, truth to tell, but dropped nevertheless.

The razor moved across his face. He watched it carefully. Gradually Bruce realized that there was something wrong with his reflection, but he couldn't fathom what it might be. Finally he noticed it: He'd stopped blinking. He was so fixed on what he was doing that his eyes were just staring, like the orbs of a serpent. Or a madman.

He blinked. It took an effort, but he did it. One blink, slow, methodical, and then open, and there were those eyes again, set in his relatively nondescript face, and *damn*, but it felt as if someone else was staring back.

You're losing it, Bruce.

Yes. You are.

He almost jumped as he once again responded to himself, in a voice that sounded like hell's cement mixer, and he nicked himself shaving.

And there was blood, blood everywhere, gushing, and it was horrible, just terrifying, and deep within something rooting around recoiled in terror and anger, all mixed together, looking at his eyes, through *his eyes, with burning hatred . . .*

It was a tiny cut. No gushing. No trauma. Just a dot. He held a piece of tissue paper to it for a moment and the bleeding stopped almost immediately.

He actually chuckled when he saw how minimal the damage was. "The dangers of letting yourself get worked up," he said aloud, although no one was there to hear.

And then, almost against his will, he saw *those eyes*, and suddenly felt as if someone was indeed there to hear. Someone other than himself.

He finished shaving far quicker than he ever had before, threw a wet towel over his face, and wiped away the shaving cream. When he lowered the damp cloth, his eyes were his and his alone, leaving him to ponder the fact that he was suffering from too much imagination and too little morning coffee.

The laboratory within the Lawrence Berkeley facility in which Bruce spent most of his time was an amusing place. Well, amusing to someone like Bruce. Whenever he saw labs in movies, the scientists' domains were always clean and polished and wonderfully organized. As a student, all the labs he'd ever been in during his school days were maelstroms of barely controlled chaos. In a way, he'd always looked forward to becoming an adult so that he could inhabit one of those movie labs and never have to be stepping in between or under or around various projects to get where he had to go.

Well, here he was, a project administrator, the lead scientist in one of the facility's most promising projects, and not only had his organizational skills not improved, but apparently they had degenerated.

His assistant, Jake Harper, was theoretically supposed to help Bruce keep on track. The operative word, unfortunately, was "theoretically," and as it happened, it turned out not to be one of Bruce's better theories. Harper was almost as hopeless as Bruce himself.

Betty could have gotten everything organized, of course. She had that sort of mind. But she had once told Bruce point-blank that if he was waiting for her to get their act together for them, then he was going to be waiting a long, bloody time, because she'd be damned if she voluntarily took on the role of token female cleaning up after the guys.

This left Bruce and Harper to make occasional, perfunctory attempts at getting the place in order, and Betty to stand in the midst of the discord, shake her head, and make disapproving clucking noises every so often. So the lab never got cleaned up, but at least everyone knew their place in the order of things. Bruce took some comfort from that, cold as that comfort might be.

Harper—with his disheveled hair, glasses perched on the bridge of his nose, and perpetually wan complexion— was several years younger than Bruce and several light-years more nervous. Certainly that nervousness came from lack of confidence in himself, which Bruce couldn't begin to comprehend. Harper's competency tested off the charts, and he'd graduated eighth in his class at MIT. His doctorate on cellular regeneration had been so groundbreaking that no less an authority than Dr. Henry Pym had shaken his hand and congratulated him on a job well done.

Yet during procedures, Harper had a tendency to move around with energized nervousness, as if concerned about his own adequacy, or perhaps about the possibility that something might blow up in his face and take his face along with it. Still, he got the job done better than any dozen men with whom Bruce had been associated, and so Bruce was willing to tolerate Harper's little quirks. Fortunately enough, Bruce wasn't of the temperament to let a great deal bother him.

Except your own reflection, he thought.

Annoyed with himself for mentally retreating to his mirror encounter—which had been elevated in his mind, much to his irritation, from a simple shave to some vast analysis of his psyche—Bruce pushed away all such irrelevant considerations and concentrated instead upon the gammasphere.

The round chamber sat glistening before him, the product of two years of meticulous planning and labor. Shielded with glass a foot thick, the lower section was lined with glittering panels, reflectors designed to process and focus the radiation that would be carefully manipulated by the scientists outside. In the center of the gammasphere, staring out passively from within a small dome atop a pedestal, was a frog. The dome was perforated with microscopic airholes that would both enable the frog to continue breathing and for gases and the like to pass through and reach the test subject. A focusing mirror was situated directly above the pedestal.

Bruce referred to the frog as "Number Eleven." This didn't sit well with Harper, who insisted on naming every damned one of the test subjects over Bruce's objections. This one he had dubbed "Freddie." Bruce considered it unprofessional. One simply didn't humanize test subjects. He'd commented rather loudly during one lunch meeting that it was pointless to expend emotional energy becoming attached to experimental creatures. Whereupon Betty, without looking up from her tuna sandwich, had commented rather pointedly that if one wasn't going to become too attached to experimental creatures or to other human beings, what *was* one going to become attached to? Harper had looked puzzled, and Betty had just smiled sweetly, but Bruce had been all too aware that the oblique observation was directed at him.

What did she want from him? Why couldn't she simply accept that he wasn't like her? What was it about women that made them feel compelled to try to change the men they loved?

Well, that was how much Betty truly knew him, he decided. Because if she knew him at all, she'd be aware that if there was one thing Bruce Krenzler didn't do well with, it was change. He was too set in his ways, too locked into the man he was, to see beyond to other possibilities. Personal transformation wasn't his forte. Ask anyone.

Bruce made a last minute check of the levels, and glanced across the room to make eye contact with Harper. Harper had just finished his own cross-checks, and nodded once to indicate that he was good to go.

"Harper," said Bruce, "release the nanomeds."

Harper nodded once, his hair flopping around like so much seaweed as he pressed a release valve. There was a hissing sound as the chamber filled with gas.

Freddie the frog glanced around in passive bewilderment. He didn't see the nanomeds, of course. He would have required eyes formed on Krypton to be able to discern them. He did, however, hear the soft hiss of the gas. He flicked his tongue out experimentally, in the off chance that there was something in the gas that would provide nourishment.

"Okay," said Bruce, taking a deep breath and then letting it out slowly. "Let's hit Freddie with the gamma radiation."

Harper punched instructions into a keyboard, muttering softly to himself something that Bruce at first didn't hear. But then he did, the words repeated softly, like a mantra: "Let it work, let it work, let it work . . ." At that, Bruce had to smile, albeit very slightly. He wondered whether Harper was so desperate for it to work because he wanted the project to succeed . . . or because he was concerned about the fate of the frog should the experiment fail.

A pinpoint stream of gamma radiation hit the focal lens above the pedestal. In a flash, it zapped the frog across the chest. The poor creature flipped over onto its back for a moment, its little arms and legs flailing before it was able to take the time to recover and right itself. Had there been any exposure to open air from the chamber, there would doubtless have been the faint smell of burning meat. Certainly the sound would have been unpleasant. But instead Bruce and Harper were conveniently isolated, and the only thing they were able to observe was the ugly gash the frog had acquired on its chest.

Freddie was still stumbling about, looking disoriented. The frog blinked furiously, probably wondering if this was the first step toward prepping it to become an entrée; perhaps it was about to lose its legs to some gourmand.

For a moment there was nothing. Bruce watched. And then slowly, miraculously, the wound began to close up. As it closed, it left a zone of throbbing, almost fluorescent green in its wake, the freshly produced tissue saturated with color.

Bruce couldn't believe it. Next to him, Harper was chortling with pleasure and triumph, and then he heard a female voice, so close to him that she was practically breathing in his ear, whisper, *"Yes!"*

He turned to see, to his surprise, that Betty Ross was standing there. He had no clue how long she'd been there, but obviously it had been long enough to observe the results of the experiment. He hadn't even been aware that she was in the lab, or else he would have held the tests up. He had thought she was out at a conference, and yet here she was in the flesh. He supposed he shouldn't have been surprised at that. Betty routinely blew off national gatherings, claiming the work she and Bruce were doing was so evolved past anyone else's that hanging around with other scientists, looking for tips and clues and guidance, was a waste of time.

She was so close that he could smell her perfume. He never quite understood why women tried to make themselves smell like flowers or palm trees or an evening rain rather than just smelling like women.

Still, it wasn't a bad scent. . . .

He caught her glance, smiled involuntarily, then went back to the issue at hand and studied the readings from the scanners mounted directly under the frog. The frog was trembling slightly, but that could be due to a dozen things, most likely sympathetic vibrations to—

The frog exploded.

Harper let out a tragedy-soaked cry as the amphibian's little innards splashed all over the inside of the container. Betty emitted a frustrated, *"Oh!"* Bruce, as was his habit, didn't let any of his disappointment show on his face, but he felt his shoulder muscles bunching up as they tended to do whenever he was faced with a tense situation. He forced himself to relax, but he could practically taste the feeling of disappointment. Other frogs had suffered "grievous setbacks," that is, died horribly, far faster, leading him to think that maybe Freddie—*Number Eleven, dammit*—was going to beat the odds.

He looked at the others in the lab, sighed, and said, "Lunch break."

"Oh, good," Harper said, sounding queasy as he surveyed the frog's remains trickling down the sides of the container, "because, y'know, strapping on the feed bag is exactly what I feel like doing right now."

There was a lab cafeteria and also some decent restaurants in the area, but Bruce usually chose to eat at his desk. Knowing this, Betty fell into step behind him as he headed toward the lab refrigerator.

"Saw my father in the news," she said.

"Oh?" The comment surprised him. Betty very rarely made any mention of her father.

"Uh-huh. Getting some medal or something from the president." She shrugged. "He's got so many hanging on his uniform already, I'm not sure where he'll put it."

"Are you going to call and congratulate him?"

"I was thinking about it."

That stopped him for a moment as he turned and saw an impish expression on her face. "Really? That would be unusual."

"Well, you know, he *is* my father, and since I actually know that, I figured maybe I might be able to lead by example."

At first Bruce had no idea what she was talking about, but then he understood. He sighed and reached into the refrigerator, pulling out a small paper bag. "Are we back on that subject again?" he asked with a tired playfulness in his voice as they walked back toward his desk.

"Yes, that subject again," she replied with a fair imitation of his voice. "Just give it some thought. Don't you want to know about your birth parents, where you come from? It's not that hard to unseal adoption papers these days. It might open you up to more feelings."

"And do I want more feelings?" asked Bruce, feeling like the tin woodsman from *The Wizard of Oz*.

Betty's response, in a surprisingly serious tone, caught him off guard. "I can wish, can't I?"

He felt a flicker of guilt when she said that, and some of that must have shown through on his face despite his best efforts, because she looked immediately contrite, as if sorry that she'd said anything at all. He wanted very much to ignore it, but it had been said, and it was out there, which meant it was going to be like the proverbial elephant seated at the table that no one could pretend wasn't there.

With great sadness and feeling more wistful than he would have thought himself capable of, he said gently, "I do wish I were someone who could feel more, express more. If I were, we'd still be together, wouldn't we?"

"I don't know," said Betty. She looked down, leaning against his desk. "I guess it's none of my business anymore. I'm just having a hard time, us being apart but still seeing you every day, working together. It makes me feel more lonely than ever." She sighed. "But what can you do?"

"I can still appreciate you," said Bruce, "admire you, be a friend—" Then he paused, thinking, *My God, you're giving her the "We'll always be friends" speech. How pathetic is that?*

Betty didn't seem put off by it; just a bit sadder. "I wish I could say it's enough," she said.

Never had Bruce felt a greater, more gaping emptiness in himself than he did at that moment. He wanted to reach over to her, to hold her, to tell her all manner of things and share feelings and emotions with her. The problem was he didn't truly know if he'd be saying things he actually felt . . . or just uttering the things he thought she wanted to hear.

Instead, he forced a smile and said, in as light a manner as he could, "Well, there is one thing."

She raised an eyebrow questioningly as, with a flourish, he opened the paper bag and pulled out a container. "Chocolate, chocolate chip," said Bruce.

Betty smiled, a smile as radiant as gamma rays . . .

As gamma rays? Good Lord, can I ever turn off being a scientist?

The problem was he knew the answer to that as soon as he thought it.

Betty hated the dog and pony show.

That's what she called the semiannual gatherings of the board of directors, when she and Bruce and whoever was working for the lab would be forced to try to explain in words of one syllable just what it was they were doing, and all the "practical applications." That was the phrase that drove her the most insane, the one she heard so often she had occasionally been known to mutter it in her sleep. They always wanted to know about "practical applications," which of course translated to, "How can we make some fast money off this latest experiment?"

They didn't understand that it wasn't that easy. Many of the most significant advances in science, the most "practical" and useful developments in the history of mankind, had been incidental discoveries that were offshoots of other studies. Experimentation was about possibilities, discovery was about "what if." While opponents of the space program were howling about the waste of money entailed in landing a man on the moon, they were utterly oblivious to the many practical aspects of everyday life that had their origins in technology developed while putting men into space. Everything from voice-responsive software to athletic shoes to water purifiers to thermal insulation for the home had all resulted from the space program.

But go explain that to number crunchers searching for some sort of mythical bottom line, as if one could put a price tag on progress.

These meetings were the only time that Betty envied Bruce his emotional detachment. She always maintained a cool demeanor when dealing with these people, but it required tremendous effort. Bruce accomplished the same thing but made it look easy . . . probably because, for him, it was. Betty gave herself a mental, if ironic, pat on the back. It took some kind of woman to find a silver lining to a character trait that effectively torpedoed a relationship.

She let none of what was going through her mind show in her presentation, of course. She was far too professional for that. Instead, she watched the fifteen or so men—all in their cookie-cutter suits and neckties—grouped around the table, studying the results and charts she had provided them on the well-founded assumption that they wouldn't have a clue what she and her colleagues did without visual aids. She was walking them through it, reminding herself that she shouldn't have any resentment toward them simply because at least half of them knew nothing about science, and only understood dollars and cents. They were . . . a necessary evil.

With a pleasant smile affixed to her face, Betty continued, "To distance the cells we subject them to gamma radiation." Behind her on a projection board mounted on the wall, there were clear color representations of the cells agitating and unraveling. "Our little molecular machines—the nanomeds—are inhaled into the organism and spread through its tissues. They remain inert until we awaken them with gamma radiation. Once awakened, they instantly respond to the cellular distress signals— from a wound, for example—making copies of healthy cells and breaking down the damaged ones." She paused to see if they comprehended. It was darker in the room than she would have liked, and it wasn't easy to discern their faces, but she thought they got it. In the meantime, the image on the board displayed the nanomeds at work.

"The main problem," she continued, "is figuring out how a living body can withstand the help our nanomeds provide so vigorously. We've yet to find anything that can survive not only the energy flux of such swift cellular replication, but the discharge of the waste products, mainly water and carbon dioxide, created as damaged cells are dismantled."

Puckishly, she'd wanted to include a graphic of an exploding frog, just to see their reactions. The humorous notion had been vigorously vetoed by Bruce and Harper, and so instead the board members only witnessed a cellular explosion. "We're trying to balance these two functions," said Betty. "If we succeed, we may someday realize the promise of near-instantaneous bodily repair." She looked to Bruce as she thought, *There. Near-instantaneous bodily repair. That should be practical application enough for them.* "Dr. Krenzler." She gestured and Bruce rose and stepped up as she moved to one side.

She found to her surprise that she had to fight a reflex to reach up and squeeze his arm. It would have been meant in the simplest "go get 'em" terms, but she was worried it might be read as more than that—and, for all she knew, it was more than that. So she kept her hand at her side and just nodded to Bruce in a vague show of support. He returned the nod and stepped up to the small podium that had been erected.

"Thank you, Dr. Ross," Bruce said, looking out over the room. He smiled slightly. Betty couldn't help but think that this was exactly the sort of situation in which Bruce was the most comfortable. No emotions, no personal interplay. Pure lecture. He'd probably make a hell of a teacher. He tapped for a moment thoughtfully on the podium, and then said, "We've been thinking a lot lately, in the lab, about memory and forgetting, about the role they play in living and dying. Death, you might say, is a kind of forgetting."

Betty glanced around the room. They seemed to be hanging on his words. Meanwhile, Bruce, warming to his topic, continued. "Each time a human cell replicates, it loses a little more DNA from the end of its chromosomes, eventually forgetting so much it forgets its function, its ability to cope with trauma, to continue to reproduce. Whereas life, life is the ability to retrieve and act on memory." He moved slightly away from the podium, leaning against it on one elbow, looking very casual. *He's so much more comfortable with science than people*, Betty sighed mentally, as Bruce said, "Now if our work succeeds, and our nanomeds begin to take over more and more of this process, you'll have to ask is it *you* that's alive, or is it the billions of artificial creatures inside you?"

He paused. The interest from the men at the board table was palpable, and Betty could almost sense their next question: *When would it be ready? When would it be available to distribute to hospitals and doctors and think tanks so we can make a ton of money off it?* Bruce apparently sensed that, as well, for he drew a cautionary line in the sand.

"For now, our nanomedical cures have been more deadly than the diseases they treat," he admitted. "Maybe that's because they remember their instructions too well. Perhaps, to stay in balance and alive, we must forget as much as we remember."

There was a pause. Then, from the darkness, one of the men said, "All right, doctors, thank you for your thoroughly professional update. We'll be evaluating the data and giving our recommendations."

Betty stifled a laugh. Oh yes, their recommendations would be ever so helpful. Why, it might open up entirely new directions that never would have occurred to them in a million years. Or, at the very least, more trees would die in vain so the board members could expend paper upon their recommendations. But Bruce, unflappable as always, just nodded and said, "Thank you. We'd appreciate that."

Moments later they were in the hallway, and Betty was looking incredulously at him. " 'We'd appreciate that'?" she asked.

Bruce just shrugged. "Why wouldn't we?"

"Bruce! They'll have nothing of use to contribute! You know that. They'll suggest things we tried six months ago. Their idea of advice is laughable."

"Very true," Bruce replied. "But laughter is beneficial in a variety of ways, and anyone who provides the opportunity for others is to be appreciated."

She tried to have a comeback to that, but instead all she

could do was chuckle when she saw the mock seriousness
on his face. She bowed slightly and said, "I am dazzled by
your intellect and insight."

"As well you should be," he said gravely.

"You coming back to the lab?"

"In a few minutes. I want to go to my office, make a
few calls. You go ahead, if you're so inclined. Or perhaps
you want to take the rest of the day off to recover from
our—what is it again—"

"Dog and po—"

"Right, right, dog and pony show." He looked askance.
"So would I be the dog or the pony?"

"The latter."

"Why?"

"Because I've always wanted a pony."

He opened his mouth, then closed it. He smiled in spite
of himself, and then gestured in the general direction of
his office as he started to back away. "I'll . . . be making
some calls. . . ."

"I'll be in the lab, blowing up frogs."

"Betty," he said reprovingly.

"I'm hoping to work my way up to blowing up other
things. Like alligators."

Bruce stared at her appraisingly. "Okay, now. That was
a joke, wasn't it?"

With a flounce of her hair, Betty said, "Drop by the lab
and find out. You may want to bring your galoshes."

And as she walked away, she heard Bruce mutter behind her, "Galoshes? Who says 'galoshes' anymore?"

She stopped briefly at the snack machine, gave it a
solid punch in exactly the right place, and scooped up a
bag of Doritos. So practiced was she that she barely had
to pause for more than a few moments before continuing

on her way. She nodded to workers as she passed, one of whom pointed at her in congratulations and said, "I heard you killed at the meeting."

"I wish," she said cheerily.

She rounded a corner, and a voice called from behind her that she didn't recognize instantly—but only because she didn't want to.

"Betty," came the voice, "Betty Ross!"

Her mind turned it over and over, refusing to believe it. Slowly she pivoted on her heel and stared. "Glen?" she said.

Sure enough, there was Glen Talbot, almost exactly as Betty remembered him. His face was a bit more full, but it added maturity and even a bit of character to him. His hair had grown out since the army-reg do he had sported back in the days when they were dating, but that canniness in his eyes—and that way he had of taking in the entirety of her with a glance which she found ever so slightly chilling—that was still there. What she was most surprised to see was that he was wearing a sharply styled blue suit, crisp salmon-colored shirt, and what appeared to be—yes, she could see the initials—a Pierre Cardin necktie.

She had no idea what to say, having had no warning that he was going to be showing up, and no clue why he had done so. In many ways, she felt as if no time at all had passed since the last occasion on which she'd seen him, and parted with him, under less than cordial circumstances. That odd sense of "just having seen him," combined with the obvious physical evidence that time had passed was very jarring. The first thing she wanted to say was, "Well, this is awkward," but that hardly seemed like an appropriate opening gambit.

Grasping at conversational straws, she commented, "What happened to your uniform?" She promptly started kicking herself mentally and walked into the lab just to distance herself from him.

Talbot looked surprised, as if she'd come up with a complete non sequitur—which, to a degree, she had. Then, smiling gamely, he stepped back, put his arms out to either side, and turned in a small circle like a model on a runway. That way Betty could admire his sartorial splendor. "I switched over," he said, following her into the laboratory. He glanced around appraisingly. She definitely didn't like the way he was looking things over. It made her want to toss drapes over everything to shield it all from view. "Still work with your dad, but you know, the military's subcontracting out all the most interesting work, and I can't argue with the paycheck. I basically run all the labs on the base now."

She in fact hadn't known that at all. It wasn't as if she chatted regularly with her father—or at all, really. For some reason she suspected that Glen was fully aware of that, but had chosen to appear oblivious to the strained relationship she currently had with her father. In the meantime, acting as if he had just thought to assess her demeanor, he gave her a quick look over and said heartily, "Hey, you're looking good."

Betty inclined her head slightly, acknowledging the compliment. No reason she couldn't be cordial, particularly until she learned just what he wanted. "So," she said, "why are you here?"

But the neutrality of her reaction and the lack of enthusiasm she bore for his sudden reentry into her life were all too evident to Talbot. Voice dripping with sarcasm, he said, "I missed you, too."

"At least you've had my father," said Betty, matching sarcasm for sarcasm. And as with all great sarcasm, there was a very large kernel of raw emotion at its base. The simple fact was that it had never been lost on her just how much old Thunderbolt had doted on Glen Talbot. It was evident in Thunderbolt's attentions and attitudes: Talbot was the son he'd never had.

And that was really the truth of it. Betty had never really fully been able to comprehend it, or even articulate it, for herself back when she had been closer to her father. Now, though, face-to-face with Talbot and possessing the analytical mind of a scientist and an adult, she knew what the real problem was. If Talbot was the son that Thunderbolt never had, what did that make her? Every time she looked at Talbot, she saw in him a symbol of everything she wasn't to her father. No "Y" chromosome. No army career. Talbot was a reminder of what Thunderbolt Ross had genuinely wanted . . . and what he'd been stuck with in return.

None of which was the least bit fair to Glen Talbot. Except Betty didn't give a damn about the fairness. All she cared about was Talbot exiting her life as quickly and unexpectedly as he'd reentered it.

Talbot, meanwhile, was feigning having been struck to the heart by her jibe. "Ouch. You don't waste any time getting back to the old repartee, do you?"

It made her think of the old gag where one guy says. "Why do people take an instant dislike to me?" and another guy responds. "It saves time." The thought made her smile slightly, and then she realized that Talbot might misinterpret her expression and conclude that he was amusing her. So she passed a hand over her mouth, covering the smile and frowning once more.

"You can take it," said Betty.

"That I can," Talbot assured her, not at all nonplussed. "But you're too hard on the old guy. He's a great man. It's an honor to work with him."

It made her want to salute. Or barf. She couldn't decide which. Remembering her train of thought from earlier, she said, "I know. And you're like a son to him. Which makes you," she added with exaggeration, as if it were an afterthought, "something like my brother."

To her surprise and discomfort, he took a step toward her. "Maybe we could make that kissing cousins," said Talbot.

His proximity, his attitude and bearing, all shouted warnings in Betty's head. Her immediate instinct was to back away, but she didn't want to appear afraid of him, no matter how nervous he made her. *Keep it light, keep it light*, went through her head, and sounding as if it meant nothing to her, she said, "Sorry, we tried that and it might lead to inbreeding, and we don't want any of that, do we?"

Talbot appeared to be trying to process what she'd just said in order to determine whether she was serious or not. She was beginning to think that he had comic instincts that made Bruce look like a stand-up comedian in comparison. Then he shrugged, as if dwelling on it was too much effort. "You're the genetics expert," he said, and then added with a barely restrained touch of impatience, "Look, I'm sorry I'm the only guy your father ever approved of. I can't help that, can I? Why don't we start this conversation over? Let's focus on the present, not the past."

He sounded sincere. Damn him. He always sounded sincere. That was how it started. Still, there was no reason to be paranoid, although the common notion was that being paranoid didn't guarantee that someone *isn't* out to get you.

"Sure," said Betty, although she couldn't help but feel that in trying to look relaxed when she was anything but, she just wound up appearing constipated.

"So how's business?" asked Talbot.

She was about to try to make small talk with him, and then realized the whole game-playing thing just wasn't working in the least. Maybe she really should endeavor to emulate Bruce. The man had a poker face that would put Mount Rushmore to shame. Giving up any pretenses, she said flatly, "Spill it. What do you want?"

He smiled ingratiatingly. That alone was enough to make her want to pop him one, but at least the games were over.

"Okay, I'll cut to the chase," he said, taking a step toward her as if they were about to have an intimate chat. "I've been hearing interesting things about what you guys are doing here. This could have some significant applications." His voice suddenly turned wheedling. "How'd you like to come work for Atheon, get paid ten times as much as you now earn, and own a piece of the patents?"

If anyone else on the planet had put forward that offer, Betty might well have turned handsprings and started going over the car ads to find that perfect BMW that she knew was out there waiting for her somewhere. But because it was Glen, there was no hesitation in her response.

"Glen, two words: the door."

And with supernatural timing, the door opened, and Bruce Krenzler was standing in the doorway.

The three of them stared at each other for one of those delightful moments that stretched into eternity. Bruce looked from one to the other, clearly wondering if he was going to be receiving an introduction to the newcomer anytime in the immediate future.

"Bruce Krenzler," Betty said politely, "this is Glen Talbot. I've mentioned him in the past."

"No, you haven't." Bruce reached over and shook Talbot's hand. Obviously his grasp wasn't firm enough for Talbot; he looked down at Bruce's hand and, although he maintained a smile, his eyes looked like those of someone who had just gotten a palm full of dead mackerel.

"Glen," Betty continued, "this is Bruce—"

"Krenzler," said Talbot. "I'm a big fan, Dr. Krenzler. And please, call me Glen. And I should call you—"

"Dr. Krenzler," Bruce replied. "Odd. I wasn't aware that I was in a line of work that generally acquired fans."

If Talbot was annoyed at the offhand rebuff, he didn't show it. With no abatement of enthusiasm, he said, "You've certainly got one here. Your studies on cellular regeneration are groundbreaking."

"Yes, they are." He looked at Betty quizzically. "You've mentioned him?"

"We . . . used to see each other socially," she said as judiciously as she could.

Bruce stared owlishly at Glen, apparently trying to place him, and then he abruptly said, "Oh! Wait. Would this be the 'army clown' you said you dated before you went to college?"

Betty covered her face with her right hand. And the cold look on Talbot's face dropped another twenty degrees.

Meantime Bruce seemed oblivious to it all. "I'm sorry. It's the lack of relevant costume that confused me."

"Well, it's Thursday, and I tend to send my clown costume out so I can have it back nice and clean for the weekend," Glen said gamely. But then, surprisingly—at least to Betty—he smiled, apparently amused by the whole thing. "So my understanding is that you and Betty work together."

"That's right."

"And does she speak for you, as well?"

Bruce stared at him in bemusement. "I like to think I'm capable of speaking for myself, thank you. What would this be about?"

"It's probably my fault, Dr. Krenzler," said Talbot, but even though he was nominally addressing Bruce, he was still looking at Betty. "I spoke with Dr. Ross about Atheon, the outfit that I work for. I don't know that you've heard of us . . ."

"You're being unduly modest . . . or inappropriately coy," Bruce said evenly. "Anyone in just about any field of research has heard of Atheon. However, your exceedingly close ties with the military . . ."

"We don't have close ties with the military, Dr. Krenzler. They have close ties with us—if you see the difference."

"I'm sure it's a great difference to you, Mr. Talbot," said Bruce. "To me, it's a mild semantic hairsplitting, but nothing beyond that."

"That may be, Dr. Krenzler. But if you'd like to hear the point I was trying to make . . ."

"If making it will enable us to get back to work sooner rather than later, I'm all for it," said Bruce.

"The point is I invited Dr. Ross to come work for Atheon . . ."

"Did you?" He looked with raised eyebrows at Betty.

". . . and what I failed to make clear," continued Talbot,

"is that naturally we want you aboard as well. Our investigation indicates that you're an excellent research team. We'd be extremely foolish to even contemplate splitting you up. The offer I made to you, Betty"—he nodded toward her—"applies equally to Dr. Krenzler. And since you've made it quite evident that you have other matters to attend to, I'll leave you to attend to them, since I'm sure Betty can bring you up to speed, Dr. Krenzler."

He put out a hand and Bruce shook it without much enthusiasm. Then he half-bowed to Betty, as if he were a German courtier, pulled out business cards with his name and the Atheon logo printed in bright red and gold, and with a flourish, presented one each to Betty and Bruce. "Betty, you doing anything tonight?"

"Sleeping."

"Alone?"

Bruce saw Betty look at him, but maintained his utterly stoic demeanor. Her lips twitched in annoyance. "You never give up, do you, Glen?"

"What man in his right mind would?" he smiled. "Look, how about a quick dinner tonight, the three of us?"

"I'm not interested, nor is Betty," Bruce said firmly, and instantly realized from the look in Betty's eyes that he had made a mistake. Still, keeping an even keel, he said, "Of course, I could be wrong about that. I don't maintain Dr. Ross's social calendar."

Without hesitation, Betty said to Talbot, "Is Atheon buying?"

"Of course."

"Might be a nice change of pace from junk food grabbed out of a machine, or occasional scoops of ice cream. Paid for by a company that I deplore. It says 'yes' to me."

Bruce knew that the words were deliberately intended to provoke him. He wasn't sure why she was doing it, but he wasn't about to be fazed by it. Instead, he simply shrugged and said, "I imagine it will be stimulating. Enjoy yourselves."

Talbot looked rather surprised for a moment, but he didn't let that distract him from the business at hand. "Well, Betty, how about I pick you up here, say, six?"

"All right," she said. "No point in dismissing new concepts out of hand, I suppose. Right, Bruce?"

He nodded, his expression as stony as ever. And not for the first time, Bruce had the eerie feeling that someone or something else was rooting around just behind his eyeballs, growling in annoyance at the way things were progressing.

He found it oddly disconcerting, and, even more oddly, comforting.

hints of jealousy

The steady squeaking of the wheels on the janitor's cart would have been enough to get on the nerves of just about any other person. But the janitor, unperturbed, pushed his cart steadily down the hallway of the Lawrence Berkeley lab facility, looking neither right nor left. People passed him by and didn't even glance at him, which suited him just fine. He had nothing to say to them, and certainly they had nothing to say to him. As a janitor, he was one of the invisible people. At most someone might nod vaguely in his general direction and then instantly forget they'd seen him at all. That also suited him.

He kept his head down, focusing his attention on the floor and his cart. Every so often he'd raise his head enough to look around, his eyes burning with a frightening intensity. Had anyone looked him square in the eyes, they would have been taken aback, perhaps even frightened. Fortunately, no one did.

He brought his cart to a halt and removed a bucket of water and a mop. He used the same bucket to both soap the mop and also to clean it, so the water within turned an unpleasant shade of gray. He wasn't doing the floor any favors by running his mop over it, but that didn't seem to matter to him.

More people were coming, and he adopted a carefully neutral, distant, and bored look as he began slathering the floor with the dirty water. Several staff members were heading in his direction, but when they saw what he was up to, they headed off down another hallway to keep clear of him.

That was exactly what he wanted. It facilitated his being able to hear the conversations he wanted to hear. Looking apathetic and nonchalant, he ran the mop across the floor as he sidled over to the lab that he knew Bruce Krenzler frequented.

"Excuse me." The female voice so startled him that he almost dropped the mop. He stepped back, keeping his gaze lowered, as that woman—that Dr. Ross—stepped carefully around the wet areas. She had her coat on, and a shoulder bag crammed with reports and such slung over her shoulder.

The janitor kept his gaze fixedly on the floor. He grunted. He didn't like this situation at all. She was noticing him, and it wasn't to his advantage to be noticed. She paused a moment more, and he briefly considered beating her to death with the mop. But he decided that might be a bit of an overreaction.

A fortunate thing he came to that conclusion, too, because she then pulled open the door of the lab and stepped through. It swung shut behind her, obscuring her from view. Obscuring her, but not her voice, nor his.

His . . .

"Mine," muttered the janitor, and he smiled, and his smile was a terrible thing to see.

There had been a little trill of warning in the back of Betty's head when she passed the janitor—as if her subconscious had been reacting to something—but then she just assumed she was, quite properly, being cautious about slipping, and gave it no more thought.

Instead she focused her attention on Bruce, who hadn't even heard her enter. He was working in the imaging room, and things didn't seem to be going well.

She adjusted the bag on her shoulder. She couldn't make up her mind about whether she should feel guilty for going out to dinner with Talbot, or feel foolish for doing so, or feel annoyed with Bruce because she'd agreed to go out with Glen mostly just to try to get some sort of damned reaction out of Bruce . . . and had, once again, failed.

She sighed inwardly, and resigned herself to the fact that things simply were what they were, and there was no use getting herself worked up about it.

"Hey," said Betty, "I'm off."

Bruce nodded. He barely glanced in her direction.

Her shoulders sagged. "You're angry," she said.

"No, I'm not," he told her. He couldn't have been more noncommittal.

"Oh, right," said Betty. "I forgot. You never get angry. Look, Glen may be a jerk, but you may want to think about it. More resources and equipment, less red tape."

"Please," Bruce told her. "I just want to stay focused. On the work. Not profits, military applications, politics. Just the work."

There was no way for her to discern whether he was talking in general terms about the direction of his career, or whether he just wanted her to shut up and get out of the lab so he could pay exclusive attention to what he was working on. But she realized that, either way, it had absolutely nothing to do with any feelings he might have about her going to dinner with Glen Talbot—provided he had any at all. Which, if he was to be believed, he didn't.

She sighed and muttered, "It's stupid," without really realizing that she was speaking loud enough for Bruce to hear her.

"What?" said Bruce, but his response was purely automatic.

"I just wish you'd show even the slightest hint of jealousy," said Betty. Naturally he didn't react. He likely hadn't even heard her. Frustrated, she moved to leave, and then paused. She went over to him and stroked his hair.

"You need a haircut," she said.

For the first time, Bruce actually focused on her. He looked at her hair clinically, as if studying a cell sample. "So do you," he announced. Then he must have realized how somber and serious-minded he sounded, because he actually smiled. Betty smiled back.

"Good night."

He nodded in response to her. She turned and headed for the door, and then she turned back to say something else to him.

He was already gone, deep into his own world. He probably didn't know if she'd left or not . . .

. . . and probably didn't care.

Shaking her head, she walked out of the imaging room, pushing through the door, taking care to do it slowly so as not to collide with the janitor.

She stopped. His back was to her, but something suddenly clicked in her mind. If she hadn't been so preoccupied with thoughts of Bruce, it would have occurred to her earlier. Addressing the custodian's back, she asked, "Hey, um, what happened to Benny? Is he still working the night shift?"

There was a pause, a heavy exhaling of breath, as if forming the words was a vast hardship that the janitor was embarking upon solely to keep her happy. "Benny's dead. I'm the new guy," he said in a voice so distant that he would have rivaled Bruce Krenzler for conveying information with the purest dispassion.

The news about Benny threw her. He had seemed healthy the last time she'd encountered him, always whistling some cheerful tune or other. And just like that, he was gone? "Oh," was all she was able to get out. Then, feeling something else should be said, she added, "Glad to meet you."

"Same."

She might have imagined it, but there was something in his voice that seemed faintly mocking. But she put it out of her mind as she headed out, thinking sad thoughts about Benny and dwelling on the fact that one never knew when one's time would suddenly be up . . .

. . . not realizing that her own time had nearly come up far sooner than she knew.

As the night shadows stretched their fingers across the length and breadth of Bruce's private office, he put down the book that bore strings of results and DNA recombinants that he was certain held the key to wherever they were going wrong. He leaned back in his chair, rubbing the bridge of his nose with his thumb and forefinger. Fatigue was beginning to play upon his mind, and he was starting to think that even if the answer to his frustrations was directly in front of him, he still likely would be too blind to see it.

He let his mind wander, which he was normally loathe to do. In this case, though, it wasn't as if he was using the damned thing for anything especially important. He thought about Betty, about her going out with Talbot, and he found it . . .

Annoying. Yes, that was it. He turned the emotion around, upside down and sideways, studying it from every conceivable angle, and yes, by God, it was annoyance.

Betty would probably have been ecstatic.

But thoughts of Betty in the present drew him, moth to flame, to thoughts of Betty in the past. In spite of himself, he reached into his desk drawer and pulled out the photo of them that the camera on the automatic timer had clicked, back in the cabin.

He stared at the photo, his mind flying back to that ill-advised weekend. They had rushed things, that was all. Tried to push a relationship through when it wasn't quite ready.

And when would it have been ready? When would you have been ready?

The thoughts moved unwanted across his mind. Unwanted because there was nothing that could be done about it, in retrospect. Unwanted because he couldn't help but think he could have done more about it at the time. There was no point in second-guessing his actions or feelings on the matter. They were what they were.

Still, her words came back to him. *You're breaking my heart.* The phrasing bothered him. It seemed to him she was making him out to be some sort of . . . of monster.

He stared long and hard at the photo, the image of two people caught forever on the cusp of a relationship that should have gone in a different direction, but hadn't.

No. No, he wasn't a monster. But maybe, he thought ruefully, he was an idiot.

Bruce put down the photo, picked up his bag, and left his office. He walked into the main hallway. It was deserted, a few lights on, some evening light drifting in. The soles of his shoes squeaked on the newly cleaned floor. He almost slipped at one point, but righted himself at the last moment.

Then he heard a whimper from around a corner. Puzzled, Bruce walked toward the sound and heard more whimpering. He turned the corner. A small, mangy poodle sat in the middle of the hallway, alone. He couldn't remember the last time he'd seen something quite that pathetic-looking.

Bruce walked toward the creature slowly, hand out. "Hey there," he said softly, encouragingly, "who are you?" He glanced around, trying to see if there was an owner anywhere nearby. No one came to his attention.

The dog, meantime, continued to stare up at him, its tail was wagging, although Bruce was having trouble remembering whether that meant a dog was friendly or tense. He'd read articles that went both ways. Its tongue was hanging out, its eyes bright.

He reached toward the poodle to pet it. Suddenly, it bared its teeth, growling and snapping. The teeth were rotting in the creature's head, and Bruce jumped back, yanking his hand away before it wound up snagged in that deteriorating jaw.

"Okay, okay!" he said, backing away. Once more he looked around, hoping to catch a glimpse of whoever might own this miniature hound of the Baskervilles, but still no one was showing up to claim the thing. He continued to back away, returning his gaze to the animal, concerned that it was going to follow him, maybe try to take a piece out of his leg. But the dog just stood there, growling at him warningly, and Bruce couldn't help but feel that he'd just had a very close call.

He emerged from the building. The sky was cloudless, the full moon hanging there like a great unblinking eye. He wondered if perhaps that didn't explain it; there was a werepoodle wandering the premises. It certainly made as much sense as anything else. Suddenly the thought occurred to him that perhaps there was some sort of pack of wild dogs wandering the area. It had to be a pack, didn't it? That was how they always traveled.

Quickly Bruce made his way over to the bike rack, keeping a watchful eye on the shadows of the buildings surrounding him. Despite the light from the moon, the darkness seemed to distend all around . . . and for no reason that he could really fathom, or at least for no reason that he wanted to, that distending brought with it associations that chilled him. He pushed them away from him as he saw a burly security guard entering the building. Between the presence of the guard and the proximity of his bicycle, now only a few feet away, he felt a swell of relief.

"Hey," he called, "there's a poodle in there . . ." and immediately realized exactly how asinine that sounded.

Obviously it wasn't lost on the guard, who gave him a look that seemed to say, *God save me from these oddball scientists*. As if addressing a child, or a moron, or a moron child, the guard replied, "A poodle. Sure. Yeah, we'll look into it."

Feeling like an utter moron—not an easy feat for someone with an IQ of 187—Bruce Krenzler climbed aboard his bike and sped off for home.

The janitor smiled as he slid the all-purpose skeleton key into the lock, and turned it with a satisfying click. As he did so, he imagined the key being a knife, and the lock being the bosom of one Dr. Betty Ross.

He could have strangled her. He had planned it so carefully, so very carefully. Benny the janitor had hardly been a twin for him, but there had been a casual enough resemblance that the janitor had been able to exploit it. A dyeing of his hair, some artful makeup had been sufficient. A casual glance between his face and his photo ID—the ID of the late Benny Goodman—would attract no attention.

Thus far it had worked. The guard at the front hadn't given him a second glance as the ID with the magnetic strip had gotten him into the facility. Once inside, he'd gone straight to the custodial closet, gotten the equipment, and proceeded to do his job. Again he had done so and garnered no notice. Why should he? He was just a janitor, a lowly worker, whose face didn't register on anyone.

And then there had been that damned Ross woman.

Bitch.

He should have snapped her neck when he'd had the chance.

Expect her to know the name of the custodian. Expect her to be paying attention. His presence was due entirely to the fact that no one knew Benny was dead. If Ross started poking around, asking questions, things could get ugly. He hoped it didn't come to that. If it did come to that, he hoped he'd have the opportunity to make her pay for inconveniencing him.

Perhaps a knife right into her, as he was imagining now. Or . . . something more creative. That was also an option. And the thing to remember was that she obviously cared about people; if she hadn't, she'd never have noticed that

Benny wasn't pushing a mop around. She hadn't spotted it the first time around, but the second time . . .

Well. Just a matter of trying to put the right spin on the situation. Rather than concerning himself with being discovered, the janitor instead decided to file away his knowledge of Ross's obvious concern for people in general and, obviously, for Bruce Krenzler in particular. That could be of great use later on, if it came down to it.

And speaking of things of use . . .

Like a passing shade, the janitor entered Bruce's office. At first he was going to leave it dark, but then he realized there was no point in doing so. He was, after all, supposed to be there. If he was cleaning up in blackness that was illuminated only by moonlight, that might attract attention. He reached over and flicked on the light, squinting slightly against the brightness.

He looked around quickly, not wasting any time. He picked up the wastebasket, examined it, grunted in annoyance, and emptied it into his cart. Then he continued to survey the office, his eyes narrowing, as direct and piercing as a laser. It didn't take him long at all to spot what he was looking for. Carefully, delicately, he ran his hand along the office chair, found a hair, and picked it up, holding it up to the light.

He smiled. He didn't do it often, and it wasn't a pretty sight.

Bruce wasn't around to see the janitor and assess his smile one way or the other. Instead he was speeding along on his bicycle, zipping down one of the Berkeley hills, a brisk breeze blowing in his face and whipping his hair back. He completed the angle down the hill and rode the momentum, going up as much as he could before he started putting muscle into it. It wasn't long before the strain started taking a toll on him, however. As he huffed and puffed his way up the hill toward his home, he started to wonder whether his hope for building up muscle and endurance was a pipe dream. Perhaps he was just one of those people who, no matter what they did, were never able to build themselves up. He might just be genetically doomed to a life of being puny Krenzler.

said of old soldiers

Thaddeus "Thunderbolt" Ross was starting to feel his age.

It annoyed the hell out of him. No one had a more demanding, more rigorous schedule of physical fitness than he. Jogging, weights, martial arts. He did so much to maintain his condition that he'd almost come to believe that he was entitled to some sort of immunity against the stresses of age, out of sheer consideration for his efforts.

God in heaven, however, didn't seem to agree.

That was doubtless the reason why he felt his eyes starting to ache as he worked into the early evening. Not only that, but he had to stand every so often and stretch his legs, because he could feel them cramping up on him. Leg cramps, aching eyes. He was starting to get genuinely angry with his body, feeling it was betraying him and not working in his best interests. He sat back in his chair, stretched his legs again, and wondered if he could have his body court-martialed for dereliction of duty.

One of his aides, Lieber, entered with a folder. Lieber had on a grim expression, which instantly caught Ross's attention, because Lieber had a fairly good sense of what was and wasn't going to irritate Ross on any given day. He definitely had his "Ross is going to be pissed off" face on.

Ross promptly leaned back in his chair, his face a question mark. "General," said the aide, "Talbot wanted you to see this. It's about a lab Atheon is targeting for acquisition and removal to Desert Base."

"Why isn't he going through NSC?" asked Ross.

Lieber cleared his throat. "It, uh, concerns your daughter, sir."

"My daughter?" That response wasn't remotely what Ross had expected. He took the folder and started to flip through it cautiously, as if concerned that something might leap out at him.

And then his face darkened to storm-cloud intensity, thereby confirming the aptness of his nickname.

"Find Talbot," he growled.

"So how do you find me after all this time?" asked Talbot.

Betty sat across from him at their table at the French restaurant Chez Robin, idly fiddling with the escargots and wondering what in God's name had possessed her to order them. Several tables over, a violinist was leaning in toward a young couple. The girl was smiling with perfect teeth as the violinist's bow moved deftly over the violin's strings, while her young escort was trying to check subtly through his pockets to see if he had a few bucks to give the guy for a tip. For some reason Betty considered the entire scene to be remarkably funny. She glanced over at Glen, realizing he had addressed her, and imagined he was Bruce as she said, "I'm sorry. What?"

He took a long sip of the wine they'd ordered, but never took his eyes off her. She had to admit the ambience of the place was really quite nice. "I asked you what you thought of me," he repeated.

She had to laugh at that. "I'll give you credit, Glen," she said, putting down the tiny utensil she was using to prize a snail from its shell and writing off the snails as an experiment that just hadn't panned out. "Most guys wouldn't be foolish enough to ask the woman sitting in front of them what she thought of them. But not you. You go right for the old, 'But enough about me, let's talk about you. What do you think of me?' ploy. That's a sure winner."

"I wasn't trying to 'win' you in any way, Betty," he said. The flickering candle from the centerpiece was reflected in his eyes and, for some reason, creeped her out. "I was, at most, hoping to acquire the talents of both you and Bruce for Atheon. I mean"—and he took another sip, then leaned back—"does part of me wish that it had worked out differently for you and me? Yes, of course. But I'm not one for belaboring the past or wishing I could rewrite it. What's done is done. I care only about the future . . . as does Atheon."

At that moment, a pager went off. Betty reflexively checked hers, but Talbot was already pulling his out from his jacket pocket, looking apologetic as he did so. He glanced at the number, sighed, and said, "Excuse me. I'll be right back."

"Do you need a phone?"

"No, I have a cell phone. I just never give the number out; only the pager's. Besides, I hate it when people sit at tables in restaurants and chatter away on cell phones, don't you?"

"I've never given it any thought," she replied.

He got up and hastened quickly to find a place where he could have some privacy. Betty watched him go, and then noticed that the middle-aged man sitting at the next table was laughing and speaking far too loudly on his cell phone. "Hey," she snapped at him, "could you keep it down? Do you have any idea how annoying that is?"

In response, the man flipped her an obscene gesture, angled himself so that his back was to her, and kept right on talking. She considered pouring her glass of wine over his head, but decided that would be gauche.

It seemed long minutes passed before Talbot finally returned. Betty looked up at him, and he seemed a bit put out. "Problem?" she asked.

"Oh, no. No," he replied, "nothing I can't handle. Actually, I got a message from someone who might interest you."

"Really." She neither felt nor sounded interested.

"Yes. Your father. He wants to chat."

Betty almost knocked over her drink. She caught the glass of wine just before it spilled all over the pristine white tablecloth. She was quite aware that Glen was trying to hide a smirk resulting from her reaction and wasn't quite doing a good job of it. "Oh, he does. How nice for you both. He hasn't wanted to chat with *me* in quite some time."

"Would you have listened, or wanted to, if he had?"

The question was a bit too pointed for her taste. She scowled as she said, "I don't see how that's any of your business, Glen."

"You're right. You're very right." He leaned forward. "You're my business, Betty. You and Bruce."

"Which one of us are you more interested in?" she asked.

He smiled. "I just want what's best for you, Betty. I always have. When you were younger, I don't think you really understood that. But now that we're both older and wiser, perhaps you do."

"You know what the funny thing is, Glen? Some people grow older, but not wiser."

"That's very true."

"So—" She swirled the liquid around in her glass. "Just what does my father want to 'chat' with you about?"

"Why, Betty," said Glen, as if he were pouncing on an opening, "I don't see that's any of your business."

She grimaced slightly, then nodded and said, "Touché, Glen. Touché."

The violinist was suddenly playing in her ear. She turned, gave him a look that would have ignited tungsten, and said in a voice dripping with honey, "If you don't move away, I'm going to shove that bow so far up your—"

He moved away.

"That's what I've always loved about you, Betty," said Talbot, raising his glass in a toast. "You always know just what to say, on any occasion."

The rest of the dinner went more or less as Glen Talbot anticipated it would, which was unfortunate but not unexpected. Betty made polite chitchat, was noncommittal about the notion of moving to Atheon, and was obviously fighting to restrain herself from asking about her father.

Glen shook his head in mute astonishment. It didn't matter how bright a woman was, or at least thought she was: They were all still very much the same, and all still very predictable, no matter how much they fancied they were mysteries to men. Well, to some men, they were. But he had solved the mystery long ago, and knew just what to say and just how to say it.

Betty declined his offer to take her home. That was acceptable to Talbot, since he had accomplished everything he needed to. He knew that originally she had rejected Atheon out of hand; now she wasn't so sure. And she was going to push that uncertainty onto Krenzler, which was exactly what Talbot wanted. And Glen Talbot was very much in the habit of getting what he wanted.

Arriving home at his apartment building, Glen pulled into his reserved space and killed the engine. He stepped out of the car, paused a moment, then suddenly reached into his jacket and pulled out a sleek blue metal Smith & Wesson. He turned and aimed it straight at a shadowy figure that had been approaching him, and now froze in its tracks.

Then he squinted into the darkness and lowered the gun, speaking in a voice as convivial as if he were encountering an old friend by chance while strolling the boardwalk in Atlantic City. "Agent Krenzler, as I live and breathe . . ."

"And as I almost didn't," replied Krenzler. She stepped from the shadows into the pool of light emanating from the overhead lamp. Her face looked a bit more careworn than when her adoptive son, Bruce, had last seen her. "A little trigger-happy these days, aren't you, Mr. Talbot?"

"One can't be too careful, Monica. There are monsters everywhere." He slid the gun back into his shoulder holster and draped his jacket over it. "So what are you doing in Berkeley? Have you been reassigned?"

"No. No, merely passing through. I just—" She cleared her throat, then came closer to him. Her hands seemed to be moving in vague patterns. "I just . . . was wondering how Bruce was doing."

"How would I know?" replied Talbot.

Her face hardened. "Mr. Talbot, don't treat me like I'm

an idiot. I know about the listening posts. I know you have his movements monitored 24-7. I know what you want of him. If Bruce gets so much as a toothache, you know about it before he calls his dentist."

"Well, tell me, Monica, if you're so anxious to find out what Bruce is up to, why not just go stop by and see him yourself? Or give him a buzz? You know he'd always like to hear from dear old Mummy."

"You know why not," she said tonelessly.

He smiled a wolfish smile at that. "I've no idea . . . oh! Wait! Perhaps it has something to do with your superiors feeling that you'd gotten too close to your assignment."

"My assignment." Monica Krenzler acted as if those were the funniest words ever spoken, except the humor involved was bleak and depressing. "You try it sometime, Mr. Talbot. You try being 'assigned' to be the adoptive mother of a child by a government organization that keeps waiting for the child to manifest some sort of . . . of aberrant behavior on a genetic level. You try caring for him, supporting him, steering him in career and life directions that are mandated not by what you feel is best for him, but by superiors who have their own agendas for him. You try doing all that without getting 'too close' and see just how successful you are."

"I just might," Talbot said without a trace of sarcasm. "It sounds like a stimulating intellectual exercise." Then he took a few steps toward her, until he was almost in her face. "You've got to learn when to let an assignment go, Monica. It's over. He's not your problem anymore. He's mine."

"His whole life has been one of having his fate determined by others acting behind his back," Monica said, her simmering anger almost boiling over. "When does he get his own life?"

"When do *any* of us?" Talbot asked reasonably. "Many people will tell you that their lives are guided and determined by God."

"You and your people aren't God," Monica told him.

Talbot's smile widened. "As far as your adoptive son is concerned, Monica, we're God, Satan, heaven, and hell all rolled into one." He started to reach up to pat her on the cheek in a patronizing fashion, but she brushed the hand away with a quick movement and simply glared. "Have a good career, Agent Krenzler," he said, and then walked off, leaving her smoldering in the parking lot.

He continued to chuckle to himself as he went up to his apartment. But instead of entering, he turned and, producing a key, entered the apartment next door to his. It was dimly lit and he saw an assortment of electronic equipment off to one side. There were boxes from pizza delivery and Chinese restaurants scattered about. There was no sign of anyone around. He called out softly, "Sitwell?"

There was the sound of a toilet flushing and moments later, a thin, blond man with oversize glasses emerged, tucking in his shirt. "Nature calls to us all," he said apologetically. "How was dinner?"

"More or less as I expected it."

Sitwell grunted as he returned to the array of electronics and slapped a pair of earphones over his head. Apparently reading Talbot's mind, he said, "Don't worry, I had a recorder going just in case anything interesting happens with Bruce. Although nothing ever seems to."

"Is he at home now?"

"A-yuh. But he's not doing much of anything. No

phone calls. No company. Typically ripping night at the Krenzler household. Or should we call him Banner?" Sitwell asked with an eyebrow raised.

"Whatever," said Talbot, shrugging. "And, yeah, I know he's not the most exciting guy in the world. Why do you think I worked so hard to get Betty into his life? Made sure she was offered a job at the same lab Banner was working at. Pulled strings to guarantee she was assigned to work with him. I practically did everything I could short of passing notes for them in study hall."

With a bitter laugh, Sitwell said, "They pay me to listen in on people, Mr. Talbot, not to figure out why people do what they do. So I never gave it much thought."

"It's very simple," Talbot told him. "We want to see what happens if Banner gets upset, as per the files his father kept on him. But Brucie keeps himself wrapped too tight. So we needed someone to get under his skin to get to him. And believe me, Sitwell, nobody, but nobody, can get under your skin quite like Betty Ross."

"I'll kill her," growled Thunderbolt Ross, pacing his office. "No, on second thought, I'll kill Talbot. No, on third thought, I'll kill both of them. Save me time."

Lieber stood there and watched the general move from one side of the office to the other without breaking stride. "Begging the general's pardon, but why is Atheon's interest in Lawrence Berkeley labs in any way the fault of the general's daughter?"

"Because Atheon's up to something, Lieber," Ross said sharply. "Supposedly we all work for the same people, but something's going on. I know it. And I'm having trouble thinking about it dispassionately because my daughter's involved. If she hadn't gone to work for those damned people, I wouldn't have this problem!"

"But didn't she used to date Talbot? Wouldn't it be worse if she were married to him by now?"

Ross glared at him. "I don't recall asking you to provide worst-case scenarios, Lieber. Dismissed." Lieber tossed off a salute, which Ross quickly returned, and then quickly departed the office, leaving Ross to stew in his own annoyance and frustration.

Well, at least Talbot would be along shortly, and perhaps they could get this whole thing cleared up. Because if they didn't, then there would be hell to pay, and Thunderbolt Ross intended to be standing there collecting the tolls.

in dreams, the knowledge he seeks are memories he cannot grasp

Once Bruce Krenzler reached his house, he parked his bike and limped inside. He considered sliding into a bath and soaking his aching legs, but his mind couldn't stop racing. He knew in a vague way that he was hungry, and the only reason he became at all aware that he had made himself dinner was because at one point—while tending a small Zen moss garden atop his makeshift desk—he suddenly realized that his stomach was full.

He put down the gardening tools, walked into the kitchen, and found an empty tray from a frozen dinner in the garbage can. Granted, a frozen dinner wasn't the most memorable of suppers, but even so he couldn't help but think he shouldn't be so much in a world of his own that he would completely forget making and eating dinner within moments of having done so.

Then, as problems he'd been having with an equation suddenly presented themselves with possible answers, he pushed thoughts of his absentmindedness out of his brain. Within five minutes, he was back to wondering why he was no longer hungry, but was so busy scribbling figures, calculations, sketches, and DNA sequences onto scratch pads that he stopped thinking about it altogether.

After a while Bruce got up and stretched, scratching

absently under his chin and wondering how long he'd been working. He'd gotten home around seven or so, and been at it . . . what? An hour? Two at most? He glanced at a clock, rubbed his eyes in order to clear them, and looked again. And the clock said the same time it had an instant before: 2:27 A.M., the numbers and letters of the digital readout glowing in the dimness.

Had time flown by that quickly? Was it possible?

Well, it didn't really matter if it was possible or not; it had, so there was no point in debating the possibilities of it. He stretched his arms, yawned, shook out the cramped muscles of his legs, and moved to the window.

One of the things Bruce had gotten used to about himself—indeed, one of his strengths as a scientist—was his ability to see patterns in everything around him. Sometimes they were utterly pointless: mundane digits in a checking account number that recombined, or sequences of letters drawn from various sources that spelled out something. At other times the result would be sudden bursts of insight that invariably led to a flurry of activity that might or might not lead to a new and even more interesting breakthrough. Betty likened the ability to that of the protagonist from that movie about the mathematician who developed psychotic behavior, a comparison that didn't exactly thrill Bruce.

So it didn't surprise Bruce at all when, while staring out at a willow tree illuminated by a street lamp, the shadows and branches of the tree seemed to form an intricate latticework of shapes and patterns. It was like nature was giving him a Rorschach inkblot test. The shapes kept changing as the wind blew: one moment they were octopus tentacles writhing through a sea of air, now they were long fingers interlacing like the hands of a silent film vil-

lain, who was rubbing his hands together in gleeful antic-
ipation of his malevolent plan reaching fruition.

And now they looked like a stairway, and now they
looked like two interlocking faces of . . . of . . .

He stared and stared, and continued to stare, and even
though the branches moved a dozen times more, the
image they had formed just a bit earlier remained in
Bruce's brain, frozen there like a gray-cell snapshot. Two
faces, ensnared in each other, but they weren't human
faces. They were like—like a pair of animals. Animals
that were . . .

An association floated through his mind, and almost
escaped unmolested, but then he snagged it and pulled it
down to him, and the thought came to him: *stuffed toys*.

Yes. That was it. The shadow imagery had born a resemblance to a couple of stuffed toys. But what kind
of toys they were precisely, and whose they were, he
couldn't say. He suspected, for no particular reason, that
they were his. But he didn't know when he had received
them and, more important, from whom.

Then he blinked, and partially turned away, only to
snap his head back and look again, for Bruce was sure
that he had seen something else that was most definitely
not a shadow. It was a figure, standing tall, shoulders
squared, and—*could I be anymore melodramatic?*—
radiating an aura of menace.

But when Bruce focused his full attention on the spot,
he saw nothing save the waving branches.

Perhaps there had never been a man there. It might have
been nothing more than his sleep-deprived mind adding
yet more shapes to the wavering shadows of the decep-
tive willow. It was certainly a supposition preferable to the

idea that someone was lurking about in the shadows at 2:30 in the morning, watching him . . .

Half past two in the morning. God Almighty.

"I've got to get some sleep," he said to no one in particular, perhaps as much to convince himself of the necessity of it as anything else. As if to underscore for him just how tired he was, it seemed that an instant later that he had tossed on his nightclothes and climbed into bed. He didn't remember the action at all. He felt as if his entire being was fading out and in, as if some of his actions were attributable to another person entirely. Which was, of course, ridiculous.

He decided to be pragmatic about it: If this were indeed the case, certainly this "other person" was benign enough if the worst he was doing was getting Bruce's pajamas on for him.

Bruce pulled the sheet up, flopped onto his back . . . and lay there.

And lay there.

He stared at the ceiling for some time until he began to count the holes in the tiles, at which point he flipped himself over and mashed his head sideways into the pillow. And as he lay there, he slowly became aware that he could hear his own heart beating, or perhaps it was just his pulse, but either way it was there, just thudding, thudding, thudding along, and he started to wonder if by picturing Betty naked he could get his heart rate to increase, and if so, how fast could a person make his heart beat through sheer willpower, and was it perhaps possible to create an entire aerobics program designed around messages or even images that would be fed directly into the brain while the subject slept, causing the . . .

He turned over onto his side, curling his legs up and up

until he was almost in a fetal position, and wasn't it interesting how many descriptions of ideas derived terms from reproduction, ranging from an embryonic idea to a notion that arrived stillborn.

Bruce looked at his clock.

It was 3:30.

He knew he hadn't slept. His mind had continued to career from one notion to the next. Perhaps . . . perhaps what he needed to do was just tire out his eyes. Yes, that might work. Clinging to that forlorn hope, he sat up and started pulling out a couple of sheets of data from the nightstand. He didn't even turn on the table lamp, instead preferring to work by the light of the moon. That seemed the ideal way to hasten the ocular exhaustion process.

In a few minutes, more data sheets joined the others, and within an hour the bed was covered with them. It seemed to Bruce that the only noise existing in the entirety of the world at that very instant was the insistent scratching of his pencil upon the pad—and unfortunately the noise was starting to annoy the hell out of him.

"Damn," he said and threw the pencil down, and decided, *All right, fine.* First he had tried to sleep, and then he had endeavored to trick himself into sleeping. There was only one thing left to do: stay awake.

So he simply sat there in bed, staring at his reflection in the screen of the television that was perched on the dresser opposite him. He was just going to wait until the sun came up and start the new day. There was nothing else for it.

He continued to sit there, fighting to stay awake, and naturally by the time the glowing numbers of the digital clock read 4:48, his eyes were fluttering closed. Reality and fantasy blurred for him and he *heard the haunting,*

*echoing sound of footsteps and a dog whimpering some-
where, and a small boy, four years old, played with a pair
of stuffed toys with long beaks, floppy ears, and oversize
feet, and his little voice squealed in innocent joy as he
lifted the toys into the air before crashing them back down
to Earth, and he continued to make noises, small shouts
of surprise coupled with his own sound effects of crashes
and skids, and as he moved the toys about they took on
lives not exactly of their own, but like aspects of his life,
and they started to move ever so slightly, winking and
nodding and smiling, and then they frowned because they,
along with Bruce, heard voices, adult, human voices, a
man and the woman in the background, but he couldn't
make out what they were saying, only that their voices
were raised to a fever pitch, and there was yelling, and
an unearthly, primal scream emerged from the boy's
mouth . . .*

And Bruce was up, out of bed, as if warned by some
inner system that bordered on the supernatural. Without
understanding why, he moved to the window, and the figure was back again.

It must have rained lightly in the intervening time, because a fog had settled over the area. Even through the
mist, though, he could see that the man appeared to be
standing a little taller, looking even a bit stronger, as if—
fanciful and ludicrous as it sounded—he had drawn some
sort of demonic psychic strength from the inner torment
rampaging through Bruce's sleeping mind.

You're losing it, thought Bruce, and he slammed the
blinds closed. *You are a rational man, a man of science,
and if there's some freak out there casing your house, you
confront him on it or call the police, but you don't start
concocting demented notions of psychic vampires.* He

took several deep breaths to cleanse his mind and his soul, and then peered out through the blinds once more, separating the metal slats with his left hand while, with his right, he reached for the telephone in order to call the police.

The mists were swirling and undulating outside as if they were themselves sentient, and in the fog, walking away, he caught a glimpse of the man once more, surrounded by three dogs of varying sizes. For half a heartbeat, Bruce thought one of them might have been that poodle he'd seen back at the lab. Or it could just have been a small dog. Whatever it was, an instant later it, along with the other two dogs and their master, had been swallowed up by the fog and were gone.

A man walking his dogs.

Bruce Krenzler, doctor, scientist, brilliant theoretician, had allowed himself to be spooked out by a bad dream and a guy taking his mutts for an early morning walk.

He wondered what in the world Betty would have thought of such a thing . . . and that turned his thoughts to Betty and to Talbot, which irked him.

So Bruce climbed back into bed, curled up with the utter conviction that attempting to get any sleep tonight was a complete waste of time . . . and promptly fell into a deep, dreamless slumber.

The dog walker unlocked a padlock on the gate of a chain-link fence in front of the small weedy yard of a run-down row house. The dogs ran in ahead of him, snapping and growling in low, unpleasant tones. Then they turned and looked at him expectantly, with an air that seemed to indicate they'd just as soon devour him as anything else if they weren't sated. But he was prepared; he knew his babies all too well. He reached into his coat and pulled out strips and chunks of meat and old vegetables from a bag that had been sealed to prevent the dogs from smelling its contents, and tossed the food to them. They snapped it up immediately, fighting with each other over the scraps that fell to the ground unclaimed. As the three canines—a mastiff, a pit bull, and a poodle with rotting teeth—busied themselves, the dog walker unlocked the padlock and entered the ramshackle house that sat like a pustule upon the face of the neighborhood. It also happened to have once belonged to Benny Goodman; it was amazing how quickly a home could go downhill.

The interior was illuminated by light from a single bulb hanging from a bare wire in the ceiling. To call the interior furnishings decor would have been an insult to the French language. There had been other furniture there before, but the dog walker had gotten rid of it all. It had borne a passing resemblance to furnishings from another time in his life, and he had no desire to be reminded of it. All that remained was a sagging, stained mattress in one corner, and on the opposite side of the room a long worn table, with stacks of papers, books, journals, and a small work area. The dog walker removed his overcoat and tossed it on a pile of clothing off to one side that included his janitor's uniform, then went to the workstation and shoved a pile of material to one side. This revealed a gleaming, superthin notebook computer.

David Banner opened the screen, pressed a button, and sat down. The light from the screen illuminated his face, causing him to resemble a grinning Halloween jack-o'-lantern. On the wall behind the computer screen was a bulletin board filled with images and clippings: various scenes from Bruce Banner's career, as well as yearbook and graduation photos.

Banner sat there for a moment, pensive, taut as piano wire, looking as if he wanted to explode out of his skin with the urgency of his many pent-up desires. Then he raised a hand and touched one of the photos.

"Bruce," he said softly, "my Bruce."

He pulled open a drawer and removed from it a small container in which a hair had been soaking in a specially designed solution. Banner held it up, his eyes narrowing as he studied it, and then grinned approvingly with a smile that would have chilled any onlooker. He placed the container down, twisted off the top, and then used a pair of tweezers to deftly remove the hair from the solution. It would have been an impressive display for anyone watching, who would likely have assumed from appearances that the old man with the graying hair and the wild-eyed look was a burned-out alcoholic who couldn't keep his hand steady if his next drink depended upon it.

Not in this case, though. There was no hesitation to his movements as, with practiced confidence, he placed the hair onto a glass plate and chopped it into tiny pieces with a razor.

He then pulled out a small test tube from a nearby rack. The tube was filled partway with a milky substance, and he dropped several pieces of the hair into it, saving the rest for possible future use.

He allowed them to soak for a few moments, then put the test tube inside a device that he called a DNA splitter. It had taken him ages to develop it from assorted parts he'd been able to scrounge, but its crude and humble roots didn't limit his confidence that it would work. He checked the connections to his computer to make certain it was plugged into the correct data port, and then turned on the splitter. The apparatus hummed and vibrated. A wire ran to the superthin notebook computer.

The night was still save for his tapping upon the keyboard, and the occasional sound of dogs snarling outside.

accident . . . or fate?

Bruce Krenzler was reminded of the old gag about the elderly man complaining that when he was a kid, his life had been so harsh that he had to make a five-mile journey to school that was uphill both ways. It was a cute joke, but a lot less amusing to him now, considering that the bike ride he undertook to get *to* work was no less daunting than the one *from* work, since he did indeed have to go uphill once again in order to get there. Granted, it was a different uphill, but his legs didn't know or care about the difference.

And because he hadn't slept particularly well, his endurance wasn't exactly up to snuff. By the time he made it to the lab, he'd developed a stiff pain in his right rib cage and felt as if the very act of taking a breath was a huge hardship. He parked the bike, locked it, then stood for a few minutes pulling himself together.

When he entered the lab, he saw something that didn't exactly cause his heart to take flight. There were Talbot and Betty, talking and appearing to be awfully damned chummy. He wondered, not for the first time, just how late their casual dinner had gone. Not that it was any of his business, of course, but still . . .

"Bruce," said Betty, "Glen stopped by—"

"What's he doing here?" Bruce blurted out, and promptly hated the way that sounded. So accusatory, so . . . juvenile. But he couldn't help himself.

. . . And why should *you help yourself? . . .* The voice within was bubbling with barely restrained anger and resentment. *She likely keeps comparing you to him. She probably thinks he's superior to you because he lets himself get worked up over every damned thing or another, whereas you, the adult, you keep control of yourself . . . and she resents you. Is that fair? It most certainly is not. Why do you tolerate it? And why in the world do you tolerate him? He has no business here. . . .*

"You know, Dr. Krenzler, we've never had the chance to get to know each other properly," said Glen affably.

Bruce felt a pounding behind his eyes. . . . *Leave. Make him leave. Show him who's boss in this facility. This is your place, not his. Make him leave . . .*

"That's because I don't want to get to know you, properly or improperly. Leave," Bruce said with a great formality that was in sharp contrast to the rage he kept buried within.

He could see from Betty's expression that she was startled by the sharpness of his tone. "Bruce . . ." she began.

. . . Now. Now, damn it. Make him leave now . . .

"Now," said Bruce.

Talbot didn't look the least put out. "Hey, no worries," he said, affecting a faux Australian accent that he doubtlessly thought was clever. He approached the doorway where Bruce had been standing like a statue. Bruce moved slightly to allow Talbot room to pass, and then Talbot turned so that they were almost nose-to-nose, safely out of Betty's hearing. He kept a smile plastered on his face, this self-proclaimed "big fan" of Bruce Krenzler, but he spoke in a rush, the words tumbling one over the other as he said in a low voice, "But let me give you a little heads up. There's a hairbreadth between a friendly offer and a hostile takeover. . . . *Kill him* . . . I've done my homework. The stuff you're doing here is dynamite. . . . *Smash his face in. Smash him* . . . Think: GI's embedded with technology that makes them instantly repairable on the battlefield, in our sole possession. That's a hell of a business." . . . *Puny bastard. Show him who's in charge. Smash him, destroy him, rip him limb from* . . .

With Herculean mental effort, Bruce resisted the insistent voice that rattled through his mind with such force that it almost made him strike out at Talbot, even though Talbot would likely have been able to break him in half. "That's not what we're doing here," said Banner, focusing with effort. "We're doing the basic science, for everyone—"

Talbot shook his head. He acted as if he were looking at some form of lower organism instead of one of the most well-established and respected researchers on the West Coast. "You know," he mused, "I'm going to write a book. I'm going to call it 'When Stupid Ideals Happen to Smart, Penniless Scientists.'. . . *You don't have to take that! Smash him! Now! Put your damned fist through his face, you pathetic loser!* . . . In the meantime, Bruce, you'll be hearing from me." . . . *And you'll be hearing from me, you vomitous little slug!* . . .

He felt a slight pain in his right arm and took several deep breaths, calming himself. Although he wasn't certain why, he was convinced that if he didn't do so, there would be a good deal more pain, and . . . and far worse things. Far worse. His vision clouded over for a moment, as if he were fighting a massive migraine. When it cleared, Talbot was gone . . . and Betty was in his field of vision, staring at him with a mixture of confusion and amazement.

"That went well, don't you think?" he said, slapped his hands together briskly, and added, "Who's for making history today?"

The helicopter was waiting for Talbot at the small, private airport, just as General Ross had said it would be. A soldier was standing there waiting for him. Talbot saluted him, snapping off the kind of professional gesture that indicated an army man, even if he was clad in civilian garb. *You can take the man out of the army*, thought Talbot as he clambered into the chopper.

The pilot nodded to him, indicated that Talbot should strap in, and, the moment that was done, the blade speed increased and the chopper rose skyward. Moments later it was angling off toward Desert Base. Talbot knew that Thunderbolt Ross was angry. That didn't bother Talbot at all. He knew the old man all too well, and knew how to manipulate him as easily as he did anyone else. Ross had his agenda and Talbot had his, and Talbot knew whose was going to come out on top.

Betty couldn't believe that she was jealous of Glen Talbot *again*, but apparently such was the case. Not enough that she felt he had more of a connection with her father than she did. Now she was confronted with the fact that, in all her time, all her involvement with Bruce, he had always remained on such an infuriatingly even keel that she often wondered if he were fully human. Yet here, after merely his second meeting with Talbot, Bruce had almost looked ready to punch the guy in the face. Not that she had any doubts about who would win a fistfight. Glen Talbot, civilian or no, was trained in combat and self-defense. Bruce Krenzler was trained in science and the arts. If it came to a witty repartee contest, or a competition to name all the elements on the periodic table, Bruce was a lock. Hand-to-hand, it was a very different story.

In any event, as ludicrous as it seemed, she was a bit envious that Glen Talbot was able to inspire such emotional reactions from Bruce when she herself could only prompt passive detachment at best.

She tried to put it from her mind as she made preparations for the next experiment. A new frog—named Rick by the hopelessly attached Harper—sat in the gammasphere place of honor that had seen so many of his brethren go *splat*. The readings were steady. She glanced across the room at Bruce, and saw that he was totally focused. . . .

No. No, he wasn't. He seemed distracted, and kept glancing toward the door that Talbot had left through. Betty didn't need to be a mind reader to see just what, or who, Bruce was concerned about. She didn't just want to let it hang there. She cared about Bruce too much. Plus, having one's head scientist not paying attention to what was going on in such a delicate environment could lead to fairly nasty consequences.

Still, maybe there wasn't time . . .

Then the time factor became moot as Harper, at his monitoring station, called out, "Okay, fifteen seconds. We're set for doubled exposure," only to mutter a curse a moment later, followed by a frustrated, "um . . . hmm . . . well."

Betty headed over toward Harper and saw a blinking message on a monitor screen that read "Interlock Negative." Well, she certainly knew what that meant: Among other things, they were going to have a brief delay before matters proceeded any further. That being the case, she had no reason not to take a few moments to speak to Bruce and get a handle on the situation.

"Hey, Harper, there a problem?" asked Bruce.

Harper sighed as Betty walked past him. "The interlock switch flaked again. It'll just be a sec."

Getting the interlock in order was certainly a priority. It was the device that automatically sealed the sphere when gamma radiation was released. It was a fail-safe device, and the prospect of having something go wrong with it was simply unthinkable.

As Harper grabbed a respirator mask and entered the airlock gammasphere chamber, Betty sidled over to Bruce, who was seated at his monitor station and watching everything occurring with hawklike intensity. "Bruce, I thought we should talk. About Glen."

"There's nothing to talk about," said Bruce. He still sounded angry. Amazing that Glen could bring that out in him. Then again, perhaps not. Glen had certainly brought it out in her enough times.

As gently as she could, she said, "Hey, Bruce. It's me."

Bruce was watching Harper through the glass window. Harper was wedged in the center of the gammasphere, testing the interlock switch. But he took the time to look at Betty and smile. He had a lovely smile. *He should do it more.*

"Sorry," said Bruce.

"Don't worry about him, okay? I'll handle it."

Bruce looked at her warily. "How?"

She knew the answer before he asked, but even so she couldn't quite believe she was saying it. "I'll call my father. He can exert some pressure."

Slowly Bruce shifted the whole of his attention to her. If she'd just informed him she'd been impregnated by the shade of Elvis while pumping gas, she couldn't have been subjected to a more cautious look of bewilderment.

"Last I heard," said Bruce, "you and your father weren't speaking."

Betty shrugged, trying to sound offhand about it, as if the concept was the most routine matter in the world. "All the more reason I should call him."

The thought of doing so wasn't exactly on Betty's top ten list of things she'd like to do. In fact, it didn't even place in the top one hundred. But her thoughts on Bruce's reaction to Talbot had caused her to reassess her feelings. Obviously she had completely misjudged the depth of feeling that Bruce had for Talbot, and she'd exacerbated it by going out to dinner with him. That had been very, very foolish. Not only had it upset Bruce, but it had also given Talbot an inflated sense of self-confidence. There was nothing to do for it now but try to make things right, and if that meant swallowing some pride and asking her father's help, so be it.

The problem was that she had no way of knowing for sure if Thunderbolt Ross would even agree to help. Her father didn't know Bruce from Shinola, so it was unlikely he would intervene just to keep Dr. Bruce Krenzler happy in his work. In fact, considering the track record of their relationship, the one that Thunderbolt Ross would most likely be worried about was Glen Talbot. Still, she felt as if she had to do something, and her father seemed the best way to go.

At that moment, Harper called out through the intercom. "Um, I think the circuit kind of fried, or—I don't know. Maybe you want to take a look."

"Okay, hold on," said Bruce.

Bruce went into the experiment area, picking up a respirator mask. He entered the clean room, mask in hand, and Betty was watching Harper's continued efforts with the interlock switch when it suddenly shorted out. Sparks jumped from it, and Harper let out a high-pitched, shrill, and startled scream. Lights began to flash and a quiet, firm recorded female voice began reciting a countdown to what would most assuredly be total disaster.

The sound of Harper's scream briefly froze Bruce in the clean room, his mask still dangling from his hand. Then Bruce saw the flashing lights, heard the commencement of the countdown, and still couldn't quite process what had just happened. *So this is how it starts*, he thought as the lights flashed as though the lab were some theater announcing to its patrons that intermission was nearing its end. He heard the countdown heading down from twenty, still figured that there was time to avert a complete and total disaster, as long as Harper got clear of the gammasphere. . . .

And it was at that instant, of course, that the panicking Harper, trying to back out of the gammasphere, snagged his mask on one of the protruding alignment rods. Such was his state of dismay that he obviously had no clear idea of what he'd just done. All he knew was that, all of a sudden, he couldn't move his head. He yanked it from one side to the other and flailed his arms, looking like a demented radiation scientist trying to hail a fleet of cabs.

Bruce didn't panic in the slightest. His heartbeat never even sped up. He did, however, allow himself to reflect on the irony of Betty's frustration with his perpetual equanimity. Harper most certainly allowed himself to be governed by his emotions, and look where it had gotten him: snagged like a hooked fish inside a chamber that was about to go hot with enough rads to flash-fry a mastodon. Three cheers for emotions, while they're busy getting you killed.

Instead of getting upset, Bruce sprinted into the gamma-sphere and pulled the snagged mask free. Harper stumbled and Bruce caught him. The last thing he needed was Harper falling and knocking himself cold. He wasn't thrilled by the prospect of trying to haul Harper's unconscious body out of the sphere.

"Bruce! The interlock!"

He whirled and instantly saw the problem. Betty wasn't panicking; she was far too professional for that. But she was barely keeping a lid on as she worked frantically at Harper's station trying to shut down a system that had no intention of shutting down, thanks to the short circuit.

"Interlock door should now be secure," the countdown reminded them helpfully. "Ten . . . nine . . . eight . . ."

The interlock door remained open, putting the entire lab facility at risk the moment the gamma cannon went off, discharging its particles into the air. She was hammering at the keyboard in a manner reminiscent of anyone who'd ever had a computer freeze up on them, except the stakes were far higher than a melted hard drive. They'd all be melted if the interlock couldn't be shut down.

". . . seven . . . six . . ."

Rick the frog watched with, at best, mild interest.

". . . five . . ."

Bruce looked at Harper, at Betty, at the interlock, at the mask in his hand . . .

And dropped the mask. There was no time, and it was just one more thing cluttering up his grip.

". . . four . . . three . . . two . . ."

In a desperate move, Bruce hurled Harper backward, sending him tumbling out of the gammasphere.

". . . one . . . zero. Nanomeds released. Engaging gamma cannon."

He heard the hissing in the gammasphere. It was louder than he would have thought, always having heard it from behind thick glass. And louder still was the whirring and clicking of the gamma canisters locking into place, the whining of the cannon as it powered up.

When he was younger, Bruce Krenzler had seen a war film in which one guy threw himself on a grenade in order to save his platoon buddies. There had been much animated discussion as the kids had all wondered whether they would have what it took to knowingly lay down their lives in that one ultimate, heroic burst of action. All of them came to the conclusion that, hell, yes, they'd be the ones taking a swan dive on a bomb rather than be one of the guys trying to run in the other direction. Only Bruce had said, "I don't know what I'd do," and had naturally been subject to ridicule for admitting it. But he had looked deeply into the eyes of the other kids, and he had fancied that in their gazes he was able to perceive fear and uncertainty. It was one thing to talk a good game, but another to act upon it when crunch time came.

With all of that, Bruce was somewhat surprised to find himself barreling forward before he'd even made up his mind consciously about what he'd do. His response was entirely automatic. He had no idea if it was even going to work: This was radiation, not shrapnel. It was far less predictable. But his mother had always had a saying: "One choice is no choice." And that was what Bruce was left with.

He slammed himself against the muzzle of the gamma cannon, blocking the opening, just as the canisters released. He heard Betty screaming, Harper crying out in alarm, heard the *scream of the gamma cannon merged with the scream ripped from his own throat, and there were other screams, people running, as a desert sky erupted in flames and a young girl was screaming and a man and the dolls were screaming and twisting and burning and he heard a satisfying click as the interlock chose that moment, after the cannon had fired, to unfreeze and seal Bruce in, and Betty was crying out his name from behind the Plexiglas and Bruce was still howling in pain except there was more than pain, there was also triumph and satisfaction and a sense of "At last!" that ricocheted through his mind for no reason and then came more screaming, and Banner thought his face was melting off and his flesh was just sliding right off his bones and puddling around his body except that maybe it was happening and maybe it wasn't, but he screamed anyway because it just seemed the thing to do, and as Bruce flopped over onto the ground like a beached mackerel, he was briefly relieved to see that his skin was still very much intact, but he felt as if something else had broken or splintered or become separated, and as he slipped away into unconsciousness, he was dimly aware that there was an odd little satisfied smile on his face, and he wondered just who was smiling.*

a daughter and son lost and found

Thunderbolt Ross didn't bother to get up from behind his desk when Glen Talbot sauntered in. Every time he encountered Talbot in recent days, it was harder for him to believe that he'd ever seen anything in the young man in the first place. Oh, Betty had seen through him. She'd been far more perceptive than her regular-army father, who thought Talbot had had the right stuff when he so obviously didn't. After all, what man in an army uniform, with a future ahead of him, would ever willingly leave it behind to enter the private sector?

"General. Good to see you again," Talbot said affably. "Very smooth ride, by the way. I appreciate your—"

"Sit," Ross told him as if addressing a cocker spaniel. Talbot blinked briefly at the tone, but obediently sat in a chair in front of Ross's desk. Ross held up the file his aide had given him earlier. "You want to tell me what this is about?" he said, and slid it across the desk to Talbot.

Talbot picked it up and flipped through it. Ross watched his face carefully, looking for some sign of weakness. But Talbot appeared quite relaxed, seeming for all the world like a man who had absolutely nothing to hide. This, of course, annoyed the crap out of Ross.

"It would appear, General," Talbot said in a leisurely

manner, "that this is a folder detailing our plans for the Lawrence Berkeley lab."

"Why?"

"Why are you showing me this folder?" asked Talbot. "I'm afraid I haven't the slightest—"

Ross slammed his open hand on the desk, causing the paperweight-and-pen set given to him by Colin Powell to jump. Talbot, for his part, didn't allow the least reaction to show. "Don't play games with me, Talbot. It's bad enough that half the time you go through the National Security Agency instead of me—"

"I try not to, General, but sometimes you leave me no choice—"

Ross spoke right over him. "—when you're trying to acquire things that I don't feel are necessary. And this is another one of those. Why have you targeted Lawrence Berkeley?"

"Sir," Talbot laughed, "I haven't 'targeted' anyone or anything. I just work for Atheon."

"The acquisition recommendations come from you, Talbot," said Ross, tapping the sheet. "Very strong recommendations, in fact."

"And I think you can see why, General."

"Yes, yes, this whole 'nanomed' business." Ross shook his head. "Science fiction tripe."

"As was Captain Kirk's communicator, once upon a time, General. How's your cell phone?"

Ross scowled so fearsomely that his brows seemed to connect in one dark line. "We both know this has nothing to do with this 'nanomeds' nonsense and everything to do with Betty."

Talbot looked as if he were doing everything he could not to laugh. "*Betty?* Betty Ross?"

"No, Betty Crocker. Yes, of course, Betty Ross. And I'll tell you something right now, Talbot," and he shook a finger at him, "I take a very dim view of your harassing my daughter by shoving yourself back into her life."

Immediately Talbot was on his feet, and although he was far more contained than Thunderbolt Ross, his own ire was no less evident. "You know, General, a hard truth for you to face is that sometimes, just sometimes, not everything is about you or your precious daughter. Now you can dismiss the research at Lawrence Berkeley all you want, but the bottom line is that I would be making the same recommendations to Atheon I'm making now, regardless of whether LB labs was employing your daughter or Wanda the Dog-faced Girl. Furthermore, you may not want to believe this, General, but I'm glad that you wanted to see me, because I'm about to do you a huge favor."

"Oh, are you?" said Ross sarcastically.

"Yes, General, and you're going to be thanking me for it."

He reached into a portfolio that he had tucked under his arm and pulled out a blue folder, from which he extracted what appeared to be several black-and-white photographs. "What I'm about to show you, General, is a matter of security, and I think it speaks to the relationship I believe we once had that I'm trusting you enough to bring you into this. I think, as Betty's father, you ought to know, and therefore I'm sharing this with you."

"Sharing what? What are you talking about? And what's the catch?"

"No catch, General. All right, one catch," he amended. "The catch is you can't ask me where I got these. I'd think you should be more concerned about what's in them than their source, anyway."

He handed the photos over to Ross. The general studied them, frowning. They were obviously private photographs of Betty with some man, taken as part of some sort of surveillance. There were several of them, walking arm in arm through a park, or relaxing together, she leaning against him in an intimate manner. This alone was enough to make him bristle.

"Talbot," he said slowly, "I don't give a damn about your catch. You will explain to me why you have my daughter being watched—"

"We're not. We're having *him* watched. Betty just happens to be involved with him . . . and that, I think, might be cause for concern on your part." He took a deep breath and let it out. "You were right that there's something more going on with Lawrence Berkeley than the nanomed program, General. But it has nothing to do with anything as relatively unimportant as my past relationship with your daughter. It's this fellow, right here."

"What's so important about him?" demanded Ross, but even as he asked he found himself staring fixedly at the young man's face. "And why does he seem . . . familiar?"

"You knew his father."

"I knew his . . ."

And then his eyes widened, and he understood. "Oh, my God. Are you telling me . . ." Talbot nodded and Ross looked back at the photos. "It's like looking at a ghost," he whispered. "A ghost of someone who's still alive, albeit locked away."

"No."

"No? What do you mean?" And then Ross was also on his feet, standing up so quickly that he banged his knee on the underside of the desk drawer. He ignored the pain. *"The father's walking around? David Banner? That lunatic? How?"*

"He was released from the hospital. He was evaluated, and it was determined he was no longer a threat."

"God save us from fuzzy-minded liberals and their evaluations!" snarled Ross. "And they've no idea where he is? Do you think he might be heading toward his son?"

"It's possible. He could also be on a slow boat to China; we've no way to be sure. But it might be that he is determined to hook up with his son again. And, if that's the case, Betty might be at risk."

"There's no 'might be' about it." He stared at the pictures again, slowly shaking his head in disbelief. "After all these years, Bruce Banner."

"Krenzler. That's his adopted name."

Ross continued to shake his head. "I said at the time having that boy simply disappear into the adoption system was madness. But at the time I was in a hellhole of hot water with a base that was on fire, thanks to the boy's father. Why should anyone listen to me?" He paused. "Does he know? Does he know who he is, where he came from?"

"I don't know," said Talbot. "It's hard for me to be sure. It's possible he knows. It's also possible he blocked it out."

"So Betty might not know, might not be aware of what she's gotten herself into. My God . . ." He looked up at Talbot, and his expression softened. "You were right. Dammit, Glen, I may not agree with some of the choices you've made in your life, but this time around I owe you."

"You don't owe me anything, General," Talbot said modestly. "Look, Betty and I may not have worked out, but that was quite a while ago, and besides, it doesn't mean I don't want the best for her. And at least I know now that someone who will be concerned about her best interests is on the job. Believe me, General, your involvement in this might just save her life."

a sacrifice too great?

*He saved my life, Bruce saved my life, my God, he's
dead, Bruce . . .*

Betty had been pacing her office frantically, only stopping every so often to see if an ambulance had pulled up
yet. She was going mad with fear, because she knew that
Bruce was lying somewhere in some room where they
weren't letting her see him. She could just imagine what
he must look like, sick and dying of radiation poisoning,
his skin puckered and burned, his hair falling out in
clumps. He was probably blind by this point, hemorrhag-
ing internally. Maybe no ambulance had shown up yet because there was no point. Maybe he was already . . .
already . . .

When her phone rang, she jumped nearly three feet and
then pounced on it. She listened to the voice at the other
end, and didn't even hang up the phone as she bolted
from the room. She just tossed the receiver in the general
direction of the cradle and wasn't around to see it bounce
off the phone and clunk to the floor, hanging by the
twisted cord.

He's asking for you.

The four words rang repeatedly in her head as she
sprinted down the hallway. She still couldn't believe that

Bruce was in the lab's infirmary. Radiation poisoning in the infirmary? They weren't remotely prepared to deal with an injury of this magnitude. It was like sending a child gushing blood from the stump of a severed arm to the school nurse so she could make him some hot cocoa.

Betty almost skidded past the infirmary in her haste, then stopped, took a deep breath, and prepared herself for the worst. She hoped she would keep it together. The last thing Bruce needed was for her to come utterly unglued or get overemotional. For all she knew, this was the last time they were going to see each other, and she simply had to maintain control. She glanced at her reflection in the glass of the door, hoped that the redness in her eyes wasn't too evident, and then walked into the infirmary, prepared to see Hazmat teams and Geiger counters clicking off the scale.

Instead she saw Bruce sitting on the edge of a bed, shirtless. A nurse was removing the blood pressure gauge from his arm while a tall, businesslike woman doctor wearing a name tag that said "Chandler" made some marks on her chart.

Betty gasped in astonishment, and Bruce heard her and turned in response. He seemed energetic, almost . . . happy.

"Bruce," Betty said, and it was more of a question than a salutation.

He nodded and smiled broadly. Betty wasn't sure which was more bizarre: that Bruce was alive and well, or that he was smiling, since he didn't smile all that much even on his best days.

"I'm going to be okay," he informed her cheerily as he stood. "Really. Barely enough for a slight tan." Then, abruptly, he sat back down, looking a little faint. "Oh," he said, sounding puzzled, as if surprised that his legs were reluctant to support his weight.

Betty looked over at the nurse. The doctor held up the developed film from Bruce's radiation detector and raised an eyebrow.

"We're double checking," said Dr. Chandler. "According to the dosimeter badge he was wearing, your friend should be the consistency of burnt toast right now. But I can't find much of anything."

She stared closely at Bruce, indulging in a flight of fancy for a moment and wondering whether Bruce might possibly have been taken over by, or even replaced by, aliens. Yes. Yes, that made perfect sense. Far more than that a human being could smother a leak of pure gamma radiation with his body and come away from it looking better than he did in the morning.

It was impossible, just impossible. It wasn't as if his body could have just healed it . . .

. . . self . . .

She stopped dead, unable to believe that it had taken this long for the thought to occur to her. She had been so filled with mental pictures of Bruce dead, the image of him splayed across the gamma cannon vivid in her mind, that the events directly preceding his exposure to the gamma radiation had been a blur to her. Only now were the full implications of what had occurred becoming clear to her, and her disbelief was gradually being replaced with growing excitement.

"Could you excuse us . . . just for a sec?" Betty asked.

"Sure," said the doctor.

She moved away, gesturing for the nurse to follow so that Betty could have some privacy with Bruce. Very slowly, Betty approached Bruce, not shifting her gaze in the slightest. Bruce saw the way she was staring at him and laughed.

Laughed. Yes, suddenly the whole alien theory was looking more and more promising.

"What?" he demanded when she said nothing at first. "Come on. That badge was probably exposed at the factory before I ever put it on."

He was in some sort of denial. That was why he was so calm, almost jovial. He clearly didn't understand what the fuss was all about, why the fact that he was still alive was nothing short of miraculous.

"You saved Harper's life," said Betty, "and all of ours."

"Don't be silly," Bruce said dismissively. "It was obviously a malfunction. I probably took a dose nothing more than a fluorescent light."

"No, the radiation was bad enough. What I'm talking about is the nanomeds. How else could you have survived it?" asked Betty.

Bruce started to laugh again, then stopped as the full weight of her observations dawned on him. "Wait, you're saying I was exposed to the radiation, but that the nanomeds repaired me? Come on, Betty," he said.

"I don't have any other explanation." It wasn't an admission Betty made lightly or willingly. She was the type of person who liked to have three or four explanations for any given phenomenon, and then spend time trying to narrow them down so she could be sure. Perceiving only one possibility just didn't seem . . . scientific somehow. It was almost like cheating.

Bruce lowered his feet off the bed again and leaned against it, looking stunned.

"But . . . if it's true, then . . . they worked. They actually worked."

She almost wanted to laugh. After all, the entire purpose of the nanomed project was to *make* them work, yet Bruce appeared amazed that it had been accomplished. Still, as pleased as she was on his behalf—on both their behalves—she knew that she had to be the voice of reason before things went too far.

"No," she said, and when he looked at her quizzically, she continued pointing out the downside. "We haven't come close to controlling them. You know it. It's . . . you." When Bruce tried to dismiss the theory out of hand, Betty continued forcefully because she knew she was right. "They would have killed anyone else. Bruce, there's something—different—in you."

She could see it in his eyes: He wasn't accepting the notion. He started shaking his head and said firmly, "We've got to start checking, doing studies, analyzing genetic makeup. Obviously we have to try and replicate—"

"Replicate!"

"We have to try the experiment again," he said matter-of-factly. "No scientific result is worth a damn if it can't be replicated. You know that, Betty. Now we have to get right on—"

But apparently Dr. Chandler had remained within hearing distance, and now she reentered the room. " 'We' aren't doing anything right now, Dr. Krenzler, except getting back in bed where we can observe you. I bent the rules to allow Dr. Ross to see you, but enough is enough. You're not going anywhere, Dr. Krenzler, and if you endeavor to do so, I will have to have you restrained. I'd rather you didn't put me in that position."

"I'd rather you weren't in it either." He looked at Betty apologetically. "Sorry. I guess we'll have to delay our research."

"Don't worry about it." She took his hand and squeezed it affectionately. "I'm just thrilled you're still alive so I can do the research with you."

His hand felt cold. Cold as ice, and a stark contrast to the ruddy complexion and air of health he had about him. Delicately she released his hand.

God . . . what's happened to him? Betty wondered. But the individual to whom she had addressed the question seemed rather silent on the subject.

Night had fallen. A nurse was asleep at her desk.

Bruce sat up in his bed, hooked to various monitors that showed nothing abnormal. He was going mad with boredom. It was bad enough when he was at home, unable to sleep and compelled by insomnia to pick up pencil and paper and start working. But here he was in the infirmary, and they were keeping a wary eye on him. It seemed as if, every fifteen minutes or so, someone else came in urging him to go to sleep. He was starting to feel as if he were a child, or at the very least was being treated like one.

He leaned back, his mind wandering over the things that had happened over the past few days. The events, the memories. He tried to force himself back into the moment when he'd been struck by the gamma radiation, and what had been going through his mind at the time. It hadn't been words so much as crazed thoughts and images tumbling pell-mell one over the other, and some seemed familiar, but others didn't. Instead they were like the recollections of events that had happened to someone else . . .

Someone else . . .

For a very long time, it had disturbed Bruce that his

early years were a blur to him. Everyone had fragments of memories, moments that were mental snapshots, and these snapshots could always be put into some sort of framework or context. That had never been the case with him. On rare occasions he would speak of them to his mother, but she never seemed to be of much help. She would just smile and shrug and offer him some freshly baked cookies. Before long he stopped mentioning those memory shards because he was beginning to worry that he'd get fat from the cookies. It seemed easier not to worry about it, and he hadn't thought of it in quite some time.

But in those final moments before he'd interposed himself between the gamma cannon and the others, his life had flashed before his eyes. Not unusual. Imminent death triggers that rush of memories, the computer of one's brain dumping all the memories like one great final purging of the hard drive. As it so happened he hadn't died, but the memories had been shaken up for the first time in ages. They floated in the river of his memory like disturbed silt . . . and also for the first time, there was a hint of . . . of familiarity. Familiarity from a most unexpected source.

Bruce's gaze wandered over to the phone on the nightstand next to him. He wondered if the thing was hooked up. Experimentally he picked up the receiver and was rewarded with a dial tone. His first attempt at dialing, however, was met with a rapid busy signal. Then he remembered he had to dial 9 to get out. *Would that getting out of any situation was as easy as dialing 9,* he thought as he dialed the phone number of the one person he felt he could talk to.

He hoped she was in. Not just that, but he hoped she

wasn't out . . . and, more to the point, he hoped she wasn't out with *him*.

The phone rang two, three times, and there was a click. Then came Betty's voice, "Hello," and Bruce paused a moment, waiting to see if it would be followed by an answering machine message. No. Just silence. A slightly puzzled Betty repeated, "Hello?" and Bruce realized that he had never been so glad to hear another person's voice in his entire life. He felt pure, raw emotion choking up in his breast, and just as quickly quieted it.

"Hey," said Bruce.

"Hey!" Betty replied, sounding cheered, even a bit relieved. "How are you?"

"I'm fine."

She paused, as if worried that he wasn't telling her something. "You sure?"

"Yeah."

He heard a small exhale of breath. She was sighing in relief. How nice. He could see her clearly in his mind's eye: her smile, the luster of her hair, that way she had of making him feel alive just by looking at him. Just hearing her voice gave him—what was the phrase?—a rush.

"What are you doing?" she asked.

"I was just sitting here," Bruce said, "thinking about you, about your dream."

"What dream?" asked Betty.

"The one of the desert."

There was another pause, this time a bit more uncomfortable. Finally she said guardedly, "And what were you thinking about?"

"I don't know," he admitted. He didn't want to say, "I thought I was about to die and while that was happening—" because she already seemed skittish and tentative enough with the entire situation. Why risk getting her worked up? So, choosing his words carefully, he said, "Sometimes, when I'm not really thinking about much of anything, I remember images from it. Did I ever tell you that?"

"No."

"It's as if—" He didn't know how else to say it. "—I dreamed it myself."

There was a soft laugh on the other end. He could tell she thought he was just being sweet, that he was trying to show just how much he shared her feelings and concerns.

Women, he sighed mentally.

"What's the number there?" she asked. "In case I'm seized with a sudden urge to hear your voice." He told her, reading it off the dial where it was printed. She repeated it, and then said softly, "You should get some sleep. Have some sweet dreams of your own."

"Yeah," said Bruce, "you, too."

He kept the phone to his ear long after Betty had hung up, hoping that he could somehow cause her to materialize in front of him through sheer force of will. After a while, though, when the dial tone changed to an irritating buzz, he hung up and settled back on the bed. The buzz remained in his head, however, fatiguing his mind. He didn't resist it. Hell, he welcomed it. It was pretty depressing to think that the only way he was able to get some sleep was to have a near-death accident and wind up in the infirmary for overnight observation.

The world blurred around him, and he released his conscious mind, enjoying the peace that slumber would most assuredly bring him.

He had no idea how much time passed. All he knew

was that, from somewhere very far away, he heard a whimpering and growling. It took him long moments to sort out the reality of the noise from his state of reverie, and then slowly he forced his eyes open. The lamp light from the parking lot spilled in through the window. It was as if his dream world had somehow leaked over into the waking world.

Sitting across the room from him was the man who had been standing outside his window the other night, the man whom Bruce had dismissed as being any sort of threat. Yet here he was, big as life, and Bruce couldn't tell whether he was dreaming up his worst fears, or whether his "paranoia" had been based in fact. And there were the dogs as well, the three of them, including that weird poodle. Seeing it close-up now, Bruce knew it was definitely the same one that he had confronted the other night.

None of them were snarling, though. They were quiet, even content to be in this place with this man. He was absentmindedly petting the head of the mastiff, which was making a soft sound in its throat, almost like a cat's purr. Bruce felt threatened, but no threat was being offered. Again it was that dreamlike quality of detachment, knowing that there was an imminent threat, but not being worried that the danger provided any long-term consequences. It was the wrong man, and certainly the wrong creatures, in the wrong place at the wrong time, and yet somehow the whole thing felt . . . right. Familiar. Even comforting in a perverse way.

And then the man spoke. Despite his outwardly frightening appearance, his voice was surprisingly soft, even gentle.

"Your name is not Krenzler. It's Banner."

Until that moment, Bruce had still half-believed that he was dreaming. But the voice was all too real, and penetrated the haze that was draped around his consciousness. Shaking off the last vestige of sleep, he sat up, fully cognizant for the first time that what he was seeing wasn't a product of his sleeping imagination. The words, however, made no sense. "What?"

"Your name. It's Banner. Bruce Banner." He hesitated and then spoke again, with an affection that chilled the scientist for no reason he could discern. "Bruce."

"How did you get in here?" asked Bruce.

"I work here now, in the labs," said the man. "The late shift. It keeps me close to you. You always work late yourself, with your friend, Miss Ross."

Bruce could see now the coat the old man was wearing, hanging partly open, and sure enough, he was wearing the clothes of someone on the custodial staff. But the man's apparel was of secondary importance to Bruce. What caught his attention was the way the old man had said "Miss Ross." The barely contained anger, even resentment. A warning rang in his head, but it was hard for him to focus on that when there was so much else vying for his attention.

Bruce started to sit up, but got tangled in the wires from the various monitoring devices, not to mention the IV drip they'd introduced just to make sure he didn't become dehydrated.

"No, please," said the man. "You're not well." He went to Bruce, unsorted the jumble of twisted wires as he spoke. "You've had an accident," he said in a soothing singsong, as if cooing to an infant in a cradle. "You're wondering why you're still alive, aren't you? You're thinking: there's something inside, something different, inexplicable."

The old man might have been crazy, but the movements of his fingers amidst the array of wires had been swift and sure. They now hung freely from one another. He stepped back and said, "I can help you understand, if you'll let me . . . if you'll forgive me."

I'm dealing with a lunatic. He thinks I'm somebody else.

"Look, mister, I'm sure I have nothing to forgive you for," Bruce said, keeping his voice calm and level. It wasn't all that difficult, really, having had years of practice at it. "So, maybe you'd better just go. Please, I'll be fine."

The old man shoved his face toward Bruce's, and an image leaped unbidden to Bruce's mind. It was the old man's face, but younger, much younger, *almost like his own, and bigger, so very much bigger, and he was shoving some sort of stuffed toys at Bruce, and the toys looked familiar, all of it looked familiar, and he was shoving a couple of toys into Bruce's face. . . .*

"You must know," the old man said insistently, his gravelly voice snapping Bruce back to the present day. "You don't want to believe it, but I can see it in your eyes"—and he was scrutinizing Bruce's face—"eyes so much like your mother's. Of course, you're my flesh and blood, but then . . ." His voice dropped down even further, and his breath was a foul thing filling Bruce's nose, so much so that Bruce had to fight the urge to vomit. ". . . you're something else, too, aren't you? My physical son, but the child of my mind, too."

The old man was between Bruce's hand and the call button that would summon the nurse from the front desk.

"You're lying," said Bruce, which probably weren't the best words he might have chosen, considering he was trying to talk sense to a nutcase. But he was understandably disconcerted by the circumstances. "My parents died when I was a small boy."

"That's what they wanted you to believe," the old man said intensely. He rose from the bed and started to pace, and Bruce could have gone for the call button at that point. But the old man's movements, the fervor with which he spoke, were almost hypnotic. In all his years, Bruce had never encountered a personality quite like this one: a true psychotic.

Despite the immediate danger, the scientist within him came to the fore, and he found himself in observational mode, intrigued to see what the old man would say or do next. Meantime, the old man continued to rant, clearly in his own world.

"The experiments, the accident, they were top secret. They put me away, thirty years—away from you, away from our work—but they couldn't keep me forever. After all, I'm sane. They had to admit it."

The dogs were starting to get fidgety. The pit bull looked in Bruce's direction and started to growl, and this was more than enough to get Bruce's hand to stray toward the call button. But then the old man raised his arm and the dogs came to attention. Bruce let the call button be, and continued to watch the old man, who had refocused his energies back on Bruce. The intruder was speaking louder, his voice growing in both volume and intensity. He sounded like the classic mad scientist from some old black-and-white horror film, exhorting whatever unseen gods were looking down on him and encouraging him in his demented endeavors. Bruce started to wonder whether this wasn't a dream after all, for the only thing the moment lacked was lightning bolts and rolling thunder as the old man declared, "You see, everything your extraordinary mind has been seeking all these years—it's been inside of you—*and now we will understand it, harness it—*"

The phone rang, a mundane sound that seemed out of place in a moment of such Grand Guignol. Bruce looked over at it, but the old man stepped quickly toward him, his voice growing softer but still at full force in its demented drive. "Miss Ross again. Don't answer! There's something you need to know about her, Bruce. Something troublesome, but I can protect you from her."

And that was, abruptly, all Bruce could take.

Starting to tremble, he fairly shouted, *"You're crazy! Get out!"*

A look of menacing hatred passed over his father's face. As if responding to the mood of their master, the dogs crouched for an attack.

But Bruce, furious over the old man's aspersions of Betty, didn't back down. At that moment he didn't care if the damned animals leapt at him and tried to tear him apart. His only concern was telling this lunatic to vacate the room instantly.

"Get. Out."

And, astoundingly, a look of satisfaction passed over the old man's face. One might have thought that he was genuinely glad to see a flash of temper. "Heel," the father ordered the dogs, and the daunting canines promptly backed off.

There was a long moment wherein the old man appeared to be sizing Bruce up, and then he said in a mildly mocking voice, "We're going to have to watch that temper of yours." From the way he said it, it was impossible to tell whether he meant it as an advisory against the dangers of giving in to anger . . . or whether he intended to keep Bruce's anger under careful observation. Nor did Bruce have the opportunity to get him to clarify, for the old man promptly departed, the dogs obediently following him with their long toenails click-clacking on the polished floor.

The phone kept ringing, but Bruce didn't notice it. He wasn't even staring in the direction that the man had gone; instead, he was fixed upon the point in the room that the man had occupied moments before. It was as if he were concerned that the man might somehow reappear from thin air, like a phantasm or recurring hallucination.

Then the phone stopped ringing, and the abrupt cessation snapped Bruce back to reality. He snatched the IV out of his arm, pulled the leads from his various monitors, and rolled off the bed. He sagged for a moment, his legs not completely ready to accept his weight, but he braced himself and forced himself forward. He stumbled once, but then righted himself and made it out into the hall. His sudden arrival in front of the nurse's station startled the nurse awake. She looked astounded to see him standing there.

"Where did he go?" demanded Bruce.

The nurse stared at him a little fearfully. "Who?" she asked uncertainly.

Bruce looked up and down the corridor.

Empty.

"Maybe it was a dream at that," he said softly. Without another word to the nurse, or even an attempt at an explanation, he shuffled back into his room. The nurse followed him and didn't say a word as she hooked him back up to the various monitoring devices. He simply lay there, staring at the ceiling, his mind far, far away. When sleep finally came for him—a total, deep sleep—he welcomed it with a sense of swelling relief.

And as he slept . . . *there was pain and hurt and a bubbling, brooding anger long repressed against anyone and everyone who had ever done harm to him or laughed at him or tried to hurt him, and a sea of faces swam before him, sneering, chuckling, and the world around him was tinted green and in the darkness of his innermost fears* . . . he awoke to discover that his bed was bent right along the frame, and the IV tube and monitoring devices had been ripped free in his thrashing.

He staggered to his feet, stumbling about in the darkness. He tried to call out to the nurse, but his throat was constricted. The idiot woman must have been away from her station, or perhaps had fallen asleep again. . . . *Useless, just useless woman. He should smash her, should* . . .

He forced the thoughts away as he lurched toward the bathroom. He knocked over a lamp in the darkness and barely registered the sound of its crashing to the floor. He made it to the bathroom with a supreme effort and clicked on the light, squinting against the sudden brightness. He stared at his face, looking for . . . well, he wasn't certain. For something. But there was nothing there.

Nothing.

He looked down at his clothes. The stitching on his T-shirt and pajama legs had ripped at the seams.

That wasn't nothing.

That was something . . . something confusing, something horrifying, something that he couldn't begin to cope with.

His gaze swiveled back to the mirror, and suddenly

there was a gray haze enveloping him. He wanted to push it away, but he lacked the will, and as he tottered toward the mirror, he thought he saw a faint hint of green reflected in his eyes. Then the gray haze overwhelmed him and sent him spiraling away into blackness.

connections

Betty Ross, moonlight filtering through the shades of her bedroom, put down the phone and stared at it long after she had hung up.

To a certain degree, she was relieved that Bruce hadn't picked it up. After all, what would she have said to him? "Hi, Bruce. Betty. Look, I had a dream that you might be in some sort of great danger, so I thought I'd call and say, 'Hi.' How's the food?" Oh, yes, that would have worked. It would have gone a far piece toward hastening him to a full recovery.

Nor could she put a face to the danger. She just had images of Bruce, and he was crying out and cringing, and, oddly enough, sometimes he looked like a little boy in her dreams. Still, Betty was a rationalist, and didn't for a moment think she was having dreams that somehow foretold the future. The explanations for the symbolism were all too readily apparent. The danger element came from the accident that Bruce had been in. The visions of him as a child stemmed from an almost maternal concern about his welfare. After all, didn't every woman sometimes mother the man she loved?

She leaned forward, her chin almost touching her knees. The man she loved. She still thought of him that way, even though he had made it clear that his own emotional stuntedness made it impossible for him to reciprocate in the way she wanted and needed. But almost losing Bruce had brought some new elements into play for her. Look what he had done: He had risked his life for others. Not just risked his life; he had actually thrown himself into what he must have believed was certain death. The fact that he had survived was pure happenstance, a freak chance, a one-in-a-million shot. The incident said something huge about the man with whom she had broken off a romantic relationship because . . . why? He wasn't good enough for her? He didn't smile enough or laugh enough or share his feelings?

She had felt isolated and distant from him, but how much of that was her, as opposed to him? If Bruce were restricted to a wheelchair, would she be angry with him because he was unable to walk? Of course not. So if he was simply psychologically unable to relate to her in the emotional manner she thought she needed, was she being equally unreasonable expecting him to do so?

Betty ran her fingers through her hair in exasperation. She couldn't get out of her head the image of Bruce splayed across the gamma cannon. Was she some sort of ingrate for even thinking that perhaps he—

The phone rang.

The ring broke the stillness and she gasped, startled. She reached over for it too hastily and grabbed the receiver up. "Bruce?" she said.

There was a pause. "Noooo. It's not Bruce. Is that acceptable?"

She sat there, confused, wondering who in the world it was. The voice was deep and resonant, and for a moment she thought it might be an obscene phone caller.

And then, abruptly, she realized who it was, and her face flushed as the notion that her father had been making lewd phone calls became not only ludicrous but downright embarrassing.

"Dad?" she said tentatively.

"Yes."

"Oh. Hi. I, uh . . . well. Heh." She felt flummoxed. "This is unexpected. I haven't heard from you in a while."

"I didn't have your number."

"Oh. Right."

"And it's unlisted."

"That's . . . that's also right. How did you get it?"

"I ordered my aide to get it."

"I see. And . . . how did *he* get it?"

Thunderbolt Ross paused on the other end. "The how doesn't matter. I told him to get it; he got it. Beyond that, it's unimportant."

She laughed humorlessly. "Nice to see you haven't changed, Dad." Then she closed her eyes and took a deep breath, because this wasn't the time to start mouthing off to her father. She hadn't forgotten her promise to Bruce, that she would get in touch with Ross and try to do something about reining in Talbot. So now, by happenstance, her father had called. This wasn't the time to be giving him lip.

"It's . . . good to hear from you, Dad. It's been . . . too long, really."

"Yes. Yes, it has." His voice sounded surprisingly soft, even concerned. "Betty, I was thinking perhaps we might want to get together. Have dinner. Are you available?"

She was caught off guard. *What's wrong? Is he dying? Am I dying?* She made sure to keep a smile on her face, though—not that he could see it, of course, but at least that way her voice would continue to sound upbeat.

"Sure, Dad! Always. When did you have in mind? Should I come there?"

"No. No, I'll come to you. I'll have my aide finalize the details and you'll hear back shortly."

She glanced at the clock. It was close to midnight. Did the man ever sleep? Probably not. And his aide, whoever that poor nameless devil was, probably didn't either, although that was likely not by choice. "Okay, that'd be fine."

"Good." Another pause. "You . . . sound healthy, Betty."

"Thanks. I've been working out."

"That's good to hear."

And the line went dead. With anyone else, Betty would think they'd been disconnected. But that wasn't the case here. Thunderbolt Ross had never developed any technique for saying, "Good-bye." To him, when a conversation was over, there was no reason to prolong it with pointless niceties.

"Why can't I have a nice, normal father?" she wondered aloud.

In the darkened home of Bruce Banner's father, the three dogs circled, silent and nervous. Containers of various sizes, marked with assorted warning stickers—all of them stolen from the lab of Dr. Bruce Krenzler—littered the room. David Banner picked up a cage from under a table. There was high-pitched squeaking as the large gray rat within the cage objected to being handled.

Banner placed the cage inside another clear container in the middle of the room, and dropped one of the nanomed canisters inside. It hadn't been easy obtaining it; it hadn't been easy getting any of the things he'd stolen. It had taken patience and cunning, but it had been worth it, particularly if it was going to provide him with what he needed.

Stepping away from the cage and the container, Banner went into the hallway, stood around the corner, and flipped a light switch. The room was immediately alive with the hum of radiation from the makeshift and far-smaller-scale gamma cannon that he had created. In terms of potency and sophistication, it was more a gamma water pistol.

Furthermore, there was every chance that Banner himself would receive a dose from free-floating rads, since he didn't have the tools available to him to create the sort of Plexiglas safe area that such devices usually required. But Banner couldn't have cared less about some incidental cellular damage. He had issues of far greater import to concern himself with.

The rat's cage began to spark and, at that moment, the nanomed canister broke open. He could hear it shatter, could hear the rat squealing in alarm, and, possibly, pain. He glanced over at the mirror set up at the far end of the room and saw, reflected in it, a cloud enveloping the rat, and a few more sparks from the metal of the cage. He hadn't realized there'd be that much discharge. It was a foolish oversight; he could conceivably burn the house down. Not that the house itself was any great shakes, but his research materials were irreplaceable. It was something he was going to have to be more attentive to in future endeavors.

He checked his watch, satisfied himself that the requisite amount of time had passed, and shut down the juice.

Gingerly he turned the corner back into the room and looked at the cage.

It was quite a sight to see. There was the rat, covered with open sores and burns and slime, all of which were to be expected from the dose of gamma radiation it had received. But it was also three times as big as it had been before. Whereas there had been plenty of room within the cage, now the infuriated creature was cramped within, tearing at it and shaking it violently.

David Banner grinned. And then he started to laugh, louder and louder, and the fearsome dogs actually cringed away from him.

Then the laughter stopped and he stared with malevolent joy at the canines.

"Hello, boys," he said, and if the dogs had had any brains at all, they would have run as fast as their legs could take them, or perhaps turned upon their master and torn him to shreds. Instead they nuzzled up against him as he stroked their heads absently while staring at the creature in the cage and smiling broadly.

mutagenic traces . . .
but of what?

Betty Ross and Dr. Chandler walked slowly down the hallway of the infirmary. Chandler was shaking her head, and her puzzlement was quite evident.

"He seems fine now," she said. "I'm afraid, since I can't quite find anything else the matter, that I'm going to have to let him discharge himself."

Betty wasn't entirely sure how to react. Naturally, that should have been good news. Bruce was going to be okay. Somehow, whether it was nanomeds or luck or a miracle from above, Bruce had dodged a radioactive bullet. The problem was it was too good to be true. And it was part of Betty's nature to be skeptical of that which seemed too good to be true.

"Well, I have a blood test or two I'd like to run on him, even if he's being released," Betty said.

Chandler looked skeptical. "Dr. Krenzler seemed rather adamant about leaving the infirmary as soon as possible, and we really don't have any standing or reason to keep him against his will or subject him to more tests. I can't say he'll want to cooperate."

"Oh, I think I can say that," said Betty, and she smiled. "I'm very persuasive."

• • •

Bruce winced slightly as Betty withdrew the hypodermic she'd used to take blood from him. The tube had filled up quickly. "Here," she said gesturing at his arm. "Press down." She put a Band-Aid on him, stepped back, and looked him over. "You sure you're all right?"

"Sure," said Bruce, trying to look nonchalant about the pain in his arm. "How are you?"

It seemed to Bruce that she was hesitant about something. He had intended it as merely a casual question, but it was obvious to look at her that a less-than-casual response was on her mind. "I got a message from my father. He's coming to see me," she said finally.

Oh, good! Let's get him together with my alleged father! I'm sure they'll get along just great! Maybe they'll get a house by the sea together and swap stories about how to rear happy, healthy, well-adjusted children!

He kept his face neutral, albeit with effort. "Your father? When?"

"He lands in an hour. Funny thing was"—she frowned, obviously puzzled—"he called me."

Bruce wasn't entirely sure why, but he considered that to be somewhat alarming. It might well have been that he was a bit on edge when it came to the advent of fathers and father figures, particularly after last night's encounter—an experience he still thought might just have been the stuff of dreams. With long practice, though, he kept any hint of alarm or concern from his voice. "You nervous?"

"Yes," said Betty matter-of-factly.

"You'll be fine," said Bruce. He took the vial of blood from her. "And I'm going to do this myself."

Betty was obviously startled. She'd told Bruce the type of tests she wanted to run on the blood sample, looking for mutagenic traces. He'd readily agreed that such tests should indeed be run . . . but he hadn't promised that he was going to have her do it. And now that the blood had been drawn, Bruce was thinking that if there was something to be discovered about his biological makeup, then he was the one most entitled to discover it. Nor was he putting the matter up for debate as he held onto the vial firmly even as Betty reached for it.

"Myself," he repeated.

She looked as if she wanted to argue the point, but finally she just shrugged her slim shoulders. "As long as it gets done," she said.

Throughout the rest of the day, Bruce Krenzler, pushing the matter of the Banner name out of his head, worked on studying the blood sample. There was most definitely something there, but the problem was he wasn't entirely sure what that something was. He felt as if he were an Aborigine staring at a model of a DNA strand, having some vague idea that there was something of importance here but knowing that he didn't have the tools or the knowledge to begin to comprehend it. Computer analysis was of little help to him, because row after row of questions and tests came back with one of two responses:

Insufficient data.

Unknown.

The "insufficient data" didn't bother him as much as the "unknown," for some reason. Perhaps it was because "insufficient data" left room for the possibility that more data would be forthcoming, along with answers. But "unknown" was vast, and could very possibly remain unknowable.

He leaned back from the electron microscope at one point, rubbed the bridge of his nose between his fingers, and cursed to himself. Then he suddenly looked over his shoulder. But there was no one there.

Or perhaps someone had been there but no longer was. "Unknown" indeed.

The Joint Tactical Force West was a sprawling base situated about thirty miles outside of Berkeley. Betty remembered it all too well. When she had been very small, she'd seen news broadcasts showing Berkeley students demonstrating outside the base, complaining or protesting about some military engagement somewhere. She remembered her father loudly cursing out the kids on TV, and she had promptly joined her father in a rigorous session of off-color language. Ross had first been startled by his daughter's word choice, but then realized she'd picked it up from him and instead let out a hearty laugh. It was one of those rare instances when she had actually pleased him, and even now—as she showed her ID to the guard at the gate before driving on—it was one of her more pleasant memories of growing up. Possibly because it was one of the few instances when she knew she had genuinely entertained her father.

She reminded herself that she was her own person, and she wasn't required to provide entertainment for her father. Yes, she certainly had the knee-jerk feminist line good to go, which didn't help her at all in terms of dealing with her dad.

Having parked the car near the building that housed the officer's club, Betty got out, smoothed her blouse and skirt, then breathed into her open palm to check her breath. Just to play it safe, she popped in a breath mint, and then headed toward the club's main entrance.

She was stopped at the door, of course, and made to

show her ID all over again. Even then they wouldn't let her enter until they found her name, and even that took longer than it should have because they had her reservation misfiled as "Ross Elizabeth" instead of "Elizabeth Ross."

Upon seeing the name, and knowing the other individual with whom it was associated, the maître d' immediately snapped to. Without a word, he pointed in the direction of her father, Thunderbolt Ross, seated at a table with his back ramrod straight and a drink in his hand. He was staring into the drink thoughtfully, but some inner "old soldier" sense made him realize that Betty was there. He looked in her direction and simply nodded in greeting. Effusive as ever.

She strode toward him and, when she got in range, he stood to greet her.

"Hi, Dad," she said.

"Betty," said Ross. He looked her up and down. She resisted the temptation to salute him. "You've changed your hair color," he announced.

No, she hadn't. "I appreciate your noticing. Thank you," she said as she sat. "It was nice of you to come out all this way."

He shrugged. "Half-hour chopper ride. Not a vast inconvenience in the grand scheme of things."

They made minimal small talk as the waiter brought them menus and, a short time later, bread and butter in a wire basket. Betty didn't push her father on what it was he wanted to speak with her about. She knew him well enough to know she didn't have to push. He was going to tell her before too long, because Thaddeus Ross wasn't one for beating around the bush if one could stomp the bush flat or level it with a bulldozer.

He didn't let her down as, in short order, he announced to her, "All right, I'll get right to it."

Betty had been considering all the possible things her father might want to speak to her about, and she blurted out what was—to her—the most obvious and most likely. "This is about Glen, isn't it? He's been snooping around my lab."

"Glen noticed some things," Ross said guardedly. "He . . . asked me to make some inquiries."

Something about the way Ross said that made Betty think that he wasn't being entirely forthcoming with her. In the end, though, did it really matter? Whichever way the information train was running, both her father and her former boyfriend were riding in the same car.

"You've been spying on me. Of course." By this point in her life, she had no idea why she was even surprised.

"Betty, listen," Ross said, obviously not paying the least bit of attention to Betty's visible unhappiness about the situation. Well, that was pretty typical of him, wasn't it? Steamroll right over her concerns. Betty put the menu down and started glancing around quite plainly, looking for the exit, and then her father reached over and put a hand on her forearm. She couldn't tell if he was doing it out of paternal feeling, or because he wanted to make damned sure she stayed where she was.

"We've turned up some surprising things," Ross told her. "This Krenzler you work with, you know who he really is? How much do you actually know about him?"

The question caught Betty completely off guard, but she made sure not to show it. His words were alarming, though. If there was one thing her father had, it was access to all manner of top-secret information. It wasn't as if Ross were saying that Bruce wasn't good enough for her, or why couldn't Betty be dating an army man. His phrasing couldn't have been more clear: He'd learned something about Bruce, something that concerned him to such a degree that he'd felt the need to contact Betty and talk to her directly, one-on-one. That alone was sufficient to underscore the seriousness of whatever it was.

Or perhaps there was something else at work here. Ross was, after all, still working closely with Talbot. As ludicrous as it sounded, this might be some sort of team effort to kill whatever interest she might have in Bruce and steer her back to someone of whom her father approved.

Cautiously, she said, "I think the question is: What is it that *you* know about him?"

Ross leaned back and cleared his throat. "Well, right now, I'm not at liberty to—"

She should have known. She really should have known. Tossing out some all-purpose, vague aspersions—just how stupid did her father think she was? Overlapping his words, she said, "Not at liberty to disclose that to me. Right." She was filled with disgust for him and anger for herself, because she had been sucker enough to let herself be pulled in. How easily duped had they believed her to be? And how dumb had she been to go along with it this far? "You know, I was really hoping, hoping that this time you honestly wanted to see me again to—"

Ross started to respond, but Betty didn't wait. Instead she pushed her chair back. "Why do I bother?"

"You've got this all wrong, Betty," Ross said.

She had to give him credit. He was maintaining the facade of the concerned father for far longer than she'd thought he would. With one eyebrow cocked, she asked, "Do I?"

"Yes. I did want to see you. I'm genuinely concerned for you," said Ross.

For a heartbeat, she hesitated. There was something in his voice, something in the way he was looking at her . . .

Then the medals on his jacket flashed at her, as if going out of their way to remind her who he was, and who she was. Science and the military had been at odds with each other for ages, and this was simply the latest skirmish in that ongoing battle. It was the oldest strategy in the world: divide and conquer. Either Talbot had been feeding her father lies about Bruce to serve his own purposes—and she could just guess what those were—or her father had some other priorities in mind involving her, or Bruce, or the project, or . . . or who knew what?

It bothered the hell out of her that she couldn't trust her own father, but that was the simple, hard truth of it. And whose fault was that? No. No, she wasn't going to feel guilty about it. She simply wasn't.

She got up to leave just as the waiter returned to take their order.

"I wish I could believe you," said Betty, trying to mask the sadness in her eyes, and then she turned on her heel and left without looking back.

She retrieved her car, drove as fast as she could until she was clear of the base, and then pulled over to the side of the road, turned off the headlights, and started to sob. She hated feeling the way she did. Here she'd dared to hope that her encounter with her father would lead to something positive. Perhaps the start of a whole second life to their relationship. Instead all that had been stirred up, like flakes in a snow globe, was paranoia and resentment.

And yet . . .

And yet . . .

Her father's words nagged at her. What if—what if he hadn't just been trying to drive a wedge of distrust between her and Bruce, for whatever reason? What if he was actually trying to help her, and her own suspiciousness was precluding his attempt?

She stared at her own cell phone, as if it were something that was out to catch her or trick her somehow. Then, ever so reluctantly, she picked it up and dialed Bruce's phone number at the lab. It never occurred to her that he would be anywhere else. She could envision him there, working until all hours. After all, he had something brand-new to explore: himself.

The phone rang several times and then his machine kicked in. "Please leave a message" was all it said in Bruce's clipped tone.

For a heartbeat she considered just hanging up without leaving a message, but her father's words preyed on her mind.

"Bruce, you there?" she asked, hoping that perhaps he was monitoring the call. No response. His answering machine was voice responsive, and if she stopped talking, it would shut off, so she took a deep breath and continued.

"I saw my father. It's like—" She hesitated, and then pushed on. "—it's like he suspects you of something." The moment the words were out of her mouth, she wished that she could retrieve them, or pull them off the recording somehow. Quickly, to make certain that Bruce knew she didn't believe him capable of any wrongdoing, she said dismissively, "Oh, I don't know. I was so impatient, as always. I should have heard him out."

Well, enough self-flagellation for one phone call. Trying to issue Bruce a warning, she said, "I just think they're planning something, with the lab, with you. Just call me, okay?"

She terminated the call, and then the headlights of a vehicle appeared behind her. A car pulled up, and she was certain that her father had chased her down to tell her more lies about Bruce, to mess with her mind.

A red light was lit on top. It was a police car. Through a loudspeaker, she heard, "Are you in need of assistance?"

She rolled down her window, leaned out, and gave a high sign. Then she started up the engine and eased herself back onto the main road. The cop watched her go. It was very reassuring . . . and it was depressing to realize just how few reassuring sights there were left in the world anymore.

It was some hours later that she returned to her home. It hadn't been an easy trip. There had been ambulances hurtling around, some sort of accident. And not just in one place; had affected different spots throughout the Berkeley area. Betty, with her supernaturally lousy luck, encountered at least three of them. She kept looking for signs of overturned cars or the similar sights that one routinely espied where disaster vehicles congregated, but there didn't seem to be any.

Instead she saw trees knocked over, a fire hydrant smashed to one side that was spraying water skyward, stop signs bent in half, and busted up pavement. It was as if some sort of major storm had swept through in isolated areas and disappeared. She'd never heard of Berkeley being prone to tornadoes, but that certainly seemed the only reasonable explanation.

When she got home, she checked her machine. She heard one message from Glen and two from her father, both of which she promptly deleted without listening the moment she heard their voices. There was nothing from Bruce. Why was it that she kept hearing from the men she didn't want to hear from, and the one man who meant anything to her couldn't be bothered to pick up the phone, despite the clearly alarming nature of her previous call?

It was ridiculously late for Bruce to still be at the lab, but she tried him anyway. When that attempt failed, she called him at home. No answer there either.

Now she was truly starting to get worried. She went to bed, but didn't manage to sleep for more than twenty minutes at a stretch before either worries about Bruce, her old nightmares, or the occasional ambulance siren woke her up.

By the time the sun rose, Betty wasn't feeling much more rested than when she'd first gone to bed. It was earlier than usual, but she reasoned there was no point to hanging around trying to sleep anymore. So she showered and dressed and drove over to the lab—and found it in a state of utter chaos.

The entire area was choked off with emergency vehicles: ambulances, fire trucks, and more police cars than she thought existed in the entirety of Berkeley. She was only able to get within a couple of blocks before finally giving up and parking her car on a side street. She then ran as fast as her high-heeled shoes would allow before encountering some police barricades and a couple of stern officers who wouldn't let her get any closer.

"But I work there!" she told them.

"Look, lady—" one of the cops began.

"That's *doctor*," she informed him archly.

He shrugged. "Fine. Look, Dr. Lady, until we get this sorted out, ain't nobody working there."

"What's 'this'? What happened?"

Then she spotted what appeared to be a gaping hole in the roof of the facility . . . and she felt a burst of alarm upon realizing that it was directly over the lab she shared with Bruce.

Suddenly a horrific scenario played itself out for her, one in which Bruce had been up late working and had inadvertently caused some sort of explosion that had—had—

She fought back rising panic. The cops weren't being of any help. She could see some of the lab security guards, but they were far too distant to hear her calling to them. Even if they did hear, they probably wouldn't be of much use. One of them was gesticulating wildly, holding his hands wide apart in the instantly recognizable gesture that indicated size. He was talking about something gargantuan, and getting clearly disbelieving looks from the police who were hearing the story. Maybe it was a huge explosion. Maybe . . .

She was accomplishing nothing by standing there and worrying herself sick. Instead she bolted back to her car, jumped in, peeled out, and sped toward Bruce's house.

Betty's mind was racing as she tried to determine just what she would do if she got there and discovered Bruce wasn't home, because that would mean he was at the lab, and he might well be dead.

Arriving at his house some minutes later, she saw his bicycle was chained up outside as usual, so obviously he had come home. That thought calmed her somewhat as she got out, went to the front door, and knocked, at first tentatively, then briskly when no answer was immediately forthcoming. She wondered whether she should be angry or concerned even as she fished around in her bag for her ring of keys. She thumbed through them, found the one for Bruce's house, and inserted it in the lock. Moments later she was poking her head into the house, calling, "Bruce?" cautiously.

No answer.

She entered, closing the door behind her, and walked through the living room. Everything looked normal, and that in and of itself made things seem even more abnormal. She walked past one hallway, then stopped, backed up and stared. Down at the far end of the hall she could see the back door. It was swinging loosely on its hinges, broken.

"What the hell?" she muttered.

She went to the door and tried to close it, and succeeded in nearly tearing the whole thing free of its hinges. She looked around. The kitchen itself was a disaster area, canned goods and napkins and whatever else had been lying about just strewn all over the place. She continued, with slowly increasing dread, following the trail of destruction to Bruce's bedroom.

And there, sleeping like the proverbial baby, was Bruce Krenzler. Bare chested, possibly naked, since she couldn't see all of him, Bruce was tangled up completely in knotted sheets. He was sleeping soundly, which was far more than she'd been able to do.

"Bruce!" she said in a far more loud and alarmed voice than she'd intended.

Bruce sat up abruptly in response to the bellow, looking around in confusion for a moment, unable to discern from what direction he was being hailed. Then, after a brief time, he focused on Betty standing there.

And then, very slowly, he said, "I think . . . I'm not Bruce Krenzler. I think my name is Banner."

what am i?

As Betty Ross was sitting down across from her father in what would be an abortive attempt at dinner, Bruce Krenzler was working—or at least attempting to—at his lab at Lawrence Berkeley. But his mind kept racing back to a time when he was quite young and had seen a very pregnant woman lying out on a beach. Disdaining more modest maternity wear, she'd been sporting a small two-piece bathing suit that had allowed her belly to bask in its full, stretch-marked glory under the sun. He had watched with fascination, creeping closer and closer as she lay there with her eyes lazily closed, and suddenly he had jumped back with a shriek.

The surface of her stomach had visibly rippled, as if something was trying to tear its way out.

The young woman had heard the boy's yelp, opened her eyes, and smiled at his reaction. "The baby's kicking, that's all. You saw it kick just now."

He knew in an abstract way that children were in their mothers' stomachs before they were born, but he'd never actually seen such vibrant evidence of it before. The bizarre concept had stuck in his head, and even as an adult, he marveled at the sangfroid routinely displayed by even the most novice of expectant mothers. They never seemed the least bit disconcerted by the notion that their bodies had been usurped by something else entirely, that everything they'd known about their bodies was out of date as they underwent massive changes. "It's the most natural thing in the world," they'd say, but Bruce was never able to comprehend it. All he knew was that he was glad that he wasn't a woman, and never had to worry about his body experiencing such odd transformations.

And yet here he was in exactly the same predicament, except it wasn't the most natural thing in the world. No, it was entirely unnatural, and the more he studied the results of the tests done on his own blood, the more his head began to hurt and flashes of pain lanced through his skull.

He checked and rechecked, stared at the cells dancing about under the electron microscope, combining and recombining in a manner that simply didn't track with anything that he'd ever studied or experienced. His thoughts were disjointed, confused, trying to make sense of it. *The cells . . . chemical bonds in the DNA . . . storing . . . too much energy. Impossible . . . impossible . . .*

His lower back was stiffening up, his temples were throbbing, and from somewhere that seemed a great distance away, he heard a phone ringing, and then Betty's voice. But he was barely paying attention, for exhaustion and fatigue were playing havoc with him. It seemed as if the shadows were moving.

Maybe it was that crazy janitor. Yes, that was it. The lunatic with the dogs was lurking about somewhere, lying in wait, preparing to . . . to . . .

He should have gone to personnel. Why hadn't he gone

to personnel? Why hadn't he had the man investigated, rounded up, fired? Why?

Because you're afraid of what you'll find out if you do. You're afraid.

I'm not afraid.

You are. You are afraid. Of us . . . of yourself. Of . . .

Betty's voice.

It sunk in that Betty was calling him, leaving a message on the answering machine. What was she talking about? Something about her father saying things about him . . . suspecting him of something . . . planning something.

He jumped up from his workstation, carelessly knocking over a rack of tubes as he did so. He lunged for the phone, heard crashing behind him as something else was knocked over, and then he stumbled, fell, landed badly on his knees, then scrambled to his feet, thrusting his hand toward the phone like a drowning man, Betty's voice promising salvation.

But she hung up just as he grabbed the phone, and he moaned. His salvation had vanished into the ether, was gone just like that.

He tried hitting redial but got a recording stating that the person he was calling was unavailable. She'd called from her cell, obviously, and now she was probably on the move again and the signal wasn't getting through.

Bruce heard another crash, turned, and saw a tube of his blood tumbling to the floor, knocked over by one of the other falling racks. It seemed to be happening in slow motion and he just sat there, transfixed, knowing he was too far away to catch it but unable to take his gaze from it. The tube fell end over end, and then struck the floor and shattered, creating a puddle of dark red liquid that oozed across the floor. He looked down, horrified, frozen, and was certain that he could hear his own heart pounding, getting faster and faster.

There was a sound in the hallway. The dogs? The janitor? Betty's father? Talbot? Or maybe monsters lurching to darksome life, spat out from the shadows.

He ran into the hallway but found nothing and no one. Yet that fact wasn't good enough for him. He sprinted through the deserted halls, around corners, looking, searching. He collided with an equipment cart and the knees, which he'd hurt earlier, flared with even more aggravated pain. But that didn't stop him. He kept running, tripped, hit the wall, and bloodied his lip, and the world began tilting around him at a forty-five-degree angle.

He was losing all sense of who he was and where he was, and as he lifted himself up, an animal cry emerged from within him. The scream echoed in the halls, images cascading through his mind, the old man and the snarling dogs and Betty's face, except it was twisted in contempt and suspicion, and there were army men with rifles aimed at him at the orders of a man Bruce had never met but instinctively knew was Betty's father . . . *and pouring copiously through all the images is blood, his blood, thick and viscous and red, except it's glowing and shifting from red to a dark shade of green . . . and fury, huge, smashing, rending, through the wall, feel it collapse, feel resistance vanish beneath strength, fury pounding animal snarl muscles knotted power surging bottled up exploding release, yes, good smash pound smash smash smash . . .*

. . . and high through the air outside the lab flew the gammasphere, ripped right out of its housing, propelled by animal fury and impossible strength. The gammasphere arced skyward for a moment, hung there as if trying to defy gravity, and then plummeted. It struck the roof of a parked security cruiser and crunched right through, causing the entire vehicle to sag on its springs. Miraculously the car's alarm system was still functioning, and lights began to swirl as the car howled as if it were an injured living creature.

. . . smash walk no walk move faster stop man small man kill man kill smash man no yes no smash destroy rip rend tear no can't no . . .

The eyes of the monster focused on the old man who stood at the far end of the lab, unblinking, unafraid. They froze there, predator and prey, except it wasn't entirely evident at first which was which. The old man smiled in the face of certain death, didn't waver under the glower of those frightening green eyes. He stepped forward, stretched out his hand

. . . rip hand smash break smash tear into pieces no no yes no no yes YES YES . . .

and the monster swiped at the hand, took a step forward, and the old man stumbled back, suddenly far less certain of his invincibility than he had been before. He tripped over his own feet, falling to the floor, and now the sirens could be heard approaching and they were

. . . Screaming noise screaming people screaming all around screaming noise make it stop go away go away GO AWAY . . .

getting closer and there were people shouting and calling out, coming closer, closer still, and the monster didn't look the least bit like a trapped animal, but instead was clearly trying to decide whether it was worth his time and effort to annihilate everyone who was approaching him and

. . . bah . . .

when the decision came, it was capricious and random

and could just as easily have gone the other way. But it didn't. Instead, it was the monster that went the other way.

A security guard in the lead barely had time to react and catch a glimpse of a mountain of dark green before the frightening mass was suddenly gone, straight up, crashing through the ceiling and causing debris to rain down, driving everyone back.

There was stunned silence, then, as the light of the moon filtered through the hole in the roof that hadn't been there moments ago. "What," gasped out the security guard, "was that? It—it was some sort of . . ."

"Of hulking monster," said the old man, and in the darkness of the shadows where he was lurking, no one could see the smile playing upon his lips. "A hulk. That's what he was. Tell everyone"—he raised his voice—"that a monstrous hulk is out there.

"Well?" he prodded when the guard just stood there, staring upward in incredulity at the damage casually left behind by the creature. "What are you hanging around for? Go! *Go!*"

The guard broke out of his stunned stupor and ran, muttering, "A hulk," urging others who were just arriving to stay the hell away from the scene of the crime, presuming he was able to figure out just what the crime was. And he left behind the old man who was feeling quite amused and exceedingly pleased with himself.

"I named him once," said the old man to himself. "Who better to name him again?"

As the emergency vehicles arrived, the shadow of the figure merged into the trees of the Berkeley hillside

   . . . leave leave leave . . .

and with deed matching thought, he leapt skyward. From time to time he landed, having no care about what damage he did whenever he struck the ground, and then off he would go again. Every so often people would spot him descending and mistake him for a falling satellite or a chunk of an airplane or a UFO, and they would run just as he hit and then stand there stupefied because suddenly the crashing object would just be gone again, and if what went up had to come down, no one was quite prepared for the reverse, and through it all, the creature didn't care, he was just . . .

. . . *free free finally free* . . .

Bruce Krenzler heard his name being spoken, and then became aware that he was in his own bed, but the sheets were completely knotted around him. Disconcerted and disoriented, he slowly twisted around, and it was Betty's voice, calling his name in alarm. He stared at her through eyes that felt incredibly sore, and there was light on his face that shouldn't have been there because it was night-time and he was in the lab, except . . . How did his bed get to his lab?

Slowly he propped himself up on one elbow, blinked several times to try to get the ache out of his eyes, and this time when Betty said his name, it was louder and filled with alarm.

And for no reason that he could readily discern, he said the first thing that came into his mind, and, oddly enough, he knew it to be the truth. He told her that he thought his name was actually Bruce Banner. He had no clue why he told her, or even if he should have done so. He only knew that in telling her that, it would make him feel better, as if he were being honest with her about something that he hadn't even known he was being dishonest with her about.

It didn't work. Instead it just made him feel more confused . . . and more frightened than ever before, as if he'd just opened a door that could never again be closed.

meetings of great portent

An hour had passed, and Bruce and Betty were seated at the dining room table. In the intervening time, Bruce had showered and dressed. "Want to make myself feel human again," he'd said, with only a vague sense of the irony of the statement. As he'd showered, he had fought to bring order to the chaotic flashes of images in his mind. But, try as he might, he couldn't manage it.

For as long as he could remember, Bruce had felt that there was another . . . mind . . . rooting around somewhere within his. But the thoughts and impulses that came from that mind were always comprehensible, filtered through his own perceptions. Now, though, it was as if a barrier of some kind had been created, cutting him off from . . .

. . . himself?

Betty watched Bruce carefully as—having showered and dressed—he drank slowly from a cup of decaf coffee, which was the only kind he ever took. He was trying to explain to Betty what had happened, but it was extremely difficult because he didn't entirely understand it himself. Betty sat and listened and nodded, but every so often her gaze would wander toward the back door, which was now leaning against the door frame with no means of attachment, the hinges hanging there uselessly. She thought about the things her father had said, and the more that Bruce spoke, the more she was thinking that her father didn't know the half of it. But it wasn't as if Bruce were some sort of sinister spy or foreign agent or saboteur. He was . . . he was . . .

God. She didn't know what he was.

All she'd previously been worrying about was that Bruce had been caught in some sort of explosion. Now, though, he'd been presenting garbled recollections of displays of incredible strength coupled with extended blackouts, as if he were trying to remember things that had happened to someone else who was also him. She would have dismissed it as fantasy, a too-vivid dream, if she hadn't witnessed everything from the devastation at the lab to the shattered door of his house. It was insane even to contemplate that he might be responsible in ways that defied any sort of scientific rationalization. She and Bruce were endeavoring to sort fantasy from reality, and having great difficulty accomplishing that usually simple task.

"It could have been him," said Bruce, speaking of the bizarre visitation he'd had from the janitor. "He said he was my father. It's like I had a kind of . . . dream of it. He was there, but I can't remember."

"Then you . . . you *were* there, at the lab?" asked Betty. It was hard for her to be certain, because Bruce's own accounts seemed so muddled. Sometimes he would refer to his being there, but at other times he indicated that he wasn't—or was there but wasn't at the same time. It was making her head swirl just to try to keep track of it.

"No, not me . . . something," he said with that same maddening vagueness. "Betty, what's happening to me?"

She was the wrong person to ask. She could barely follow the conversation, much less offer anything vaguely approaching a rational explanation. There was one possibility although, given the circumstances, she was loath to suggest it. But it was the only thing she could think of. "Maybe . . . maybe *he* could tell you," she said.

He stared at her for a moment uncomprehendingly, and then she saw the understanding appear in his eyes. Understanding . . . and fear. She was broaching the idea of going to a man whose very presence was daunting to Bruce, calling up all manner of associations that he could barely begin to comprehend, much less deal with. Still, if this janitor wasn't insane—if his claims were legitimate—then maybe . . .

There was a loud, repeated pounding at the door. Bruce and Betty exchanged confused looks as Betty got up and opened the door, not knowing what to expect.

Two members of the military police filed in, followed by Thunderbolt Ross and several other MPs. His gaze swept the room as it routinely did whenever he entered a new place, the better to identify any potential threats. His eyes widened when he saw Betty; he was clearly taken aback by her presence. She wondered if he was considering her some sort of traitor, perhaps having given aid and comfort to an enemy, because the way he was looking at Bruce clearly indicated that he thought of Bruce as just that. But Ross recovered quickly, clearing his throat and saying to one of the MPs nearby, "Mitchell, escort my daughter out. I'll join her shortly."

My daughter. Not "Dr. Ross," not "Betty," not "the young woman." No, he had to establish right up front just who was in possession of whom, that she was a piece of his property. It rankled Betty no end, and she started to say, "But—"

"Now!" Ross interrupted her. "Betty, this is serious," he said, and he was sounding far more like a father than he was a general.

She looked to Bruce, determined to stay by his side if she thought for even a moment that her continued presence would be of help. She was perfectly prepared to force them to drag her out if she had to.

But then Bruce said, very softly but firmly, "I'll be okay."

Bruce's condition at that moment seemed far removed from any reasonable definition of "okay." However, when Betty still exhibited reluctance to leave, he nodded in a more firm manner, which clearly indicated that it would be best if she left.

She cast one final, contemptuous glance at her father—just to let him know whose side she was on, and that she wasn't leaving because *he* desired it, but because Bruce did—and then she walked out. It wasn't anything that could remotely be called a moral victory, but she reasoned she had to take what she could get.

He could see Betty in Thunderbolt Ross's face.

Bruce thought that was amusing. After all the times that Betty had spoken so angrily about her father, had expressed again and again the belief that they were nothing alike, Bruce could nevertheless instantly see the family resemblance. Oh, granted, Betty was far prettier. But around the nose, the general shape of the face, and the eyes—lord, they had the same eyes, including that inner conviction that they were absolutely right about, well, everything. In Betty, he chose to find it a charmingly endearing feature. In her father, he found it . . . less so.

Ross had something in his hand behind his back. For a heartbeat, Bruce wondered if it was a gun. Was Ross so far gone that he was prepared to shoot Bruce right then and there, that he was just waiting for Betty to leave the room so he could do the deed?

"Bruce Krenzler?" asked Ross.

It seemed an odd thing to ask. Obviously Ross had to know who he was. He wanted to play some little game with Bruce. A sort of cat-and-mouse thing. Mentally, Bruce shrugged. The man's capacity for showing off his strength in a situation seemed boundless, but if that's what he wanted to do, Bruce wasn't going to prolong it.

"Yes," he said flatly.

"My, my. So this is Bruce Ba—" Ross paused deliberately, apparently looking for some sort of reaction from Bruce as he "caught" himself saying a different surname. Bruce's poker face remained immobile. "Krenzler," finished Ross, and there was a fleeting look of disappointment on his face. Bruce hadn't given him what he wanted, and that failure didn't bother the scientist one whit.

But Ross wasn't finished. Indeed, he'd barely begun. "I think you left something at your lab last night." He held up the torn seat of Bruce's jeans; from the ripped back pocket, Ross produced Bruce's wallet. Then he said nothing, just looked at Bruce and waited.

Bruce simply stared at it, inscrutable. He could see what Ross was up to. Some people, when faced with an awkward situation accompanied by silence, would blather out explanations and, in doing so, make things worse for themselves. Ross clearly was hoping that Bruce would try to come up with some way of explaining why parts of his clothing had been found back in the laboratory. Three or four explanations immediately occurred to Bruce that would seem nice, reasonable, "normal" rationalizations of this odd happenstance, but none of them would be the truth, since he wasn't entirely certain what the truth was. Furthermore, it would just give Ross an excuse to start hammering away at everything Bruce was saying, and that would be of no benefit to Bruce at all. So, instead, he kept his silence.

Several long moments passed, and then annoyance flickered over Ross's face. "Keep him under observation," he snapped at the MPs. "I'll be back."

Ross turned and walked out of the room. Banner looked mildly at the MPs, whose faces were so serious that they could have been etched out of marble.

"I'm sure he's very sweet once you get to know him," Bruce deadpanned.

Their expressions suggested otherwise.

When Betty Ross was a little girl, she'd always felt as if her father could read her mind, that no matter what she was thinking, somehow those eyes of his could just bore straight into her head and pick out whatever bits of information he wanted. So as Betty approached her car, the little girl within her jumped when she heard her father call to her from behind. Her adult mind assured her that there was absolutely no way her father could discern what she was thinking at the moment—that she possessed information to which he had no access.

Nevertheless she did freeze for a moment, with the knowledge of what she was going to do and whom she was going to seek out uppermost in her mind, and she worried, however unreasonably, that he was going to be able to tell.

You're an adult. Act like one, she thought as Ross came up behind her. She drew in a deep breath and turned to face him.

"What?" she asked.

"Stop and listen," he said. He started to reach out to take her by the shoulders, but her body language made it clear that such a touch would be unwelcome. He stood there awkwardly for a moment, his hands extended, and then he lowered them. But his voice was fervent as he said, "I need you, even just for a few days, to trust me. I'm going to do everything I can to sort this out. And I promise . . . your friend in there, no matter what kind of a mess he's in, I'll make sure he's cared for."

The assurance almost made her want to laugh. Thunderbolt Ross hadn't particularly cared about his own daughter for years, but the milk of human kindness was going to be spilling over for his daughter's erstwhile boyfriend? She wasn't exactly convinced.

Her father continued, even more firmly, "But as of right now he's incommunicado. And for the next few days, at least, you're going to stay away from here."

The urge to laugh grew exponentially. Who the hell was she to think that—?

Then she saw the MPs all around, armed to the teeth. And she realized that nothing short of obtaining a lawyer for Bruce was going to get her anywhere near him again. And that was what she was going to have to do, as soon as she attended to another problem. A problem that, if solved, might provide answers to many questions about Bruce Krenzler, or Bruce Banner . . .

She shrugged, not giving her father so much as the

benefit of a reply, and then climbed into her car and sped away.

Her plan was formulating in her head when her cell phone rang. She picked it up absently, knowing it wasn't going to be Bruce and not caring all that much who else it might be if not him.

"Yes?" she said.

"Pull over," came a sharp voice.

"Who . . . ?" And then she recognized it, and she was angling the car over to curb even before her mind fully processed the information. "Is . . . is this . . . ?"

"Yes."

"How did . . . ?" She glanced around quickly, looking for some sign of him, suddenly nervous that he might be looking over her shoulder or standing near a tree with one or more of those bizarre dogs that Bruce had described. "Are you . . . watching me?"

"No, Dr. Ross, my spy satellite is unfortunately on the fritz," he informed her with dry sarcasm.

"How did you get my cell phone number?"

"You called the lab last night. Caller ID is a wonderful invention, don't you think?"

"You were there last night when Bruce . . . ?" She stopped, suddenly worried about giving something away.

"Yes," he said silkily. "I was there. Quite a show. And you want to know all about it, I'll wager. As a matter of fact, you were about to seek me out. You were going to drive over to the lab, check personnel records, that sort of thing. And please don't bother to deny it."

"I'm not denying it," said Betty firmly. "Although I am interested in how you figured that out." She was perturbed to find that she was clutching her phone far too tightly, practically jamming it against her ear.

"Because I'm brilliant, Dr. Ross. As brilliant as Bruce is, I'm more so."

"And modest."

"It's a curse I live with," he said sadly, and then chuckled. How charming to know that he amused himself to such a degree. "Doctor, I'm going to save both of us some time, particularly since you'll never find the information you seek in the manner that you're seeking it. Believe me when I tell you that the personnel records would be less than helpful. I've been far too thorough in that regard. But we can be of service to each other, because we both care very much about Bruce—it's just that each of us does so in his or her own way. If we are of one accord, however, one mind, then all can benefit. Do you have a pen and paper?"

"Yes."

"Then write down the following address."

She did so. It was an address on Jones Street over in Oakland. She knew the area of town; it wasn't a particularly good one. She'd once gotten a flat tire there, and the fifteen minutes she'd taken to change it had been among the longest in her life. So she wasn't entirely sanguine about the prospect of heading out there again voluntarily. But she didn't see that she had any choice.

"I shall see you when you arrive," came the voice. "And Dr. Ross—"

"Yes."

"You're an explorer. This will be a voyage of discovery. So . . . smile."

The line went dead.

She hoped she wouldn't be next.

crossing purposes

The area was exactly as unpleasant as she'd remembered it. *You're insane; you're going to die; get the hell out of here,* her common sense kept warning her, even as she turned off the ignition and got ready to step out of the car. Just to play it safe, she placed a lock on the steering wheel for additional security. Even as she clicked the bar into place, she decided that locking up the car was morbidly amusing. Her body could be lying in shreds in the backyard of this horrible house for weeks, picked clean by ravenous pooches and chortled over by a psychotic old man, but, hey, at least her car would still be here, impervious to robbers. Yes, wonderful. It'd probably be stripped as clean as her bones.

She'd briefly considered bringing someone with her, but couldn't figure out who to ask. Her father? One of the MPs? Not bloody likely. The police? On what grounds? No one was accusing this man, even if he truly was Bruce's father, of any crime. The police had nothing to question him about, and there was no way she was going to be able to explain it all to them.

What she needed was some big burly private detective, like the one the heroine was always able to find in mystery novels. The kind who was a sucker for a damsel in distress. But Betty wasn't exactly inclined to think of herself in those terms, nor did she have time to start flipping through the Yellow Pages to try to locate someone who filled the fictional bill. Too much was happening too quickly, and Bruce's future, his very life, might be hanging in the balance. So with that uncomfortable, if slightly overwrought thought festering within her, she walked slowly up to the front door.

She paused, took a deep breath, and was about to rap on the door when it swung open before she could knock.

Sure enough, there he was, the janitor who had brusquely informed her that Benny had passed away. *I wonder if he killed Benny*, she thought, and then banished the notion from her mind as simply being too paranoid.

She was startled to see that he had a genuinely nice smile. Betty would have thought there was a bit of Bruce in him, except Bruce rarely ever smiled, so it was difficult to find a basis for comparison. He bowed slightly, as if she were a duchess, and said in a quiet, almost gentle voice, "Dr. Ross. Please." He gestured for her to step through, and for a moment she could hear a Transylvanian voice utter those famous words, "Enter freely and of your own will." But the man known as Banner simply smiled once more and again indicated that she should cross the threshold.

She did so, and glanced around, but the light was dim and her eyes hadn't yet adjusted. Dispensing with small talk, she said, "So. You are . . . his father."

"He told you." It was hard to tell whether he was pleased by the revelation or upset.

"He . . . mentioned you'd talked to him," said Betty, deciding it would be best for the moment to provide Banner with as little information as possible. She still had no idea whether to trust the man, and her instincts were leaning toward the negative. "And I was interested, because I've always thought, if he could reconnect to the past, to himself . . ."

". . . he would be a more suitable partner for you," said the father.

There was something electric in the air, a palpable hostility that hovered there for a heartbeat, and then it was gone as she turned to look at Banner. He was maintaining his gentle, even-tempered gaze.

"Well, maybe, yes," she admitted.

His tone was singsong and slightly wheedling—very likely it was what Satan sounded like while trying to convince a sucker that a soul was a burden that was useless in the long run. "Yes, but first you want to know what's wrong with him; you want to fix him, cure him. Change him."

"I . . ." She paused, not wanting to be pulled into a discussion of trying to remold Bruce into something other than what he was. It was an internal struggle she had fought many a time before, every time she'd felt a bout of guilt for wanting Bruce to be more open, more emotional. Opting to avoid that tar baby altogether, she said, "I want to help him."

"And so you've brought your father down on his head." There was bitterness and contempt in his voice, and Betty couldn't entirely blame him, because she felt it herself. She had to admit that he was absolutely right. Her interest in Bruce, her work with him, had led to her father's—and Talbot's—interest in Bruce, and look where matters now stood. She wasn't blaming herself entirely. She had a sense that there were far greater forces at work. Nevertheless, she did indeed feel some degree of culpability, and Banner was just clever enough to play upon that.

"How little you understand, Miss Ross. And how dangerous your ignorance has become."

She blinked, lost in the train of logic. "I'm sorry?"

He gestured for her to sit. She did so. The chair wasn't the most comfortable, and her eyes were beginning to adapt to the dimness. She was able to make out what appeared to be some sort of workstation, and there were pictures, pictures of Bruce. There was also a smell in the air that caused her to wrinkle her nose. It was definitely canine in nature. She didn't hear any growling, didn't feel that dogs were advancing on her, but the aroma of the animals was indisputable, and simply verified for her that Bruce's descriptions of the man were more or less accurate. The air was hot, even oppressive, and Betty removed her coat and the light scarf that was draped around it, laying them back on the chair.

The old man didn't sit opposite her, since there was no other chair. Instead he crouched, and in doing so bore a striking resemblance to a gargoyle. His eyes narrowed, and now they didn't look remotely gentle or benevolent. Instead, there was something . . . frightening there. Something hidden.

"My son is . . . unique," he said, lowering his voice as if someone might be listening just outside. He sounded concerned and even paranoid. His tone was not dissimilar to the slightly desperate air that Bruce had displayed earlier when he'd first told Betty of his encounters and experiences of the previous nights.

She wanted to ask Banner about what had occurred last night, what sort of . . . of bizarre change could have seized hold of Bruce, endowed him with power enough to become a one-man tornado. But she said nothing, spell-bound as she was by the increasing fervor of the man's words.

"And because he is unique, the world will not tolerate his existence. I'm afraid we're both too late to help him. There's nothing I can do for him, or for you. And besides, he's made it clear he wants nothing to do with me. His choice." He rose, his knees creaking. "Now, if you'll excuse me, Miss Ross, I have some work to do."

That was *it*? That was why he wanted to see her? To tell her that Bruce was effectively doomed? It seemed so insane. . . .

And then she saw the look in his eyes, and it occurred to Betty that insanity wasn't only the name of the game, it was the only game in town. For half a moment, he had let slip what truly lay behind his eyes, and it was every nightmare, every collection of disgusting bugs that had ever been seen squirming around under a rock. It was right then that Betty abruptly realized that if she didn't get the hell out of there, she wouldn't be going anywhere, possibly ever.

"Of course," she said, and rose quickly, grabbing up her coat. She did it so fast that she didn't notice the scarf fluttering off the coat and landing on the floor. She was about to say something pointless such as "Good-bye" or "Have a nice evening," but the inane social niceties froze in her throat and instead she just headed out the door as quickly as she could.

She heard a soft chuckle as she swung the door shut behind her, and fully expected someone or something to leap out at her as she sprinted for the curb, but nothing came. Betty hopped into her car and counted herself lucky as she gunned the engine and drove away. She had waltzed with the devil and survived for another dance, utterly unaware that the devil had her dance card.

Bruce felt a great swell of anger as he saw the contemptuous and doubting looks on the faces of Ross and the other officers. It was only his long practice at keeping his feelings firmly in control that enabled him to prevent that anger from being anything other than momentary.

The situation was so clichéd that Bruce would have laughed had he not been the subject of the interrogation. They'd even brought in a lamp with a high-powered bulb that they were shining on him, so that he would . . . what? Tan?

Ross sighed extremely loudly, in that way that one does to announce that one is reaching the end of one's patience. "You guys buying this repressed-memory syndrome thing?" he asked the other officers.

"I *don't* remember," said Bruce, maintaining his equanimity. He didn't in the least indicate that he was annoyed by their obvious skepticism. They were effectively calling him a liar. That didn't bother Bruce. He'd been called far worse, under more trying circumstances than this. "How many times do I have to tell you? I'd like to help you, but I don't know." He almost sounded apologetic.

Ross leaned in toward him. "You know who I am, right, Banner?"

"Don't *you*?"

"Banner . . ." Ross said warningly.

But Bruce simply smiled inwardly. "Perhaps you're suffering from repressed-memory syndrome. Nasty, isn't it? But you'll learn to live with it. I have."

"Banner!"

Bruce wasn't exactly accustomed to answering to that

name, but he knew that he'd pushed things as far as he could. "You're Betty's father," said Bruce. "A high-ranking general."

"Let's cut the crap," Ross snapped, circling Bruce, coming closer and closer in on his personal space. If he was trying to intimidate Bruce, it wasn't working. Last Bruce had checked, there was no law against not knowing something, and at that moment, that was all Bruce was sure he was guilty of. Ross, however, didn't seem deterred by Bruce's lack of offenses. "I'm the guy who had your father tossed away, and a lot more like him. And I'll do the same to you if I feel so disposed. You understand?" asked Ross.

Bruce had to admit to himself that that interested him. "My father. You say his name is Banner?" he asked, all too aware that it was the name the janitor, or dog man, or whatever one wanted to think of him as, had claimed was Bruce's own. This simply couldn't be coincidence.

"Now we're getting somewhere," said Ross, mistaking Bruce's desire to clarify his own thoughts as an anxiousness to cooperate. "But then you say you've never known your parents."

"I never did," Bruce insisted.

"Don't play me! You were four years old when you saw it—"

And those words caused something to freeze within Bruce. Abruptly he felt as if he were standing on the other side of a door, which, if swung open, would lead him toward things that would clarify so much, things that would fill the great gaping hole he'd always carried within him. The problem was he wasn't sure he wanted to step through that door, for he knew instinctively that there would be no going back. And the old saying about ignorance being bliss had some merit to it at that.

He wrestled with the prospect of asking, but finally couldn't help himself. "Saw what?"

Ross stared at him incredulously. "You were *right there*! How could anyone *forget* a thing like that?"

"Like what?!"

The general missed the rising ire in his subject, and instead simply said with unbridled contempt, "Oh, some more repressed memories?"

And Bruce saw himself jumping from his chair . . . *leaping upon Ross, bearing him to the ground, pounding on his face, and his fists becoming larger, more powerful with every blow and Ross's face was a horrible mess but Bruce didn't care for he was howling with fury and laughing and smashing, just smashing . . .*

Bruce sank further into his chair. He closed his eyes, desperate to shut out the vision that his own imagination had given him. He started to tremble, the repression of his anger becoming literally a physical thing. "Just . . . tell me," was all he managed to say, his voice strangled.

There was something in his voice, something in his manner, that actually seemed to get through to Ross, at least a little bit. The slightest hint of empathy crossed his face. "I'm sorry, son," he said with a heavy sigh, casting a frustrated glance at the other officers. "You're an even more screwed-up mess than I thought you'd be."

Bruce looked up at him, realizing that this was about as close to sympathy as he was likely to get from Ross. He wasn't sure if the general accepted his protestations of ignorance, but at the moment, at least, he appeared disinclined to continue harassing Bruce about what he was supposed to know but didn't.

Ross harrumphed loudly and squared his shoulders. The brief instance of sympathy was gone.

"Until we get to the bottom of this, your lab has been declared a top military site, and you're never going to get security clearance to get back into it—or any lab that's doing anything more interesting than figuring out the next generation of herbal hair gel." Then he came very close, practically thrusting his face into Bruce's. When he spoke his breath stank of cigar. "And one more thing," he snarled. "You ever come again within a thousand yards of my daughter, I'll put you away for the rest of your natural life."

Bruce said nothing. There didn't seem to be a whole lot of comebacks to that.

My life is spinning out of control.

It was a hard admission for Betty to make as she walked toward her front door, digging in her purse for her keys. Her entire job as a scientist was to find ways to master her environment, to reduce it to quantifiable units, to study it, measure it, and develop reproducible experiments that others could use as yardsticks for their own research. Just as Bruce valued his ability to control himself, Betty valued her ability to have a thorough grasp of her world and understand what made it tick. Not only did she no longer understand what made it tick, she didn't even know what kind of timepiece it was.

Before she could insert the keys into the door, it swung open. She jumped back, startled and terrified. Then she gaped as a pair of military police marched out of her home as if they had every right to be there, taking out her computer and a box of papers for good measure. One of the MPs looked a bit embarrassed that they'd been caught. The other didn't seem to give a damn, but just stared at Betty as if she were presenting an inconvenience to them.

"Just what the hell do you think you're doing?" demanded Betty.

"Sorry, miss," said the embarrassed-looking one. "Orders. Anything related to the lab, we've got to impound." He actually sounded a bit apologetic.

She noticed another MP, sitting in a car across the street, eating a doughnut. "And him?" she asked.

The one who didn't seem to give a damn spoke up. "For your own protection, miss," he informed her in a monotone. Robo-Military Cop.

"I should have known," said Betty sharply.

She wasn't in the mood to be protected by her father. At that instant she wanted nothing more than for him to do her the courtesy of lying down in the street behind her car so she could back over him.

Betty turned on her heel, hopped back into her car, and drove off. She glanced in her rearview mirror and, sure enough, the MP in the car was following her. Apparently her father's priorities superseded even the desire for a doughnut.

"Good," she muttered. She was in a stupendously foul mood, and finally here was someone handy on whom she could take it out. The sun was setting, which was always the most hazardous time to drive. She welcomed it.

Betty cruised along, approaching an intersection, slowed down as the light turned yellow, then floored the accelerator just as it turned red. She hurtled through the intersection just as two cars began to enter it, and they both slammed on their brakes as she blew past them.

The sudden switch in acceleration caught the MP off

guard and he automatically started to follow her. But the intersection was now blocked by the other two cars, and they were honking furiously at him. Betty watched in her rearview mirror, saw the car dwindling in the distance, and then increase in size again as it maneuvered around the two cars and came after her.

Good, she thought. *I'd hate for it to end too soon.*

Her car was a sporty model with manual transmission, and she'd been driving her sporty manual car in second gear, just to warm up. She switched it over into third, lead-footed the accelerator, and took off like a jackrabbit. It was the most fun she'd had in ages. In fact, it was the *only* fun she'd had in ages.

When she was fighting for her life several hours later, cursing herself for having ditched the MP in the kind of deliriously enjoyable auto chase that one usually only saw in films, the fun would seem very far away indeed.

unwise provocations

Glen Talbot was in an exceptionally good mood.

As the sun sank low on the horizon, Talbot drove up to the home of Bruce Banner, for such he knew him to be, and jovially greeted the MPs standing outside. "How's our boy?" he asked.

One of the MPs nodded toward Banner's window. And Talbot didn't like what he was seeing, because he didn't understand it. The blinds were opening, closing, opening, closing again, each time revealing and then shuttering light from within the living room. It was as if Bruce were trying to send a signal to somebody via some sort of code. But Talbot knew Morse code, not to mention sema-phore, for what that was worth, and Bruce wasn't blink-ing the blinds in any pattern he recognized.

Maybe it was another code altogether. That might be it. Bruce Banner might have invented a completely new version of an already existing transmission code, and was using it now to send a desperate message to a con-federate.

Either that or it really was meaningless, and Banner was just doing it to mess with their heads. Talbot started to relax, but then realized that might be exactly what Ban-

ner *wanted* them to think, which would mean that . . .
that . . .

Glen Talbot was no longer in a jovial mood. He was suddenly very, very irritated with Bruce Banner—and was certain that he was going to take that irritation out on Banner
himself.

Bruce wondered what they were hoping to accomplish
by leaving him alone in his home. Probably they wanted
him to sweat, to wonder what horrible thing was going to
happen next.

They didn't understand, had no comprehension. Sitting
around in his house couldn't begin to worry him. What
they were going to do to him was of no consequence. The
notion that they were going to yank his security clearance, ban him from plying his trade, was meaningless; all
their threats were meaningless.

His worries were far away from their priorities. His worries centered around the voice in his head, and a pounding
rage that seemed to be taking on a life of its own. Their
threats to the life he knew were inconsequential, because
Bruce already sensed that the life he knew was over. The
only matter remaining to be decided was precisely how
over it was.

At that moment, he heard the faint ringing of a telephone.

It confused him because it didn't sound like the ring of
his own phone. He wondered if Ross or one of the MPs
had left behind a cell phone, but he didn't see any. Just to
make sure, he picked up the receiver of his telephone, but
the ringing continued unabated. It would actually have
been rather surprising had it been his phone, considering

he could see now that the cord had been cut. Very thorough people, Ross and his boys.

That didn't alter the fact that the ringing was going on, and Bruce was starting to get more and more annoyed. He looked for its source and found it under the cushion on his chair. He pulled out a tiny cell phone, looked at it, pressed a button, and held it to his ear. "Hello?" said Bruce tentatively, certain that the phone must belong to Ross or an MP, and that was who the caller would be asking for.

He was stunned when he heard the voice of the man who had purported to be his father saying in a softly dangerous tone, "Bruce?"

When Bruce didn't answer, the old man just continued talking, as if Bruce's participation in the conversation not only wasn't mandatory but might even slow things down. "So they think they can just throw you away as they did me?"

Banner walked to the window and checked. The guards were milling about, unaware of his conversation. "What's wrong with me?" Bruce was almost whispering. "What . . . did you do to me?"

David Banner—if that was truly who he was—chose not to answer. Instead he said blandly, as if delivering a weather report from Guam, "I got a visit today. A very unwelcome visit. I'm afraid my hand is being forced."

Bruce wasn't going to let himself be distracted. "What did you do to me?" he persisted in asking.

An unpleasant laugh came from the other end. "You so much want to know, don't you? But I think no explanation will ever serve you half as well as experience. And, in any case, I still don't quite understand it myself," he admitted. "If they had only let me work in peace—but, of course, my 'betters' would have none of it."

"So you experimented on yourself, didn't you?" Bruce guessed between gritted teeth. Except it wasn't much of a guess; he'd had plenty of time to figure out exactly what had happened, presuming the old man's claims of patrimony were true. And as of now, he had zero reason to think otherwise. He paused, afraid to ask the next question and afraid not to. "And passed on to me . . . what?"

There was a silence on the other end that seemed to stretch to infinity. Bruce began to think that the connection had been lost, and then the old man spoke, making Bruce realize that his "father" had just been enjoying stringing him along.

"A deformity. You could call it that. But an amazing strength, too," he added, and Bruce could practically hear him smiling over the phone. "And now unleashed, I can finally harvest it."

There were few things David Banner could have said that would have been more alarming than that. "You'll do no such thing," Bruce said sharply. "I will isolate it and treat it myself. Remove it, kill it—before it does any real harm."

This time there was no deliberate pause or smugness. David replied immediately and angrily, his voice dripping with bile and bitter sarcasm. "Oh, I bet you and your Betty would love to destroy it. But would you *really*, even if it meant killing yourself? I don't think so."

Bruce wasn't so sure about that. He was slowly becoming aware of just what it was that was moving through his bloodstream, brought to full life by the combination of the nanomeds and gamma radiation. Had Bruce been left to his own devices, it was possible that—with his tendency to repress his emotions and fears—he might well have led a normal life—a life full of loneliness and emotional deprivation, but normal nonetheless. Well, relatively normal.

But it was becoming clear that the nanos and rads had had some sort of catalytic effect on him, triggering biological shifts and changes of which he could only guess. But if they had caused some sort of revision of his biological makeup, then perhaps it was possible to find a way to reverse the effect. Anything that was done could be undone. It didn't seem much more complicated than that.

And then David Banner said something that complicated things very, very much.

"And as for Betty," he told Bruce with a chortle, "I'm sending her a little surprise visit from some four-legged friends of mine."

The room, the world, seemed to go dark around Bruce Banner, seemed to skew at an angle. Suddenly there was a thudding pulse in his temples, and he had to fight to hear the words from the other end of the phone. "You see, I've managed to culture some of your very own DNA, Bruce, and the results, while unstable, are powerful," said David Banner.

"What *about* my DNA?" demanded Bruce.

His father ignored the question. "Let's just wait and see what Betty makes of the results!"

"No!" shouted Bruce. "You're crazy! I won't let you! You—!" But then he looked at the small readout on the phone and saw that there was no longer a connection. His father had hung up.

Utterly frantic, Bruce ran to the front door, pulled it open, and found Glen Talbot standing there, a smile on his face.

"Inside, asshole. I want to talk to you," said Talbot.

• • •

David Banner whistled a late 1950s pop tune called "Betty My Angel" as he removed the headset and went into the yard. Everything was moving so perfectly, falling into place so ideally, that it was one of those moments where he couldn't help but think that there was some higher purpose to all that had happened to him, some higher power that was moving in most mysterious ways. It was odd; he'd never thought of himself as a particularly devout man, or even a believer. But with all that was occurring and falling his way, perhaps—perhaps there was something to this God thing after all.

Well, why not? Man was, after all, supposed to have been created in God's image. That being the case, man should be as deft and adept at creating as that which had brought him into existence. And certainly David Banner had been holding up his end in that regard.

As he walked out into the yard, he was greeted with growling so vicious that it bordered on the obscene. Three feral voices snarled low and deep, sounding more like huge semis with busted mufflers than anything alive. He continued to whistle "Betty My Angel" even as he contemplated Betty becoming a genuine angel. It gave him a satisfied feeling. Let her be God's problem instead of his.

He held up Betty's scarf. Since she'd left it, he'd been careful to keep it isolated in a plastic bag so it wouldn't get any other scents mixed in with it. Now he waved the scarf, teased the dogs with it, kept it just out of their reach even as the waving caused them to go into berserk fits of barking.

When he'd gotten them sufficiently worked up, he let fly the scarf. Huge teeth powered by great, green muzzles tore into it as flecks of jade spittle flew from their maws.

"Now, fetch!" said David Banner, and they understood

what he wanted, for they had been well trained to start with, and the processes he'd inflicted on them had only made them more intelligent—not to mention more ferocious. "Fetch and let nothing stand in your way!"

The sun had not yet quite set, but the full moon was already visible high above the horizon. The dogs, like gigantic gamma-irradiated wolves, leaned back on their haunches and bayed at it.

If Glen Talbot had heard the chorus of canine ululation, he might well have joined in.

Everything that he'd done—the planning, the maneuvering, the precise and far-reaching Godlike manipulation—everything from striving to put Bruce and Betty together, to arranging for Bruce's nutball father to be kicked loose from the hospital so that the screws could be jammed in ever more tightly, everything was coming together precisely, like cogs in a great machine. In his mind's eye, Talbot could see Bruce Banner being mashed between those cogs, and in so suffering, unleashing tremendous untapped energy.

Talbot couldn't, of course, have anticipated the accident that sent the nanomeds and gamma radiation coursing through Banner's bloodstream. But that was the true beauty of a really great plan: When something unexpected occurred, it played perfectly into the overall scheme without causing the plan to miss a beat.

So now, when faced with the frantic scientist, it was all Talbot could do not to laugh in Banner's face and tell this brilliant researcher—who unquestionably thought that he was so much brighter, so much more intelligent than Talbot—that he, Banner, was just a pawn in a vast chess game. With Talbot moving all the pieces.

"Talbot, listen! It's my father. We don't have much time. I think he's going after Betty," Bruce said, the words spilling over one another.

Talbot stepped inside, kicked the door closed behind him, and approached Banner. He made sure to display a proper amount of ire, throwing a total non sequitur at Bruce to keep him off balance. "So, you think you can go behind my back, get Ross to cut me out?"

Banner blinked, an owl caught in the wash of a spotlight. "What are you talking about?" said Banner. "I'm trying to tell you, we need to get help—"

With a swift maneuver. Talbot kicked Banner's legs out from under him. Banner dropped on his back to the floor and Talbot pressed a shoe into his face. "You pathetic freak," he said tightly, his jaw twitching with an anger that came all too naturally. "Tomorrow, after I convince Ross, you'll be carted off to spend the rest of your life in some tiny, solitary hellhole. And I'll take over your work. But in the meantime," and his voice became more and more intense, "you're going to tell me what the hell happened to your lab. You didn't happen to steal anything important from it last night, did you?"

Talbot's heel was crushing Bruce's mouth. Even Talbot had to admit to himself that he was impressed by Bruce's tenacity, because all he could talk about was the woman. *"I swear to you, believe me, Betty is going to be killed."*

Unsure of whether he believed Banner or not, but certain that he didn't especially give a damn, Talbot pushed down harder. "If I can state the obvious, it's *your* health I'd be worried about right now."

Bruce desperately grabbed Talbot's leg with both hands, grunted, struggled, but couldn't overcome Talbot's strength and skill as Talbot ground his shoe into Bruce's face. He did so with a cold calculation that even an experienced scientist might have envied, provided that experienced scientist wasn't busy getting his face kicked in.

Talbot had studied the records concerning Bruce Krenzler, aka Banner, far too thoroughly to be engaging in such brutality simply for its own sake. Granted, he was enjoying it, but that was merely a bonus. The bizarre incidents involving young Banner's form had involved, according to all evidence, stress situations—so much so that Banner himself, in his psychological development, had locked away anything in his makeup that might trigger a response to stress. Now, though, the course of events had taken on a life of their own. Talbot had helped set the roller-coaster in motion; all he had to do was hold on for the ride.

He began to worry, though, that Banner might lapse into unconsciousness rather than provide him with what he wanted. So, satisfying himself with a final kick, he removed his foot from Banner's face. Bruce rolled over in pain, and propped himself up.

"Talbot—" he grunted through swollen and bleeding lips.

Talbot raised an eyebrow, amused. "Yes?"

"You're making me angry."

And Talbot really, really wanted to laugh at that. "Oh, am I?"

Banner managed a pained nod, then made what undoubtedly passed for a threat when coming from a ninety-pound weakling who was literally getting his head kicked in.

"I don't think you'll like me when I'm angry."

At which point Banner staggered to his feet, and Talbot took a quick step forward to drive a punch into Banner's gut.

It didn't land.

It was at that moment, that terrifying moment, as Talbot found his fist immobilized by a strength that dwarfed his, and was only growing exponentially with every passing second, that he fully and truly appreciated the wisdom of the old axiom: "Be careful what you wish for. You might get it."

. . . Hurt me hurt us hurt me pain make him pain hurt smash crush him let out out get out smash yes yes . . .

As the sweat poured down Banner's body, it soaked his shirt, and then the shirt ripped and there was

. . . pain so much pain good out stretching bending ripping rip tear smash . . .

exhilaration and a feeling of release, and Bruce Banner was a man who had been blind his entire life and was suddenly blessed with vision, and it was a vision filled with rage and anger and joy and lust and fury, pure unbridled fury, a volcano of fury exploding, an ocean of fury that wouldn't be held back anymore, and there was Talbot shaking and clearly terrified and he didn't matter anymore, nothing mattered anymore except

. . . Betty . . .

and the name, that name slammed through the pain, cut across the hot wires of Banner's wrath like a great pair of pliers, giving the transformation form and purpose and direction.

. . . smash him smash SMASH . . .

Talbot, a grown man, was whimpering like a child.

For all his research, for all his conviction that he had covered all the angles and anticipated everything that could possibly happen, he had never come close to truly guessing just what it was that he'd had a hand in.

All at once, he had an inkling of what it was like for those first scientists testing atomic bombs, and coming face-to-face with the potential for unprecedented destruction they had helped unleash.

The major difference was, in this case, that the face involved was green and snarling and filled with undiluted rage.

The face still bore some resemblance to Bruce Banner's, but it was widening and flattening out. It was like watching *Homo sapiens* devolve, tumbling down the evolutionary ladder and enjoying every rung of the plunge. There was rending and tearing of cloth, the shirt splitting down the back, the sleeves becoming mere rags. He'd been wearing a pair of sweatpants, and they at least were stretching somewhat, but the lower legs were being torn apart.

Banner was screaming, but it was hard to tell whether it was in pain or in release. His skin tone was changing completely, skewing from pink to light green and then to a deep jade. Insanely, he let out a loud, primal, vibrant laugh, then more screams of pain, more transformation, bigger, bigger, then a deafening roar.

Talbot hadn't come straight to Banner's home. He'd gone to the lab first, and he'd heard a word bandied about by some of the security guards. A word whispered in fear and dread by men who'd claimed they'd caught a glimpse of a slope-shouldered, slouching beast of a creature. Talbot had discounted much of it as fish stories, these tales of a hulk. He'd been sure that Banner had gained some sort of strength, undergone a transformation, but one had to allow for exaggeration even in the cases of eye-witnesses.

There had been no exaggeration. What there had been was the Hulk.

. . . kicked hurt hurt when kicked kick him smash kick . . .

Talbot fell back onto the couch, throwing his arms up as if such a pathetic defense could even begin to ward off the advancing green Goliath. The Hulk, not even slowing down, delivered a furious kick to the couch that sent it, and Talbot, crashing through the front window and out onto the lawn.

. . . out out Betty out . . .

Driven by imperatives he couldn't begin to articulate or comprehend, the Hulk exited the house by the most expeditious means possible: He simply walked through the front wall. It didn't slow him down for a millisecond. Wood and plaster shattered before him, sending debris flying everywhere, and then he stood there covered in white powder and howled into the darkness like a great primal ancestor of mankind, spat back up from prehistory.

The MPs barely had time to react to the sight of Glen Talbot making his explosive appearance on the front lawn, propelled via a couch, before they were confronted by a howling monster. It looked around with feral intensity, as if seeking something to tear apart with its massive bare hands.

Acting as one, they whipped out their guns and started firing. The Hulk flinched, more from the noise than anything else, and perhaps propelled by a residual memory that these little flying pellets were supposed to be lethal. They were, as it turned out, anything but. At most they were vaguely irritating, bouncing harmlessly off his green hide, and the Hulk made wide, sweeping gestures with his arms as if brushing away a swarm of wasps.

... hurt little hurt hurt them ...

Somewhere within the primal recesses of his brain, the Hulk make the connection between the small, stinging bits of lead and the men who were standing there with hunks of metal in their hands pointed at him. They were a good ten feet away, but the distance afforded them no protection at all as the Hulk vaulted it in one jump and plowed through them, tossing them aside with a swing of each arm. One went down with a loud crack, breaking several of his ribs. Another tried to leap out of the way and got caught in the sweep of an arm that was like a tree trunk, only harder, and was sent flying across the lawn to land in a heap some yards away.

Talbot said nothing. Curled up on the broken couch, trying to make himself as small as possible so as to avoid being noticed, he wasn't even breathing. To him, the pounding of his heart was too loud.

He needn't have worried. With the end of the immediate attack, the Hulk forgot about them completely. Instead his nostrils flared as he sniffed the air

... Betty Betty Betty ...

as her name pounded through his mind. There was no longer any connection to the immediate threat from his father, no clear comprehension that a woman named Betty whom he loved was in mortal danger. Instead it was simply a word he associated with a certain feeling, like hunger or pain or anger, and it was a feeling that was uppermost in what passed for his thought processes

... Betty ...

and it would have been impossible for Bruce Banner, with all his analytical ability, to decide whether the Hulk knew what to do next because—his senses hyperaccelerated by the transformation—he was actually able to pull Betty's scent from the air, or because he was functioning off some rudimentary memory of a happier time.

Ultimately, Bruce's talent for analysis had about as much relevance to the Hulk's actions as a remora's presence might have on which direction a shark decided to swim. The creature glanced around for a moment as street lights lit up around him. The lamps startled him for a moment, but just as quickly they too were forgotten.

The ground beneath the Hulk's feet began to rumble, as if an earthquake was approaching, and the Hulk's breathing began to increase. His entire body tensed, he crouched, threw his head back and let out an explosive howl of unfettered primal joy. And then he was airborne. The launch itself occurred with concussive force. All up and down the block, houses trembled and dishes shattered and people staggered around thinking that there had been a seismic shift of some kind.

And there had been. But it had been a shift in the very nature of what man was capable of achieving. It had been the unleashing of a force that was, in its own way, as devastating as the dropping of Fat Man and Little Boy on Hiroshima and Nagasaki. They had lived through it, and didn't even know what it was that they had lived through, nor did they understand just how lucky they were.

Nor did the Hulk understand anything, as he arced through the air for two miles at a clip, before angling downward, striking the ground at some new and equally vulnerable location—highway, delta, railroad track, wherever—then hurtling skyward once more. Only two things registered in his mind:

... *Betty* ... *smash* ... *Betty* ...

But whether that meant the Hulk was going to destroy anything that might be threatening Betty or whether he was intent on smashing her himself, no one could have said.

The starlight played across his skin, causing bizarre patterns to emerge as he melted into the night.

PART THREE: SUPEREGO

dogs of war

The thing Betty Ross loved most about the cabin was the quiet. No sirens, no babies crying or people shouting. All was calm and serene. The only thing around were the noises of the wildlife, and admittedly there had been a time when that had been disconcerting. Many were the nights when she was startled awake by screech owls or howling coyotes. Perhaps "quiet" was something of a misnomer at that, for the sounds of life in the forest were almost constant. Before too long, however, Betty had not only adjusted to them, but she'd come to appreciate and enjoy them. In fact, the steady backdrop of animal noises routinely lulled her to sleep, and this night was no exception.

She had built a nice, roaring fire in the fireplace and then, tossing on sweats and a T-shirt, had curled up on the rug to watch it and think about all that had occurred. She knew it was entirely possible that an MP might show up outside the cabin at any time. It wasn't as if her father didn't know about the place. But considering that she had ditched her unwanted shadow in a spirited car chase that involved extensively ignoring the speed limit and, most entertainingly, a high-velocity blast through a railroad crossing just under the descending barrier, it was entirely possible that she had sent a message to the army even they were capable of comprehending.

Her thoughts didn't stray far from Bruce and his father as she lay there, contemplating the flames. She remembered when she and Bruce had been up here, and she had nestled in his arms, during that brief time when anything in their relationship seemed possible. Amazing how quickly it had all come unraveled.

She also kept running through her mind her encounter with David Banner. She couldn't help but feel that she had experienced a narrow escape, but not quite. That was to say, she hadn't quite escaped. But even she couldn't quite wrap herself around the notion that there was something she was overlooking, some bit of business that could come back to bite her.

Betty tried to come up with some definitive plan of action, but her thoughts were simply too scattered, too unfocused. Before too long, the mesmerizing effect of the fire tired her eyes, and she settled into a deep sleep.

It wasn't the noise that woke her some time later.

It was the lack of noise.

She didn't realize it at first. All Betty knew when she awoke with a start was that something was wrong. The fire had burned down, but there was still some light filtering through the window from the full moon. Light, warmth, a secure place . . . everything was as it should be, but something was still off.

That was when it occurred to her. There were no noises coming from the forest at all.

At all.

At. All.

Everything, every small creature trying to avoid being eaten, every predator rummaging for prey, everything that walked or flew or crawled through the underbrush had ceased making the slightest sound. It was as if they had all fled the area, or else had become completely quiet, withdrawing into themselves so as not to attract the attention of . . .

. . . of what?

Then she heard a noise, and felt relief for a brief second because it seemed to indicate that everything was normal after all. The noise, however, was a rustling that sounded as if it was being produced by something—bigger—than was normally the case. As big as a bear, or perhaps still larger.

Other than that rustling, she couldn't hear a thing.

Betty thought about every horror movie she'd ever seen, where the idiot heroine mindlessly thrusts herself into the midst of danger by walking guilelessly toward it, waving a flashlight. Growing up, she'd seen such films and shook her head at the stupidity. "Idiot plots," she had muttered while her friends watched, enraptured.

So she was vaguely surprised to find herself scrounging for a flashlight, gripping it firmly, shoving her car keys into her pocket, flipping on the outside lights, and stepping away from the cabin to try to discern what was approaching. On the surface of it, her actions were utterly mad. But she couldn't really just stay cowering in the cabin; if there was, indeed, some sort of extremely large animal out there, it could easily be able to smash through the windows and corner her within. In her car, at least, she would be mobile.

That would also be the case if the animal were an extremely dangerous type—such as a human being. So after running all the options through her mind, she was forced to conclude that the action she was now taking—as demented as it might seem—was the best one available to her.

Nothing leapt upon her as she emerged from the cabin, playing the beam of the flash across the woods. Perhaps it was indeed just some dumb animal, frightened by the brightness of the beam. Nevertheless, just to give herself an out, she made her way toward the car, consistently turning 360 degrees as she did so, in order to see as much around her as she possibly could. When she made it to the car, she put her back against it and studied the dark forest edge and the black dense water of the lake, both of which lay in front of her.

"Hello?" Betty called softly.

She paused, listened. The wind whispered gently, and other than that there was no sound at all, not even the rustling she'd heard earlier. The pale beam of the flashlight slowly arced across the trunks of the massive redwood trees that surrounded the cabin. Still nothing.

Betty began to laugh softly to herself. Here she was, getting ready to jump into her car and speed away lest she be harmed by nothing at all.

She began to walk back inside but then stopped and turned. She'd caught something out of the corner of her eye just as the flashlight was making a final pass over the trees. She wasn't sure what it was, but it was something that wasn't quite right. Not when compared to the trees around it.

She frowned, keeping the beam steady. "What the hell . . . ?" she murmured, and took several steps forward.

There were two broad-trunked redwoods, but there was something else—a bizarre tree or vegetation—in between them. It was as massive as the trees themselves, but the surface was smooth rather than rough, like bark. And it was the most curious shade of green, and it . . .

It breathed.

It . . . was alive.

Impossible. Get in the car, run. Impossible.

Her feet, however, refused to move. She was literally rooted to the spot. Her arm, however, was still functioning, and slowly she angled the beam, moving it up and over what Betty was beginning to realize, to her horror, was the chest of a living, breathing creature. Up went the beam, over pectorals the size of children and arms the size of cannons. Up toward what would be the face, but at that point Betty had no idea what to expect. If the beam had revealed a creature laughing dementedly while waving a flaming pumpkin head, she likely would have taken it in stride.

The face of the green-skinned individual was lost in shadow. She could, however, see the general outline of the creature, and more than that she saw the beam reflected in the glowing green eyes. Those eyes narrowed in suspicion and mild confusion. It stared at her in a way that seemed to reflect a rudimentary degree of recognition—most likely, she thought, because it was recognizing her as a late-night snack.

At that point, Betty screamed, stepping slightly backward, and dropped the flashlight as the monster turned and approached. And "monster" it most certainly was. There was no disputing that this beast was something unknown to, and outside of, nature. An abhorrent, lurking thing that would just as soon rip her apart as waste any time at all on her.

As she backed up, she stumbled over a tree root. Her arms flailed out as she fell backward, and the creature was

right on her, grabbing her before she could hit the ground
so that it could rend her limb from . . .

And the monster held her.

That was all. Just held her, at an angle. They looked, insanely, like a pair of dancers caught frozen in the midst of
a graceful dip. But there was nothing the least bit genteel
about the beast that was holding her in the palm of one
hand.

She tried to move, but couldn't. The creature wasn't
holding her immobile; she was simply too terrified to
budge. And the monster was staring into her face, as if
whatever the beast wanted was hidden in her eyes.

They remained that way for a long moment. Then, as
gently as a mother easing her child into a crib, the creature brought Betty up so that she could stand on her own
two feet. And still it never looked away from her. It appeared to be . . . recognizing her somehow. But from
where? Betty wasn't exactly in the habit of spending in-
ordinate amounts of time with huge, green, forest-
dwelling monstrosities.

She gave out a small, startled gasp as the creature lifted
her gently onto the top of her car. She sensed the strength
in the arms; the monster could have crushed her with no effort at all. Instead it was handling her with almost touching
delicacy.

Once she'd been set down atop the car, the change in al-
titude provided her with a new perspective, namely one of
eye-to-eye. The monster stared fixedly at her, almost as if
it was trying to determine something.

Abruptly Betty saw the creature's face fill with a mixture of terror and anger. It turned and sniffed the air. It
was ludicrous of her to even think of addressing the monster, and yet she started to ask what was wrong. But it

swiftly placed its hand over her mouth. Reflexively she started to struggle as she realized that the creature might try to strangle her. But it didn't even seem to notice her resistance as it just held her, and then it lifted her up, holding her in an embrace that could only be seen as protective.

There was total silence, just as there had been earlier. It seemed as if the rest of the world had come to a complete halt, leaving just the two of them.

Betty saw them before the creature did.

All the blood drained from her face as they seemed to materialize like green specters at the edge of the forest. Three dogs, but they were only dogs in the broadest sense of the word. They were huge, hulking green creatures, heads lowered, jaws hanging down, eyes blazing hatred at a world that would allow such atrocities as they to exist. Saliva dripped down in a steady stream. From each of their throats came low growls that sounded like passing freight trains, but they were most certainly not passing. They were staying right there, and they were utterly terrifying.

And then they attacked.

Operating in concert with one another, the three animals took several quick bounds toward Betty and her unlikely protector, then vaulted through the air, covering the twenty feet between them in one impossible jump. Betty barely had time to register their advance, when her protector sprang backward, landing on the other side of the car. He did so with such facility that Betty realized he could probably escape from the charging monsters with very little difficulty, perhaps even enable both of them to get away.

But the low growl of anger she heard rumbling within

his breast said it all. She realized that running away was simply not in his nature. She also realized that she had suddenly stopped thinking of him as an "it."

The monstrous dogs overshot their target as if they were still unaccustomed to using their bodies and were unfamiliar with what they could do. The moment they passed, the giant shoved her against the car, and Betty automatically yanked the door open and thrust herself inside, offering herself a modicum of protection. He shoved the door closed, and the metal crumpled under the impact. Then he whirled to face the monsters, and issued a full-throated roar that seemed to dare them to take their best shot. The dogs thudded to the ground a few feet away, spun to face him, and snarled back, obviously accepting his defiant challenge. He crouched, looking as if he were going to jump at them, and suddenly he was airborne, heading straight up like a missile. Betty craned her neck, trying to peer through the windshield and keep track of him, but he was gone.

The dogs tried their best to follow. They jumped straight up, but quickly fell back to earth. Instantly Betty understood why: Their bodies were designed to cover horizontal distances, not vertical. Human beings were upright creatures, and it was Betty's strongest indication that—whatever her mysterious savior was—he was somehow far closer to human then she had initially thought.

The three canines circled in confusion, unsure for a moment what to do. Then, as one, they swiveled their attention to the car, and her heart froze in her chest. Their thick lips pulled away from their rotting teeth, their eyes glowered, and they started to advance.

And then, from overhead, the jade giant descended

once more, and landed squarely on the back of one of the three dogs. He drove it straight down to the ground, crushing its body beneath his feet. There was a deafening snap and the creature let out such a cry of anguish that for an instant Betty actually felt sorry for it. But only for an instant. The other two dogs converged on the green monster, but he was already up and gone again.

Betty watched with a combination of horror and fascination as the crushed dog's flesh began to steam and melt away. It was as if nature was anxious to dispose of this abomination. The remaining two terrifying animals circled with even greater agitation, for they had absolutely no idea where to focus their attention: upon the prey in the car, upon their obviously deceased fellow, or upon their airborne green tormentor, who might return at any time.

Suddenly one of the creatures darted quickly to the right, for no apparent reason that Betty could see, but then the reason became evident. The giant landed again with a resounding impact. This time, however, his target had sensed him at the last second and barely avoided meeting the same fate as the first.

Now the battle was truly joined. One of the dogs clamped onto the giant's ankle. He let out a thunderous bellow that seemed capable, on its own, of leveling trees, and indeed it seemed to Betty that the redwoods were trembling as a result. He tried to shake the dog loose, and its fellow lunged straight at his neck.

Betty screamed. It was unthinkable how quickly everything had turned around. Less than a minute ago, she had regarded the bizarre green intruder as some sort of incredible threat ripped from the deepest recesses of her nightmares. Now she was seeing him as a defender, her only chance of getting out of this insane situation in one piece.

But it was hopeless. He was outnumbered by his inhuman attackers, and one of them had a death grip on his throat.

The giant staggered. With a snap of his leg he shook the one dog loose, then managed to pry apart the other dog's jaws. Betty saw mangled flesh at the base of the giant's neck, and green blood began oozing from it as the behemoth swung his arm around and sent the dog tumbling. He grabbed at his neck, probably feeling the pooling warmth, and looked in what was obvious surprise at the thick green liquid that collected in his palm.

The dog who had been at his ankle turned its attention to Betty, and she screamed once more. The giant tried to respond, but the other dog was blocking his path. He staggered back, his rage momentarily taking a backseat to his primal urge to survive, then vaulted backward, ricocheting from the top of the cabin to the top of a nearby tree.

The dogs quickly lost interest in their opponent, and circled the car. Betty shoved her hands into her pockets, looking for the keys . . . and spotted them outside, ten feet away, glistening mockingly on the ground where they'd fallen. "Oh, perfect," she grated, realizing that her temporary haven was little more than a hunk of inanimate glass and metal that would fall very quickly to any concerted attack from these . . . these . . .

Gamma irradiated . . . displaying tremendous strength and resilience . . . they were manufactured somehow, similar to the experimentation we've been pursuing. If it was only possible to perform studies . . .

She was stunned at herself. Stunned, but also a little

proud. Here she was, her life probably about to end, but she was going to go out thinking like a scientist. It was cold comfort, but it was better than nothing.

And suddenly she jumped, jammed back against the seat, as a huge paw thudded against the windshield. Then her view was entirely blocked by snarling fangs and a long, dangling tongue. Another paw joined the first, slamming against the glass and leaving long scratches with ear-splitting shrieks. The windshield began to crack, spiderweb designs ribboning across it.

Then there was a thump, and the dog's face was mashed flat against the windshield, thick rivulets of blood dribbling everywhere. At first Betty couldn't comprehend what had just happened, but then she saw it.

The behemoth hadn't been running from the dogs at all; he had simply been seeking out a weapon that would prove effective against them. What he had chosen proved devastating in its simplicity: an uprooted redwood tree. He had swung it with the precision of a baseball player at the plate and mashed the attacking canine flat.

Straining to see through the streams of blood that were obscuring her view, Betty caught a quick glimpse of her protector looking around, clearly trying to see where the third dog had gotten off to. Then he found out as the mastiff leaped from behind, landing squarely on his back. The giant swung the tree around futilely, trying to reach the dog and having no luck. He tossed aside the lumber and instead tried grabbing at the dog. The beast eluded his questing hands, and so the giant simply threw himself backward, hoping to crush the dog by hitting the ground flat on his back.

It was good in theory but failed in execution as the dog scrambled around to the front just as he struck the

ground. It tried to drive its massive jaws toward the
giant's throat once again, but the behemoth caught it just
in time, and they rolled across the forest floor, a combination of howls and snarls and green-muscled fury locked
in a deadly embrace, biting, mauling, choking.

And suddenly the dog that had been smeared to within an
inch of its life on the windshield managed to retreat from
that final inch. The light dying in its eyes stoked back to full
fire. It smashed through the glass in a final, desperate lunge,
and just as it did, Betty's hand yanked on the seat release.
The upper section of the seat slammed back and Betty fell
flat as the beast's jaws crunched together just above her. She
closed her eyes, partly to avoid getting broken glass in them,
but also because she couldn't stand to see that horrific face
crunching into hers.

She braced herself, hoping against hope that it would
be quick.

It wasn't.

She froze that way for a few seconds, then looked up.
The dog's head had gone limp; its jaws were hanging
open. Its final attack had been, indeed, its final attack, as
it succumbed to the damage the giant had inflicted upon
it. Its body began to sizzle and melt as the other one's had,
and Betty scrambled backward, getting her legs clear. She
wasn't sure if the goo would have any toxic effect upon
her, but she wasn't inclined to take the chance.

From across the clearing, she heard more snarling and
howling, and it was impossible for her to discern what
was coming from the animal and what from the giant. The
dog was most certainly not human, but it was still hard for
her to believe that the giant ever had been.

The sounds escalated as the ferocity of the struggle
increased, until there was a high-pitched whimper that

could only have come from the throat of the dog. Betty
tried to see past the shattered glass, but was reluctant to
touch the dead dog in order to get it out of the way.
Through the blood and gore she saw the outline of the
giant, holding the third dog at arm's length, and it seemed
impossible but somehow the giant appeared larger than he
had before. Yes . . . yes, it was true, for his fist was large
enough to encircle the entirety of the beast's throat, where
it hadn't been before. And suddenly the fist squeezed and
the dog's whimper became a high-pitched squeal of alarm,
followed by a pulpy bursting of flesh and bone.

Had Betty been processing information in anything resembling a normal fashion, she would have felt sick to
her stomach. As it was, she was so much into the realm of
mental overload that she was starting to think that nothing could ever shock her again.

*. . . Dead dead smashed no more dog done Betty safe
Betty Betty . . .*

. . . Safe . . .

. . . Done tired so tired but . . .

. . . but . . . but . . . Betty . . . is . . .

. . . is safe . . . Betty is . . . safe . . .

"Betty . . . is safe. . . ."

He spoke the words, and didn't fully comprehend what
they meant. The urgency, the need had been so deeply
within him that it had lost all context or sense.

His mind still in a fog, he was stumbling forward and fell
to the riverbank, catching himself with his powerful arms
before he could tumble headfirst toward the water. He stared
blankly at his reflection, his thoughts fighting through the
white noise of his consciousness, and there was an image in
the water, and the water was wavering, except . . . it wasn't.

The water was still save for the rippling being caused by raindrops. It was his face that was wavering, except it wasn't his face because it was large and green and distorted, except it was, because every man knows in his heart the face of darkness and rage that he carries within him; he simply chooses to ignore it.

But there it was, staring back at him, except it was shrinking and shifting and undulating and turning into a face of weakness and bewilderment, and the sight of that face both angered him and filled him with a greater relief than he had ever known. The green tint to his skin mottled and then dissolved away into his normal flesh tone.

And a voice sounded within his head, and it was his own voice and it was another, guttural voice. But, for one, brief moment, both voices had exactly the same concern:

Betty . . .

The rain splattered against what remained of the windshield, causing the blood to smear and run. Some of it was beginning to wash away, enabling Betty to see a little better. A little, but not much.

She thought the giant was staggering toward the water, and she was worried that he had been mortally wounded. But he was no longer clutching at his throat where the skin had been torn away. That injury alone should have been enough to kill him, but instead, remarkably, it seemed as if the blood flow had been halted, as if the rip had just . . . just healed itself up somehow.

. . . healed . . . gamma radiation . . .

Oh, my God.

Oh. My God.

Even as she watched the giant sink to his knees, the truth of what she had just witnessed, the insane reality that her world had become, made itself known to her. Even as she watched the skin ripple and shift and retract in on itself, defying all the known laws of physics, as the behemoth's mass just melted away like butter in a skillet, she denied it while accepting it.

My God, what have we unleashed? she thought with a combination of revulsion and fascination.

The world stopped as the man staggered to his feet, swaying in the rain, as if it had washed away the form of the monster to leave only the man. A baptism, reestablishing his humanity. And when he turned to face her, when Betty saw the face she knew she would see, the delicate line separating fantasy from reality blurred and twisted and then broke apart. Dancing through her head was the child's song about rowing a boat, purely because of its refrain, "Life is but a dream."

He staggered toward her like a drunken man, and when he got to the side of the car, he pulled on the door that had been crushed in when the monster had shoved it closed. So strong he had been, so strong, and yet now he was standing there dripping with rain and pulling with all his nonexistent might, pitting his meager efforts against the giant's almost casual display of power. Finally, after much struggle, he managed to pry it open, and Betty half staggered, half fell out of the car. She saw blood smear across him and panicked for a moment before she realized it was hers, blood from cuts caused by the shattered glass and the final desperate swipe of a dying beast's claws.

They sank to the ground, which was becoming muddy from the now-cascading rain, clutching each other, mutually seeking anchors of reality in a world made deliriously unreal. She held him tight, cradled him in her arms, and then he looked at his hands like a newborn child seeing them for the first time. It was only at that point that it really, truly seemed to dawn on him that his towering green alter ego was gone, that he was himself again. How horrifying the realization must be for him, to know that he was rage incarnate, power out of control.

And then he laughed.

The response wasn't at all what Betty expected. It not only caught her off guard, it made her feel—as strange as it sounded—even more uncomfortable than when she was being attacked by the gamma-irradiated dogs. He shook the fist that he'd been staring at, the thrust coming perilously close to Betty's face, and the shocking thing was that he didn't seem to notice. Rain poured down his face, into his eyes, slicked down his hair, and it didn't seem to matter to him. He laughed again, this time sounding almost maniacal, like a . . . like a mad scientist.

Betty winced and reflexively drew back. He didn't seem to care, caught up in his delirious chortling and self-satisfaction. He wasn't shocked, he wasn't terrified or appalled or frightened by what these events portended. He was happy. *Happy!* Happier than she had ever seen him. Worse . . . happier than she'd ever made him.

"Am I awake?" said Bruce. Betty nodded hesitantly. "Was it me? I *killed* them, right? *I killed them!*"

Bruce Krenzler, for all his emotional repression, had always been deeply considerate of Betty's feelings. But the man known as Bruce Banner didn't seem to care about them in the least, because he clamped his hand over her mouth without thinking in order to demonstrate what he was referring to. "Like that! I snapped their necks!"

Driven by nearly frantic energy, Betty shoved him away. He seemed startled.

"Bruce!"

He looked at her, blinking against the rain, then squeezed the bridge of his nose between thumb and forefinger as if to force himself to fully concentrate on who and where he was.

Tentatively, fearfully, Betty leaned forward and whispered, "You can't control it, can you?" She wasn't just talking about the transformation, and she had a feeling he knew that. He couldn't control the giddy euphoria that seized him and filled him with joy over the prospect of having crushed living creatures to death. Best, though, to focus on the change rather than his current emotional state. "Do you remember . . . how it comes?"

Finally a true look of fear appeared in his eyes. The full weight of what had occurred became clear to him, an eclipsing shadow of the moon moving away from the sun. He looked again at his hand, his fist, and this time there was no joy in contemplating the power of life and death that hand had held.

She took it gently in her own hands.

Slowly Bruce shook his head. "I don't know," he said, with no trace of the mania that had gripped him so thoroughly. "It's just the anger, the rage. I don't know. I'm just . . . tired . . . afraid and so tired."

She held him again in the rain. He closed his eyes and sagged against her. She helped him up and brought him into the cabin, and as she did so, the noises slowly returned to the forest.

As Bruce slept, Betty sat there and watched him. She thought of the creature. She thought of the power he had displayed, the way he'd reveled in it. And she thought that rage, in its most fundamental form, was uncontrollable.

There was no way for sure to know what direction his anger would take, or against whom he might next turn.

She was shaken to the core by the way he'd clamped a hand over her mouth, and she thought of the way the hulking behemoth had crushed the skull of that glowing green mastiff. She stared at Bruce's hands and could only see them large and green, and subjecting her to the same fate as the dogs. She looked at his bare chest, slowly rising and falling, and saw instead the massive chest of the awesome jade monster as she'd first spotted him in the woods.

The single most devastating, destructive, and unpredictable force to be created in the last half century was sleeping on her couch.

It was no wonder, really, that she panicked. No wonder that she picked up her cell phone, scrolled through the saved numbers, found the one for the Joint Tactical Force West. But now she found there was no signal on her cell. Hardly a shock. She tiptoed into the kitchen, picked up the phone, and dialed as quietly as she could.

It took them no time at all to track down her father, and when she whispered, "Dad?" into the phone she did so with the tentativeness of someone entering a confessional and trying to determine if a priest was on the other side.

"Betty!" came her father's voice, and she couldn't recall the last time she had been so glad to hear it. Or glad at all, really. "Are you all right?"

His booming tone was a sharp contrast to Betty's hushed whisper. "I'm scared, and I . . . we need your help. I need to . . ." She paused. It was the most difficult thing she'd ever said, and she was saying it as much to herself as to him. "I need to trust you."

"Where are you?" said Ross.

She pressed the phone more tightly against her ear. "It's not Bruce's fault. You have to believe me. His father, he tried to kill me and Bruce. . . ."

Bruce stirred slightly and Betty paused, watching him.

"Yes? Betty? Betty?" said Ross.

"We're at the cabin," she said abruptly. "We're not going anywhere. Take your time. Make preparations. And Dad, whatever you do . . ."

"Yes?"

"Don't piss him off."

betrayal or salvation?

The rain from the night before had had a cleansing effect on the forest. Come the morning sun, it would have been hard to believe that there had been any sort of altercation at all. The downpour had washed away the blood and gore that had been splattered about, including the dissolved corpses of the killer dogs. The fallen tree was there, but trees fall all the time. As for the bashed-in car, well, there wasn't much to be done about that, really.

Bruce was sitting up on the couch, a blanket wrapped around him since he had no clothes there to change into. He was still having trouble processing all that had happened. So much of it was like a dream, and not just the over-the-top changing into a monster aspects of it. He remembered the entire event in the same manner that one does a dream, with quick impressions here or sense memories there. The only difference was that in a dream, you're entirely within your own head and limited to whatever visual elements you can recollect. But here, Betty had witnessed it, and she had even spoken with Bruce's lunatic father, who purported to be behind at least some aspect of what had occurred. So she was able to help him piece it all together.

She sat in a chair opposite him, hands resting in her

lap. She was taking all of this far better than he would have been able to, if the circumstances had, somehow, been reversed. She smiled at him, spoke to him gently, did nothing to get him the least bit worked up. A certain amount of that came from pure self-preservation, sure enough. It definitely wasn't in her best interests to get him worked up. The fortunate thing, though, was that Betty was concerned about Bruce, about what had happened to him, and what most likely would happen to him if the situation were allowed to continue unchecked.

Betty was in his court, though. She was one hundred percent on his side, and as long as that was the case, Bruce couldn't envision any scenario they couldn't overcome, any conundrum so difficult that they wouldn't be able to solve it.

The morning sun created a small corona around her hair. She appeared almost angelic as, with a beatific face, she went over everything that had happened, trying to connect the dots of the puzzle in order to bring it into clearer focus.

"Your anger," she was saying, "it must trigger some kind of signal, and if the DNA strands break open that quickly there must be a tremendous release of energy."

"Which I somehow absorb," said Bruce thoughtfully.

"And transform. Like you did with the gamma rays. It's just . . . inside of you." Then she paused, trying to figure out the answer to her next question even before she voiced it. "But then . . . what stops it?" she asked.

"Yeah, what stops it from going on and on, into some kind of chain reaction?" he wondered aloud. "Maybe the next time, it'll just keep going."

The notion caused Betty to shudder. Bruce couldn't blame her, really. The prospect of becoming . . . what?

King Hulk, stomping through town, knocking over buildings and threatening airplanes while clutching a screaming beauty in his oversize hand. What a wonderful mental image to carry. Better that he should explode, like Freddie.

He paused. There was something else he wanted to say, but it was a difficult thing for him to admit. He had no idea how she would react, and his instinct was to keep it to himself. But he was trying to be honest with Betty, to let her know everything that was going through his mind. If he stinted on that now, she would know. He didn't know how she'd know, but she would.

And the bottom line was she wanted to help him. She cared about him, loved him. How could she possibly aid him if he kept things from her?

He leaned forward, gesturing for her to do likewise. She hesitated a moment, and then did so. He spoke in a low voice, like a wizard about to utter a chant. "You know what scares me the most? When it happens, when it comes over me, when I totally lose control—" They locked gazes, and he reached deep into the truth of his soul and admitted it to her, and to himself. "—I like it."

There was a moment of silence. Clearly Betty had no idea how to react, and that was understandable. Bruce was exploring new territory himself. There was no reason that Betty shouldn't be daunted by the prospect. Indeed, the fact that she'd taken as much as she had in stride was nothing short of . . .

At that moment, Bruce heard a noise outside. It sounded like a garbage can being knocked over. Perhaps a raccoon was foraging around.

He gestured for Betty to remain exactly where she was. She watched him with limpid eyes as he went to the window to ascertain just what it was that was rooting around outside. He wasn't expecting to do anything more than shout loudly in order to frighten off some creature foraging, looking for a snack.

So it was that when he leaned out the window, he was caught unawares by a soft pop of air and a sudden sharp pain squarely in his gut. He stared down uncomprehendingly to see a tranquilizer dart still quivering in his stomach.

He knew it immediately for what it was, and sought to yank it out of his belly. However, when he informed his right arm of what he wanted to do, his right arm simply hung there like a lifeless slab of meat. His left arm was, rudely, no more cooperative than his right, and then he sank to his knees and managed to get out the word, "What?" Which was about all he could think of to say.

The world started to haze out around him, and then Betty was there, her face filling the entirety of his field of vision. Betty went to him, helped him to the ground. He stared up at her uncomprehendingly as she murmured, "It's going to be all right. It's just going to make you sleep." He tried shaking his head, but he couldn't even force his neck muscles to respond, and she continued, "You'll forgive me, Bruce. I know you will. I didn't know what else to do."

That was when he realized what she had done. He hadn't associated the dart with Betty, because the magnitude of such a betrayal was too great for him to comprehend. But now that he did realize, he felt the beginnings of a green haze settling upon him. He could see it, floating there, bringing with it fury and release and the ability to avenge this wrong, to strike back at his attackers, at his betrayers.

Forgive her? *Forgive her?* He would . . . would . . .

"To help you, okay?" she continued, although he could

barely make it out, for the haze was enveloping him, but it was also beginning to dissipate. He realized it was a race, the narcotics coursing through his body even as his mind tried to fight them off, to send him to a place where the anger would carry him through. Nourish him.

"We're going someplace safe, where nothing can go after you. You understand, I didn't know what to do. I couldn't just let you go."

But he was going to go . . . go . . . He would show her, show them, whoever they were . . . and . . . whoever he was . . . *hard to . . . focus . . . just . . . have to . . . remember . . . remember . . . something . . . what was . . . ?*

The door burst open and a uniformed tactical team entered, weapons drawn. Although he could no longer move his head, his eyes shifted toward them and the world became a great blur to him, a great, large green blur. That seemed somehow amusingly appropriate to him.

He looked up at Betty once more, and she was taken aback, because she saw it then in his eyes, the hint of glittering anger, pure as a newborn, and if he had been able to remain conscious for even another three seconds, he might have been able to fight it off, fight through it, and become that which he knew would be able to solve this problem, something that would mow through the mass of green bodies in front of him like a thresher and he would . . .

. . . *smash . . . smash them . . . smash . . . sleep . . . sleep . . .*

And a blackness tinged with green claimed him.

Betty Ross had never felt so utterly torn in her life.

She told herself that what she had done was good and right and proper, that she'd had no choice, really, none whatsoever. And she kept saying that, right up until the soldiers grabbed the unconscious Bruce as if he were a sack of meat and bones.

"Hold it!" she shouted.

"One side, we'll take it from here," one of the soldiers said brusquely, and another strong-armed her out of the way.

They were throwing him around, slamming cuffs and locks and restraints on him, bruising him. Bruce moaned in his drug-induced sleep, and she saw the beginnings of a large bruise on his bare shoulder from where one of them had thoughtlessly banged him into the edge of the sofa.

"I said hold it!"

"Ma'am," one of the soldiers said with that sort of feigned politeness that was really nothing of the kind, "step aside or we'll be forced to—"

"Shut up, soldier, and stand down right now! All of you! *Now! Unless you're that anxious to screw with the daughter of Thunderbolt Ross!"*

She derived some faint intellectual amusement from the fact that she had something sounding very much like her father's voice coming out of her mouth. Certainly the soldiers looked stunned, and the entire operation crashed to a halt as they froze where they were.

Betty didn't hesitate, because to do so would have indicated weakness, and she could afford to display none. "Now listen up! I'm Dr. Elizabeth Ross! Ranking officer, identify yourself."

One of the soldiers stepped forward, looking at her suspiciously. "Lieutenant Simmons."

"Simmons, this man here is my find and my responsibility, and I will see him handled with kid gloves or I will see the next man who so much as uses harsh language on him hauled up on charges. He's got more power in one arm than you have in your entire armory, and if you cause that power to be unleashed, then God help you, because no one else will, including your mama. Do we understand each other?"

Speaking very stiffly, but with proper restraint, Simmons said, "Yes, doctor."

"Now," she said with brisk efficiency, "show me what you've got."

He frowned. "Ma'am?"

Rolling her eyes, she clarified, "For transportation and containment. And let's remember, soldier, this man was eight feet tall and green not all that long ago, and all you troops still couldn't find him, which makes me think you couldn't find your ass with both hands and a flashlight. You're here because I called my father and told you where to come and what to do, which means we play this my way. Got it?"

"Yes, doctor," he said again.

Inwardly, Betty felt like a complete sham. These weren't her own words flying out of her mouth, her own personality in force. She was deliberately channeling her father. On the other hand, as the soldiers proceeded to treat her with complete deference and she watched them handle Bruce's insensate body as if he were a carton of eggs, she couldn't help but feel like the most glorious sham in the world.

And for just a moment, she had the faintest idea of what it had been like for Bruce to be almost giddy with empowerment. She liked it.

unbalance of power

The quiet of the sky over Desert Base was shattered by
the powerful engines of the Sikorsky H-60 Black Hawk
helicopter, escorted by a pair of smaller Apache choppers
that flew high above. On the ground at the base, there was a
mad scramble that might have looked to the untrained eye
like total confusion, but was in fact highly organized. A
transport truck drove up just as the Black Hawk descended
to several hundred feet, and the 'copter's loading bay
opened up to disgorge its cargo on a crane—the cargo con-
sisting of a large container that looked like an oversize tube,
or, perhaps, a high-tech coffin.

The transport truck joined other vehicles to form a convoy, then headed away from the main section of the base,
the place with the obvious hangars and barracks and all
sorts of places that congressmen or assorted inspectors
might poke through at any given moment in order to im-
press constituents. But this particular transport's destination was someplace a bit more . . . secluded.

Back in the early days of Desert Base, there had been
some additional property adjacent to it that was privately
owned and featured a drive-in movie theater. The theater
had served as a popular gathering place for army personnel, who'd park with their honeys and kick back to watch

the latest grade B horror flick. Curiously, when the base blew up years earlier, the theater was one of the few things left standing. It wasn't, however, in good condition.

Over a period of time, the deteriorating remains of the theater became a front for all the research that was considered a bit too delicate for normal venues.

The convoy rolled up to the dilapidated screen and then stopped. Nothing happened at first, and then slowly, with an audible grinding of gears, the ground itself began to move. The first panicked thought of an observer would have been that it was an earthquake, and that a crevice was opening up directly in front of one. But seconds later, a huge door lifted clear, revealing a deep, sloping tunnel, and there was the glint of a track in the early morning sun.

In no time at all the soldiers off-loaded the metal tube from the truck and onto the rails. Interlocks engaged, and the tube slowly but steadily descended into the hidden recesses of the underground facility. A small mountain range sat in the near distance, and it would have been impossible for anyone to guess that entire sections of the range had been hollowed out to serve as hidden means of access for aircraft. And, once the entry ramp sank back down into the desert soil, no one would have known that there was anything underground at all.

A short time later the tube was unloaded in the vast underground arrival hall, filled with military personnel, scientists, and technicians moving in and out of various tunnels that radiated outward from the main hub. A command and control center was perched high above the hall, with windows overlooking the hive of industry that began surrounding the tube, like worker and drone bees bustling around the arrival of the queen.

And from high above, looking out one of the windows, Betty Ross watched as the tube slid along its track toward a spherical containment cell into which the unconscious Bruce would be loaded. She bit her lip, fighting to keep down the grief and uncertainty that raged through her with as much emotional force as the Hulk had displayed in disposing of the dog attackers.

The Hulk.

That was the name she'd heard bandied about, the name people had started using. She was unable to figure out who had first called him that, but the name seemed to have stuck, and now she was using it too.

Well, that made a certain amount of sense. That was the scientific tendency, wasn't it, to find names for things, all the time? No new discovery was really legitimate until it had a name slapped on it. So why not the Hulk? The creature certainly bore more of a resemblance to a hulking beast than he did to Bruce Banner . . .

. . . and yet . . .

. . . and yet when she had looked into his eyes, she had found more emotional purity and honesty there than she had ever seen in any other man. Thinking men kept their thoughts hidden behind layer upon layer of civilization and subtext and second thoughts. But the Hulk, he looked at the world with pure emotion, and no sense of anything beyond his immediate wants and desires. In many ways, it was a more honest way to exist. She almost envied him having so immaculate a worldview.

She heard a throat being cleared behind her, and knew who it was before she even turned.

General Ross was standing there, looking as if he

hadn't slept for a very long time. Then again, Betty didn't think she looked much better. They saw the fatigue in each other, then both managed a brief but pained smile to acknowledge it.

"Now what?" she asked.

"Now," said her father, "we talk. Not about the things we should have all this time," he admitted. "But we talk. Not here, though."

"Lead the way," she invited.

"I always do." And he preceded her as she walked away from her view of the containment cell, the large door just slamming shut, locking away the most dangerous ninety-pound weakling in history.

Ross paced his office as Betty sat in a chair, perfectly still. It wouldn't do to have both of them tromping around, she thought, so she stayed put while her father moved like a caged cat.

"What do you really know about this?" he asked her.

Betty, seated with her legs delicately crossed at the knee, gave the question a moment's consideration. "In principle," she said, "I can explain the nuclear chemistry of the transformation, and I have some ideas about how his cells can store so much energy."

"Principles and ideas. I hear you," said Ross, obviously trying not to sound dismissive, but making it clear that he wasn't concerned about comprehending the mechanics. "But we don't have all that much time here. And if he poses some kind of imminent danger . . ."

Betty supposed it was a valid enough concern, and her father's priorities weren't exactly out of whack. If some-one had a gun pointed at them, they didn't have to know how the firing mechanism worked. They just wanted someone to make the gun go away.

"Then help me get right to work," Betty said briskly. She sat forward, interlaced her fingers and tucked them under her chin. "First, you have to understand, the triggers are somatic, but they're also emotional. He needs to connect those emotions with the memories to which they are linked. And there *are* memories here, aren't there? About his father?"

Slowly Ross nodded. "Yes, Betty," he said, clearly not happy to acknowledge it, "there are. But frankly it's not the *memory* of his father I'm worried about right now. It's the fact that he's still out there, and he may know as much about this, if not more, than we do."

"Then he can't continue to be out there."

Again her father nodded in agreement. "All right," he said briskly. "Here's what we're going to have to do. We'll have to assign troops—at least a hundred—to comb the Berkeley area, turn the place upside down, see if we can shake him loose. Get the latest pictures we can of him, show them to every neighbor who might have seen him. Investigate the lab where he was posing as a janitor, and see if they have an address for him, or some sort of lead—what's that?"

She was holding up a piece of paper. "It's his address. You can just go to his house."

Ross took it from her hands and stared at it.

"Yes, that might work, too," he said, and then actually smiled at her. She returned the smile and was surprised to see just how easy it was to smile at him.

The FBI agents burst into the house of David Banner, guns drawn. Their eyes quickly adjusted to the darkness, even as they waved flashlights around and shouted warnings that anyone in the house had best present themselves hands up, ready to surrender.

The warning made no difference to the small creature that streaked across the room, emitting high-pitched squeals that briefly froze the blood of the nearest man, Agent Lee. His mind told him that whatever was letting out those screeches couldn't possibly be human, but for a heartbeat he thought he was being charged by a small child. His survival instincts overwhelmed him, however, and he fired off a fast shot at the fast-moving form even as he thought, *Oh, my God, oh, my God, I shot a child.*

It thudded to the floor and shuddered and twitched, and the agents moved forward hesitantly. The agent who had fired let out a sigh of relief, even as bewilderment swept through him. It definitely wasn't a child; rather, it seemed to be some sort of rat. But it was indeed as big as a two year old. He'd never seen anything like it—and was even more stunned to see it dissolve into a hissing puddle of goo. "Man, Willard's been smoking some serious steroids," he muttered.

"Who the hell is 'Willard'?" another agent, Special Agent Thomas, demanded.

"He was a rat in an old movie."

"Oh. I remember that," said Thomas, and frowned. "I thought Willard was the guy."

"No, Willard was the rat."

Thomas shook his head. "No. Willard was the guy who trained the rat. The rat was named 'Ben.' "

Lee stared at him. "Thomas . . ."

"Yeah?"

"Search the damned house before I shoot you next."

• • •

David Banner was smiling.

He loved being one step ahead of his pursuers. He was certain that, at that moment, someone—soldiers, Feds, whomever—were bursting into his house, hoping to arrest him. But all they were going to find were some wrecked remains of his work—wrecked because he himself had chosen to wreck it. The only thing of any interest in the house would be an oversize rat or two: early subjects for experimentation he had used.

The wheels of the janitor's cart squeaked steadily down the hallway. The place was fairly deserted; small wonder. The rumors about what had happened had morphed and twisted, and now the popular belief was that terrorists calling themselves the Hulks had detonated a bomb at the lab to protest nuclear experimentation. As a result, 90 percent of the staff had called in sick for the rest of the week, and management wasn't prepared to press the issue. So David Banner had the place more or less to himself, which was, of course, exactly what he wanted.

He parked his cart in front of his son's lab and pulled out assorted tools from a case within. Stepping through, he found that the door to the gammasphere was open. The place was still pretty much a shambles, just as it had been when he'd been face-to-face with the green hulking creature that had been his son.

A sizable chunk of the sphere had been evicted through the roof, courtesy of the Hulk's unearthly strength. But enough redundant systems were still in place that the equipment was still functional. There'd likely be radiation leaks throughout the lab, but David Banner didn't give a damn about that.

Banner wasted no time, since he had no idea how much time he had. His babies, his glorious hounds of hell, had not returned to him. That led him to suspect that their assault on Betty Ross had not gone successfully. It had, however, succeeded as far as David Banner was concerned, because their failure meant that his son had managed to take on all three of the creatures single-handedly. His son, having assumed the great and glorious shape that was his birthright, had more than lived up to his father's expectations. No father could have asked for more.

And as the son had beaten the path, so now would the father follow it.

Swiftly, with the focused drive of someone who has been waiting for this moment his entire life, he rigged up a series of makeshift reflectors around the edge of the vacuum tubes protruding into the room. Fine beads of sweat built up on his forehead, and his breathing came faster and faster. He caressed the mirrors as he set them into place, ran his hands lovingly over the instrumentation as he brought the power on line and set the dials.

As he walked into the midst of the chamber with the mechanisms on a time release, he felt as if time had slowed down, as if the world had turned to liquid and he was moving through it in a dreamlike state. Everything, everything had built to this moment, and he stood there, mentally counting down the moments, waiting, waiting, and finally there was a loud *click* that told him everything had come together, fallen into place just as he had planned it—hell, better than he'd planned it. He spread wide his arms and bathed in the light and radiation that filled the wrecked gammasphere, the open canister emitting gas filled with nanomeds, while the gamma radiation bathed him in its glorious light.

Images spun through his head. He was living and dying all at the same time, his life flashing before his eyes as if he were about to die—and in a way he was. The man he had been was dead. He would bear as much resemblance to normal men as normal men did to the lower primates. For, unlike his son who had the strength but not the resolve, he would harness the forces now rampant in his body and use them to accomplish . . .

. . . anything.

He would be able to do anything. He would be more powerful than God, because God was so afraid of his creation that he hid in his heavens lest he be seen. But David Banner would have the powers of a God, and yet would walk among his subjects, and his vengeance would be great and powerful.

A blissful smile filled his face, and then abruptly the gammasphere shut down. The light was restored to normal. Slowly he opened his eyes, looked around, and sagged to his knees. He held up his arms and studied them. No signs of radiation poisoning, no blistered skin, no nothing. No outward signs of physical distress. That alone told him everything he needed to know, for he wouldn't have been able to survive the gamma ray exposure if it had not worked.

But it *had* worked.

"Yes," David Banner said in low triumph. He grabbed the edge of a metal table to help him stand, and looked down at his hand. It had been cut slightly on the edge of the table when his hand had brushed against it, leaving a tiny rip, a thin strip of blood. He took a handkerchief, and held it to his hand . . .

. . . and the tissue around the cut began to take on the characteristics of the cotton cloth.

David Banner gasped and yanked the kerchief away. He gaped at the point of contact, shook his hand out, and looked again. Upon second inspection the skin now seemed utterly normal. He frowned, wondering if he had imagined it.

Then, out of curiosity, he pressed his hand against the silver metal table. At first nothing happened, but then he felt an odd tingling, the blood and flesh and tissue beginning to alter their composition. They took on a distinct metallic glow, and this time when he moved his hand away, it maintained that silver look.

Wasting no time lest the absorbing effects fade again, he whirled and smashed his hand into the wall. It went right through with a crunch, and not only did it do so easily, but he didn't even feel the impact.

He had expected nothing like this at all—but in the world of science, one must always be prepared to allow for variables. His mind was already racing, considering the possibilities, and he laughed loudly in delight as he yanked his hand clear and studied it, holding it up to the light. The metallic properties were still there. The absorption had been retained far longer this time. Would it remain this way? If he touched something else, would those new properties replace what he already had, or supplement them? Would the retention time increase each time he used it, or was there a maximum?

Questions, dozens of questions, tumbled through his mind as he flexed his metal hand and envisioned it squeezing the world in a viselike grip.

At that moment, the door to the lab opened. He turned and saw a befuddled guard standing there. The guard was slightly paunchy, an older man, squinting in the light of the lab and looking in confusion at what appeared to be a regular janitor who, for some reason, was laughing like a madman.

"What's happening here?" he asked.

Banner took a step forward, practically thrusting the hand into the guard's face. "Look! My hand," he said with escalating excitement. "You see, the strength of my son's DNA, combined with the radiant energy, it's transformed my cells, allowing them, after exposure to other cellular structures, to absorb and replicate them. . . . "

He should have realized that it was pointless to share such a scientific breakthrough with a pathetically normal individual who couldn't begin to appreciate it fully. Indeed, the guard responded in what should have been a woefully predictable fashion. His hand started to drift toward the butt of his holstered gun. "I'm gonna have to ask you to put your hands up, pal. Okay? Nice and easy."

David Banner thought this was just about the funniest damned thing he'd ever heard, and his peals of laughter obviously rankled the irritated sentinel. He didn't pull his gun, however, since both of Banner's hands were empty and, aside from his erratic behavior, he didn't yet seem a genuine threat. This turned out to be a mistake although, in the final analysis, it probably wouldn't have made much of a difference if he'd yanked out his revolver and pulled the trigger.

Still laughing, Banner stepped forward, quick as death, and swung his metallic hand. There was another crunching noise, not dissimilar from the one the wall had made when he struck it. He moved his hand quickly away from the side of the guard's head, not wanting to get any blood on it lest he absorb that, as well.

It didn't make any difference to the guard, who sagged to the ground with blood welling up from the large, smashed-in section of his skull. Banner didn't know whether the guard was still alive or not, and didn't especially care. He was far too busy staring at his metallic fingers, pleased with the fact that they hadn't yet reverted to flesh and blood and wiggling them like a puppeteer enjoying a new creation.

The world was swirling around Bruce Banner, bizarre images that he couldn't sort out colliding with one another. He had a feeling he'd been incredibly angry, but he couldn't remember why or where or what it had all been about. There was a sense of disorientation, similar to what he'd experienced when he had transformed back to normal by the side of the lake, but different as well. His nostrils flared and he knew he was no longer in the forest, for the smell of trees and leaves and fresh rain were all gone. The air was sterile and odorless, like the interior of an airplane cabin only worse, and as his eyes opened to slits, the world was blurred and glaring and there was a sense of the metallic.

And then something was stroking his hair, smoothing it, and he caught a whiff of a familiar scent. Her scent. That wonderful perfume of hers, and he'd never been so happy to smell it as the aroma filled his nostrils now.

"You still need a haircut," she said softly.

He tried to sit up, but his muscles didn't want to cooperate. Betty sensed the desire, but was able to keep him down with a single hand on his shoulder. "I bet you're wondering where you are," said Betty. He nodded. As gently as she could, she said, "You're home."

At first he didn't know what she meant. This wasn't the bedroom he'd grown up in, under the close watch of his adoptive mother, Monica Krenzler. So what could she mean . . .

Then he realized, and the full import sank in. He

ceased trying to sit up, and instead stared at the ceiling of what he now realized was some sort of containment unit. Tears began to well up in his eyes. Bruce Banner had spent as long as he could remember working to suppress his feelings. Now he was in a place that was part of the hidden section of his life, with all the answers and all the possibilities of a full and comprehensible existence being dangled in front of him—and he had no clue how to feel.

Betty saw the moistness in his eyes, saw the tears trickling down the side of his face, and looked as if she was going to start crying at any moment. She reached over and brushed the tears away from him.

"Would you like to see it?" she asked.

He couldn't even manage a nod. But she knew what he wanted. More than that, she knew what he needed.

going home again . . . or not

"Out of the question."

In a hallway outside the containment chamber, Betty Ross faced her father, who had a cigar jutting angrily out from between his teeth. The "No Smoking" sign nearby didn't seem to make the slightest impression on him.

"Dad," she began.

But Thunderbolt Ross continued to shake his head, spraying cigar ash in a semicircle. Betty stepped back to avoid having some fall on her. "I said out of the question! That containment unit could restrain a herd of elephants. You let him loose from that, and he turns into the jolly green giant in a heartbeat, we've got a major scuffle on our hands! Provided he doesn't just leap out of here and go . . . go destroy Tokyo or something!"

"Dad, the transformation only occurs when he's filled with uncontrollable rage. . . ."

"And who knows what could cause that?" insisted Ross, folding his arms and glaring down at her firmly. "The other day I found out the price of milk went up a quarter; I hit the damned roof! We don't know what might set him off."

"I'm reasonably sure a trip to the grocery store isn't going to send Bruce Banner off the deep end," Betty said, although she was still having trouble dealing with the notion that Bruce's name seemed to have changed overnight. She rested a hand on her father's forearm. "Dad, the other day, when I called, I said I needed to trust you. That was . . ."

"Difficult," he said with a low sigh. "Yes. I know it was. I appreciate that you were willing, and able, to make that request. That was . . . a huge step forward. For both of us."

"I know. The thing is, Dad, trust has to go two ways."

"Betty," he moaned.

"Send as much backup as you want, Dad," she said quickly. "Have troops following us with a dozen stun guns set to knock Bruce cold if he so much as starts humming 'It's Not Easy Being Green.' But I'm telling you that this place, Desert Base, particularly the area that was never rebuilt, is a huge, gaping hole in his life. The . . . the 'Hulk' side of him . . ."

"Hulk," snorted Ross. "That's what they're calling him, isn't it? Me, I call him 'Angry Man.' Helps to remember just what it is that gives your enemy his power."

"He's not your enemy, Dad, and not mine. What I was saying is that the Hulk represents the emotional gap in Bruce's life caused by his lack of memory of his early years. If he has any hope of ever controlling the Hulk . . . of controlling himself . . . of living anything vaguely resembling a normal life, he needs to see and experience the part that was lost to him for so long. Dad . . ."—she wrapped both arms around his one—"I know you hold his father responsible for a lot. God knows I do at this point, as well, starting with the fact that he tried to turn me into Purina gamma chow. But please, I'm begging you, don't punish the son for the sins of the father. The son saved me. He may not have been himself, but he saved me. That's got to count for something."

Thunderbolt let out a long, unsteady, and frustrated breath. "You, young lady, had better be right about this."

"I'm your daughter, Dad." She smiled. "How can I ever be anything *but* right?"

One of Bruce's earliest memories—he knew his memories didn't go as far back as most people's—was from a time when he was about nine years old. His mom had taken him on a road trip, and they'd stopped at a place that billed itself as a genuine "ghost town." Young Bruce had found the notion terribly appealing, envisioning spooks and shades drifting from one building to the next, caterwauling and "*ooooooohing*" as they went. He'd been disappointed to discover that it was a tricked up, touristy Western theme park, with cheesy employees decked out in even cheesier costumes. He'd kept a resolute face and told his mom that it was well and truly a nifty place, and even fooled his mother into thinking he was scared a couple of times.

But it had been something of a letdown, and he'd become convinced that the concept of a "ghost town" was charming, but no more based in reality than any other mythic notion.

It turned out he was wrong. As he and Betty walked through what had once been the bustling commercial district outside Desert Base, he knew that he was in a genuine ghost town. In his imagination, he could actually see and hear people long gone walking around and chatting and enjoying life, linked by the army family they all shared.

That was no longer the case. The base had been rebuilt

over the years, but things were different now. Everything was kept low key and under cover, so as not to alarm the skittish residents of nearby cities who dreaded the thought of research at the base. At least, that was how it was explained to Bruce.

Their first moments together, once Bruce had fully recovered his ability to communicate, had been awkward. "I'm sorry," she had started to say to him.

But he had cut her off almost immediately. "No. You're not," he had said flatly. "You knew what you were doing, calling in your father and his people. And given the exact same circumstances, you would do exactly the same thing again, wouldn't you?"

She had begun to protest . . . then looked down, unable and unwilling to respond. That alone had told him that she knew he was right. And then, to Betty's surprise—and, to some extent, his own—he had reached a finger under her chin and tilted her head up to look him in the eyes.

"All this time you've been telling me that I'm too rational, that I don't let my emotions just take me," he had said to her. "If I gave in now, let myself feel anger, betrayal, hurt, what purpose would it serve? What's done is done. The fact is you did what you felt you had to do. I may not be thrilled by it. I may have been the victim of it. But I can respect your decision. So you see, Betty, that aspect of me, which you felt was detrimental to our relationship, makes it that much easier to get past being shot with a tranq gun and carted away. Double-edged sword and all that, I suppose."

"So, we're okay?" she had said.

"Betty," and he had actually laughed, but it had an ironic sound to it, "when were we *ever* okay?"

He had seen her flinch a bit from that, but it was the truth and she had known it.

Now they were walking through one of the deserted, ramshackle streets. At a not-too-discreet distance, troops armed with various high-tech containment weapons and lightweight attack vehicles moved slowly behind them. Bruce got a mental picture of what they must look like viewed from overhead. Just a guy, a girl, and the troops. The ludicrousness of the situation caused him to laugh again, this time to himself.

"It used to be so full of life here," Betty said from beside him. Then she noticed he was laughing, and obviously couldn't quite understand what was so funny about her last statement. "What?" asked Betty.

"Nothing," he said, gesturing toward the troops shadowing them. "Just what do you think those boys would do if I leaned over and gave you a kiss?"

"I'm not sure either of us would survive," said Betty smiling.

They stopped, faces close, but Bruce hesitated and then pulled back. Betty looked slightly disappointed, but didn't press the matter. Bruce sighed. "I must have seen you or known you," he said. "If only I could remember."

"You will," Betty assured him. "It'll be painful, but you will."

His face darkened. "I bet *it* remembers," he said, and there was obviously no doubt in Betty's mind as to just who "it" was. "It must have been a child here, too, inside of me." He started rubbing his temples. Although he wasn't intending to, he looked like a mentalist trying to get in contact with the dead. "I feel him now, watching me. Hating me."

"Hating you?" Betty asked. "Why?"

He lowered his hands and leveled his gaze on her. "Because he knows, one way or another, that we're going to destroy him," said Bruce. He sounded determined. He also sounded a bit afraid.

Betty shook her head. "We're going to understand him."

"It's the same thing, isn't it?" asked Bruce.

Clearly she didn't comprehend, but Bruce did . . . all too well. The creature drew its strength from rage, and rage came not from what one had, but from what one didn't have. Rage was the lack of control, of compassion, of love, of understanding. Any of the softer emotions, anything that sought to incorporate the creature into the minds and hearts of humanity, was anathema to it, a crucifix to a vampire. Love drained it of hate, compassion drained it of rage, and without those, it was literally nothing. It was a gamma-irradiated genie released from its lamp, and all the Aladdins in the world weren't about to stuff it back in. Not if the Hulk could help it.

Banner walked a few steps away, falling into a reverie. Betty continued to follow, but at a distance. Perhaps she was respecting his need for space, or perhaps she was just afraid of him. Well, why not? *He* was afraid of him.

They wandered among the broken down, deserted houses, the wind stirring up dust and bits of detritus, and carrying with it an almost mournful sound. The image of the ghost town came to his mind again, and then he heard something that triggered a recollection, something just beyond his ability to grasp, so close he thought he could touch it. It was a steady, rhythmic squeaking, and he turned to see that Betty was sitting on an abandoned swing set, absentmindedly swinging.

He noticed a particular house nearby and paused. Deep

in the recesses of his mind, there were long shadows that suddenly seemed to have faint light cast upon them, all from the sight of this ramshackle house. He started to walk toward it. He heard the squeaking behind him stop, Betty's feet treading again on the gravel walk. She was following him, although she likely had no idea why. The blind leading the blind. It didn't get more ironic than that.

Banner entered the old house, paused, and looked around. Betty entered behind him and Banner froze.

"What is it?" she asked very quietly, as if worried that a loud voice might disturb the long-gone occupants.

Pictures . . . images . . . running . . . screams and hatred and a pounding . . .

He turned to face her, pushing the mental images violently away. "Why did you bring me here?" he asked, suddenly angry. "What's the point of it? You saw what I am. You know as well as I do it's no use." His voice was filled with loathing and self-pity.

"That's not true," said Betty.

"It is true," he fired back. He paced the front hall of the house, stepping over some debris, moving quickly, as if he could outrun the thoughts in his head. He spoke in a voice dripping with sarcasm. "Come on. I'm supposed to have some sort of emotional breakthrough now? Reconnect to my inner child, exorcise my inner demons, find my true self, and everything will be just fine and dandy? Don't kid yourself."

"And don't you kid yourself!" Betty replied. If he'd thought that she was some sort of shrinking violet, that she was in some way intimidated or reluctant to stand up to him, then clearly he was mistaken. She was willing to be sympathetic, patient, loving, but she obviously wasn't going to be pushed around. "We don't have any options, remember? At least here we have a chance—"

"A chance to what?" Bruce demanded in exasperation. He felt like pain incarnate. "Don't you understand? Whatever it is you want me to remember, there's a good reason I can't. It . . . might just kill me," he said, and he refrained from adding, *or you*.

For that was really his greatest fear. As much as he was capable of understanding Betty's actions, of forgiving her, he was also certain that the hulking beast within him was equally *in*capable of doing so. What she was showing him now was stirring up not just memories, but the monster within. It was scrambling forward on its knuckles toward the uppermost regions of his mind like the rough beast, its hour come at last, slouching toward Bethlehem to be born, as Yeats had written in "The Second Coming." If it got loose again, if it did, it might kill her.

"The centre cannot hold; . . . The blood-dimmed tide is loosed . . ."

It couldn't know, of course, that to kill Betty was to kill itself, because if it harmed Betty, then Bruce would undoubtedly take his own life the moment he was back in control, rather than live with the knowledge of what he'd done. That, of course, would be the ultimate way to stop the monster.

He just hoped it didn't come to that, for all their sakes.

He kept looking away from Betty, but she wouldn't permit it. "It might just kill you," she repeated his words, and then added, "or save you."

"And what if I don't want to be saved," he said darkly.

"You don't have to try. You can choose, Bruce. But me, I don't have a choice," she said sadly.

He was genuinely puzzled by her response. "Why?"

"Because I love you," said Betty.

The truth was he was surprised to hear that. With all that had happened, he hadn't even thought that a possibility anymore. He couldn't help but wonder how much of what she was feeling was genuine, and how much of it was wishful thinking, that she was trying to make herself believe she was in love with him because, considering the circumstances, the notion that it had developed naturally just seemed absurd.

"How is that possible?" he finally asked, giving voice to the doubts he harbored. "You—neither of us—we don't even know who I am." There was a pause and he turned away, kicking through the rubble. He was beginning to think he had no clue what love was anymore, or what the purpose of it was—and certainly he didn't know whether he was worthy of it or not. He didn't even feel like a man. More like a half-man, his psyche splintered into so many pieces that just having someone look at him made him feel unclean.

She went to the broken window and stared out at the desert.

"We'd better go back," Bruce said finally.

"Yeah," was all she said in reply.

Their journey back was remarkably silent. On the trip out, Bruce had studied the ways in which the army kept the facility hidden, finding them to be a fascinating distraction. Coming back, however, he couldn't dwell on anything but the empty feeling he had inside. She loved him. He wanted that to mean something. He wanted to love her. He thought he did, but he'd always thought that in the past and it hadn't been enough. Was it enough now, particularly considering what it was he had to overcome?

An armed escort led Banner and Betty down the hall.

At the door to his containment cell, they paused. Betty turned to Banner. "I'll see you," was all she said. Hardly a deathless protestation of impassioned love. *What the hell do you want from her*, part of him scolded. He had no answer. He was starting to wonder if there was a damned thing in the world he did know. She gave him a little wave as she left, like a chum from school dropping him off at his house at the end of a busy day learning readin' and writin' and 'rithmetic.

The door to the containment unit slid shut behind him. Just before it closed completely, he turned and watched Betty vanish from sight on the opposite side of the door. She wasn't looking over her shoulder at him. That was smart. Never look behind you. It was pointless to dwell on what was past, and it left you less prepared for whatever might be heading your way.

Betty walked briskly down a corridor toward the central control room, convinced that Bruce thought she didn't love him despite her protests to the contrary. And she was reasonably sure he didn't love her. That alone was enough to make her heart sink to somewhere in her gut, but that wasn't the biggest problem.

Her biggest problem was that her attempts to get through to Bruce, to help him reconnect with the world, had so far failed miserably.

She was certain that the main reason Bruce changed into the Hulk was his feelings of isolation. Everything—from the kids who had made fun of him as a child, to Talbot and his frankly abominable actions of a couple of days ago—served to feed into the Hulk's perception that the world was a battleground and he was but a piece moving through it, a piece that was hated and despised by everyone else.

Betty placed her thumb on a biometric reader at the door to Command and Control, also known as C and C. The door remained locked. She tried it again, and still it didn't respond. She blew air impatiently between her lips, rubbed her thumb against her blouse to try to remove whatever random dirt or oil was causing the picky lock to malfunction, then tried yet again.

Then she looked more closely and saw that there was a red light on the lock. It wasn't just failing to identify her. It was outright rejecting her thumbprint.

"What the hell?" she murmured, then she heard loud voices from within. The door slid open to reveal her father. She looked at him with a question on her face, and received the answer in the very next second.

Glen Talbot was standing just inside C and C. He looked a bit weary, wearing a dark blue suit and a crisp white shirt with the tie loosened; he had the sort of haggard expression one usually has after having undergone a sustained argument with Thunderbolt Ross. He looked as if he had been roughed up, as well. But he also had, most dangerously, a smug look on his face.

"Hey, Betty," said Talbot, "I would love to chat, but I'm pressed for time. I'll let your dad deliver the news."

She turned and again looked questioningly at Ross. With a quick shake of his head, he said, "Not here," took her by the shoulder, and guided her down the hallway. With every step they took, a sense of dread rose higher and higher within her.

The last time she could recall Thunderbolt Ross looking this upset was when she was a kid and insisted he take her ice skating. Her father had fallen on the ice so many times that he had point-blank told her if she ever spoke of it to someone else, he would disown her. She'd asked him about it years later, and he'd sworn that he absolutely meant it . . . and that it still held.

When he told her of what had just happened, however, that incident paled in comparison. He dropped into the chair behind his desk and came right to the point. "Your access has been revoked. NSA has decided to hand over study of the . . . the threat . . . to Atheon, and they have explicitly limited my jurisdiction," said Ross.

"You're the head of this base!"

"Yes, I'm aware of that. Just as they are aware," he said sharply, "that I am the father of the chief scientist attached to the situation, who, in turn, is romantically involved with an atomic bomb on two legs. Talbot apparently sold them on the notion that my close relationship to the principal players in this little drama presents a conflict of interest, since obviously I won't have my priorities in place."

"But . . . that's ridiculous! 'Close relationship'? You and I haven't spoken for close to a decade, and Bruce told me you threatened his life if he ever came near me again!"

"Well, it's one of those odd circumstances where my failures as a father aren't working in my favor. Ironic, I know. Usually my parental shortcomings reflect so well on me."

"All right, I'm sorry." She sighed. "I didn't mean to—"

He waved it off. "Betty, this old skin has developed so much armor plating over the years, you couldn't get under it with anything short of dynamite. The bottom line is I don't set policy." He shook his head, looking as if he'd been personally betrayed, which was probably exactly how he felt. "I had no idea Glen would go around me like this. I—I miscalculated what he was capable of, and I failed you."

She fixed a look on him as she shook her head, sagging into the chair opposite him. "You didn't fail me." She sighed. "I wasn't counting on you in the first place." Then she frowned. "You know, believe it or not, that was meant to be consoling, but it didn't come out that way at all, did it?"

"Not in the least," he agreed, his mouth twitching into a smile beneath his mustache. "Don't worry about it, though. You're likely just out of practice when it comes to me."

"Very likely, yes. So, what am I supposed to do now?" she asked.

He shrugged one shoulder. "I would tell you to go and say good-bye to Banner, but I've already been informed that's out of the question."

She couldn't believe it. The only reason she had contacted her father—aside from the fact that she'd been scared out of her mind—was that she felt by going through him, she would be able to maintain some control of, and involvement with, the situation. Instead, through Talbot's duplicity, the one person who might be able to prevent the entire predicament from spiraling out of control was being banished like a dissident Russian to a Gulag.

"All I can tell you, Betty," Thunderbolt Ross informed her with what he likely thought was reassurance, "is that I'll be watching every move that Talbot makes. At the slightest hint of a breach, I'll make the case to pull him out of there."

"It will be too late," she said flatly. "Whatever Glen does is going to make matters so much worse, so quickly, this place will be coming down around your ears. You're going to be busy filling out paperwork requisitioning a new barn door while a herd of horses will already be ten miles away." She stood. "I'm going to see Bruce. Right now."

Ross shook his head with a resigned sigh, but she didn't quite understand the message until she opened the door and saw two burly guards blocking her way.

"Betty, I'm sorry," said Ross, and he really did sound apologetic. "It's time for you to go home."

Barely five minutes later, Betty was looking down from her seat in a chopper at the desolate desert floor as she flew home.

She thought bleakly, *This is the last time I'm looking at this while it's in one piece. They'll never be able to handle Bruce. Never. Putting Glen Talbot in charge of Bruce Banner is like using a sledgehammer to open a bottle of nitroglycerin.*

playing with fire

Bruce was beginning to remember.

As he lay on his bed in the containment cell, pieces, fragments of what he'd seen, were starting to fall into place like the parts of a jigsaw puzzle. He was starting to realize that it was simply a matter of being willing to accept what was being presented to him, that it wasn't just that he didn't remember; his mind was doing everything it could to block it all out. He couldn't help but wonder how much of that was as a result of the ... other ... within him, the other that would do whatever was required to keep those recollections at arm's length.

How ironic, mused Bruce. How remarkably ironic that a being who was the living incarnation of strength, who feared nothing physically, was repulsed by something as ephemeral as memory. It made Bruce feel strong in a way, as if he—

A number of small openings mechanically appeared in the walls around Bruce. He sat up and saw gun barrels pointing at him from everywhere, enough guns to Swiss cheese him before he took another breath. And they were accompanied by laser sightings. There were so many red laser targeting dots on him that he looked like he'd come down with a sudden case of measles so massive that the spots had actually broken out on his clothing.

The door burst open, startling him. *What the hell is going on?* Bruce wondered, and even as he did so, he felt something else, deeper within him, stirring and readying itself, like a child in utero responding to a loud noise. Bruce didn't know what to do first. He couldn't decide whether to work on quelling the small but dangerous uprising he felt rooting around in his brain, or to focus on what was apparently a change in the status quo.

Then Glen Talbot walked in.

At that moment, with a burst of clarity, Bruce Banner knew precisely what was going to happen. The exact details were open to debate, but the outcome wasn't in doubt. The only thing left to ponder was just how long it would take, and Bruce Banner—ever the scientist— couldn't help but think that it would be interesting to find out.

Talbot was sporting what appeared to be some sort of electrified walking stick. Bruce took note of it in a distant, almost analytical manner, as if the ramifications of the device were of no immediate concern to him. He also noticed, with a bit of smug amusement, that Talbot was looking a bit banged up. The right side of his upper lip was swollen from a cut, and there was considerable bruising on the entire left side of his face. He was also wearing a brace on the first two fingers of his left hand. Considering the pounding that he had given Bruce in their previous encounter, Bruce could only consider it just desserts, a beating well deserved. He only wished he could remember some of the details of it. He seemed to recall something vaguely about a couch, but he wasn't exactly sure how that fit in.

"Hi ya, Bruce," Talbot said with the sort of false joviality usually exhibited by a bully who's convinced he has the upper hand. "How you feeling? Grub okay here for you?"

"You're looking a little worse for the wear," Bruce observed. He didn't sound any more sorry about it than he felt.

Talbot shrugged it off. "I'm fine and dandy. Might need a little reconstructive work on my left index finger. Insurance'll cover it."

Bruce nodded as if he cared. "What are you doing here?" he asked, knowing the answer before he posed the query.

"Good question," said Talbot. He took a step toward Banner, but didn't get too close, not wanting to put himself in the path of even one of the red targeting dots. "See, I need your cells to trigger some chemical distress signals—you know, so you can get a little green for me again—and then I'll carve a little piece out of the real you, analyze it, patent it, make a fortune. You mind?"

Well, there it was. One almost had to admire Talbot for his bluntness. But there was more to this than just some powerful company interested in patents. Because if Talbot was marching around here, and Ross *père* and *fille* were nowhere to be seen, then that indicated a major shake up in the status quo.

"Who are you really with, Talbot?" asked Bruce silkily.

Talbot blinked. "You know who I represent, Bruce. A private research corporation called Atheon. Pity you didn't cooperate with us when I first arrived. We could be on the same side right now."

"I somehow doubt that," Bruce replied. Considering he had several dozen target sights upon him, he was sounding remarkably relaxed. They weren't going to kill him; he knew that now beyond question, because they wanted something he couldn't provide them if he were dead. So here was Talbot, ready to throw twenty gallons of kerosene on a campfire while laboring under the delusion that he wasn't going to get burned. A blind man during an eclipse had more vision than that.

"Just as I doubt," Bruce continued, "the notion of a 'private research corporation' pushing around the military. That's just not flying for me, Talbot. Which means, to me, that there's another branch of the government involved. Atheon is a front for something far more covert than any of Ross's people, and far more highly placed as well. What are you, Talbot? NSA? CIA?"

"M-O-U-S-E," grinned Talbot. He actually seemed amused by Bruce's speculations. "I'll tell you all about it later, Bruce. Just, right now, let's bring the big boy out to play, shall we?"

"I'll never let you," Bruce said. He meant it, too, even as a plan was forming in his mind. The re-emergence of the Hulk was inevitable. Banner was too intelligent not to see it. Talbot would never stop until he got what he wanted. The problem was that if the Hulk came out in half measures, the various targeting devices would let fly before Bruce was impervious. Then Talbot would quickly acquire the cell samples he wanted, and leave the riddled and vulnerable body of the partly formed Hulk to die on the floor of the containment unit.

So instead Bruce had to bottle it up, bottle it up as hard and as deeply as he could, and then let fly with the transformation all at once. Which meant he had to endure all that Talbot dished out and more. He had to let Talbot push him and push him and push him until he was ready to push back in all his unadulterated fury.

"I'm not sure you have much of a choice," said Talbot. With that, he took his stick and jabbed it into Banner's stomach. Sure enough, the stick had electrical properties, and a vicious jolt sent Banner flying backward against the wall. He threw his arms out to either side, braced himself against the wall, steadied the frantic beating of his heart. Despite the gravity of the situation, the irony was also evident. Repeated electrical shocks might, sooner or later, cause his heart to stop. If that happened, then the entire business was going to be moot.

"C'mon Bruce," he said, "aren't you feeling a little angry? After all, you only have me to play with, now that Betty's dumped you and gone back to Berkeley."

Bruce didn't buy that for a second. If Betty was gone— and she might well be—it was due to pressure from Talbot. Love and dedication aside, Betty Ross was a scientist above all else, and the Hulk was simply too interesting a project to leave behind willingly.

"You're lying," said Bruce with conviction. Then the strength in his legs started to go, a delayed effect from the electrical jolt, and it was all he could do not to slide to the floor.

Talbot stayed where he was. "You know, for me this is a win-win situation. You turn green, all these guys kill you, and I perform the autopsy. You don't, I mop the floor with you, and," he added in a conspiratorial whisper, "maybe by accident I go too far and break your neck." He paused. "Bad science, maybe, but personally gratifying. Come to think of it, you are looking a little green— around the gills."

Bruce, using the wall for support, fought back to his

feet. He continued to stare resolutely at Talbot, and he heard it then, the beginning of the rage within him, the desire to smash this little cockroach flat, to stomp on him and crush his body beneath his feet like packing peanuts. *Smash smash* echoed in his mind, and *Not yet* fired across the gulf of his neurons. His brain felt bifurcated, one half arguing with the other, but he kept himself together despite the best efforts of that growling inner voice to seize control.

"C'mon. Just a love tap," said Talbot, thrusting out his chin, daring Bruce to take a swing at him. "Let's see what you got."

"Never," Bruce said weakly. He tried to move and stumbled, the strength still gone from his legs, and Talbot—obviously displaying a confidence that Bruce knew to be misplaced—tossed aside the electric cane and pummeled Bruce with his fist. Bruce's flesh shuddered and shook beneath the pounding, and he threw his arms up in front of his face and head, ultimately unable to accomplish anything defensively. Talbot stepped in through his guard and planted a right hook on Bruce's chin and he went down. As the world darkened around him, he decided that perhaps he'd done too good a job of suppressing his angrier half, because this strategy hadn't worked out exactly the way he'd hoped.

Then again, at least he was alive, so hey, major points for Bruce, and *Mom, can I have some ice cream? I promise I'll do all my homework*, and then he teetered on the edge of insensibility.

From very far away, he heard Glen Talbot mutter, "You know, consciously you might control it. But subconsciously I bet that's another story." And Bruce, from his place on the edge, could almost sense the creature within, watching him but constrained by the constant rationality, the morality, the upper brain functions—in short, the superego of Bruce Banner. But if Bruce was out of the equation, then that opened up possibilities, which was obviously what Talbot was hoping.

"Anybody home?" he inquired, right before kicking Bruce's crumpled body.

The door opened and Thunderbolt Ross barged in with the sort of unexpected arrival that suited his nickname. *"Talbot, that's enough!"*

"All in the name of science, sir," Talbot said with a shrug. He moved back and walked out of the room past Ross. Ross followed him out, and as he did so, Bruce Banner opened an eye and watched them leave.

One for you, Talbot, he thought, pain wracking his body, *but a war isn't won with one battle. Don't have to be a soldier . . . to know that. . . .*

And then he was out cold.

In one of the lab facilities at the base, Thunderbolt Ross was expressing his personal annoyance to Glen Talbot who, in turn, didn't give much of a damn just how worked up Ross was. Workers went on about their business, making a great attempt to pay no attention.

"What I'm saying is deliberately provoking an incident *is* my business," Ross told him flatly.

"I've got every kind of active denial system in place," said Talbot, sounding rather bored with what he obviously saw as an unwarranted interrogation. "We will contain or neutralize according to procedures." Then he folded his arms and looked like the most smug SOB in the world as he addressed his former commanding officer with barely restrained condescension.

"The fact is unless we get this thing in vivo, we have little or nothing to build on. The secret's in him and I'm going to extract it." As an afterthought, he added, "Sir." Then he raised an eyebrow, daring Ross to say something else, to try to continue the argument.

Ross stood there for a moment, his mustache bristling, and then he turned on his heel and left. Talbot watched him go and almost had to chuckle. To think that he had once held Thunderbolt Ross in such high esteem. Hell, he'd practically worshiped the man. And now look where the two of them were. Ross seemed so . . . so small in comparison to Talbot's recollections. To Talbot it was a distinct reminder of the danger of putting people on pedestals.

He waited another minute or so to make sure that Ross wasn't on the other side of the door, preparing to sandbag him or come at him with some other inane argument. Then one of the Atheon workers caught Talbot's eye, and he turned.

"Subject is in the tank, sir," he told Talbot.

Talbot nodded once and then headed out the door. Ross was nowhere around, thankfully. As he headed down to the immersion lab, he could only guess at the personal agonies Betty must be enduring, yanked away from her favorite experiment and boy toy.

Still, the fly in the ointment was Banner. Not only had he resisted the pounding Talbot had given him, but he had made some annoyingly accurate guesses about Atheon's true nature. Talbot was going to have to have a talk with his superiors, to discuss ways in which Atheon and its parent organization could tighten things up so no one else would be able to put two and two together.

As he considered the possibilities, he entered the

immersion lab. There, deprived of sensory input, wired up to so many machines he looked like a Christmas tree, was Bruce Banner.

Talbot smiled, went over to the monitors to study the readouts, and called, "Let's fire up those brain waves, shall we?"

Electrical probes shot into Bruce's body, stimulating specific centers of his brain, trying to jolt a reaction from him. His body twitched slightly.

Start small, Glen, Talbot reminded himself. *Don't want to use a sledgehammer to pound a flea, not before we've got the big dog in our sights.*

Betty wasn't at all surprised when the van that had dropped her off at her house parked at the curb. She turned and stood in the doorway, staring at it in grim annoyance. They were probably busy setting up a listening center of some kind, to make sure Betty didn't start calling newspaper or TV reporters to try to tell them what was going on. Not that anyone would believe her, of course. An underground army research base? Studying her boyfriend who was capable of turning into a half-ton of rampaging fury, if someone pushed him far enough? Oh yeah. That would fly.

And then, as she entered her house, she froze. Something felt wrong, although she wasn't sure what. She flicked on a light and gasped.

David Banner was seated in a chair square in the middle of the living room. He looked rather comfortable, as if he'd sent Betty out to pick up some cigarettes and was wondering what had taken her so long.

"My dear Miss Ross," he said, "welcome back."

Betty started to back toward the door. She didn't even

bother to ask how he had gotten in. A man who was capable of turning three canines into slavering engines of destruction shouldn't have had any difficulty with a door lock.

"Look," she warned him, "there are two MPs parked right outside. I scream, and—"

He waved off whatever concerns she had, or that he thought she might have. "You don't have to worry. I'm not angry with you, not anymore."

These were hardly the most comforting words she could have heard from someone who was, essentially, a lunatic. She didn't continue her retreat, though, freezing in place just within the door frame. She could still bolt if need be. Both of his hands were plainly visible, so it wasn't as if he could produce a gun and shoot her down.

David Banner continued. "Please, just hear me out," he said soothingly. "I can guess why you're here. Your father betrayed you, didn't he? You should have expected it. They did the same to me."

She wasn't listening to the things he was saying, although she hated to admit that they did interest her slightly. Instead, she demanded, "What do you want?"

"That's the thing. I don't really know anymore," he said with a shrug. He leaned forward in the chair and Betty reflexively flinched back. But his hands remained unthreateningly in front of him. The odd thing was that he didn't even seem to be addressing his remarks to her, even though they concerned her. He seemed to be talking more to himself. "I know what you want. The same thing you always have: You want to understand him, don't you? But you'll never understand him," he told her sadly. "There is no scientific language yet that could ever account for him."

She licked her lips, which had become remarkably dry. He wasn't sounding like a crazy man at this point. Instead, he was surprisingly lucid. Perhaps she might even be able to communicate with him in a common language, about a common concern. That wasn't too much to hope for, was it? Even madmen had their saner moments. If this was one of his . . .

"But there is a cause, isn't there?" asked Betty. She cleared her throat, speaking with the delicacy of a police officer trying to talk a jumper in off a ledge. "At the very least a chain of events I can reconstruct. I have some idea of your research, of the experiments you performed on yourself. I think that Bruce—"

He interrupted her brusquely, but it seemed motivated by anger aimed more at himself than her. His voice laced with sorrow, he said, "Of course Bruce is the outcome, the mistake . . . my mistake. And you think I haven't lived a day since without regretting it?" He sagged back in the chair, as if making the admission had drained him of whatever energy he had.

"No, I don't think that," said Betty. "But now you can do something about it."

"But what could I do?" said the father, not paying attention to Betty. "She so wanted a baby. And I was so in love with her . . ."

the devil you know

His memories floated in an abyss, scattered about, and he saw them dancing past him, taunting him, ready to be reclaimed. . . .

Connections—wires to his brain, his brain to his past, his father, his mother—the connection was there, long forgotten, long unemployed, but it was there, sucking him in. His past was one large vacuum, and nature abhorred a vacuum, which meant nature abhorred him, and it had turned its sights upon him now and drawn him down, down through a vast neural network of reticulated nets which formed floating, liquid screens of unconscious images, memories, an uncharted chorus of voices and sounds inside him, and he almost felt as if he could hear his father's voice, that's how connected they had become . . .

"I could feel it, from the moment she conceived," said David Banner, as Betty listened with rapt attention. "It wasn't a son I had given her but a monster. I thought"—his voice rose with desperate urgency—"maybe if I could make this one mistake go away, I'd give everything up, even my work, take it back, just take it back to when it was just she and me."

• • •

And his mother was smiling at him, except it wasn't Monica Krenzler, it was his mother, his real mother, and she was glorious and beautiful and she bore a passing resemblance to Betty, which made perfect sense somehow, perfect sense, and the floating image of his mother collided and mixed with the image of two dolls, overlapped with the vision of his mother, and she was smiling and reassuring, and a door opened, flooding her image with light. . . .

"I remember that day so well," said David Banner. "Every sensation, as I walked into the house. Felt the handle of the knife. It must have been destined, just like Abraham and Isaac, the son, sacrificed by the father."

Betty didn't comprehend what he was saying at first, for the mention of the knife came from nowhere, and then she did, and she cringed back in horror.

His mother cringed back in horror at first, and then she saw that her husband was eyeing their son, and the horror was replaced by the fierce determination of a mother fighting for her child's life, and she backpedaled, occupying the door frame between them, and young Bruce clutched the stuffed toys to his chest as he tried to see around his mother, thinking that it was all a game and she was hiding some sort of surprise, that was it, she was suddenly going to turn around and she and his father would yell, "Surprise!" except she wasn't turning, she was still facing his father, and there was yelling, but it wasn't "Surprise," it was a bunch of bad words that he wasn't supposed to say, and anger, and suddenly there was a shriek and somebody must have been holding a bottle of ketchup between them because red liquid was spilling down the side of her dress. . . .

"But she surprised me. It was as if," and he spoke in a singsong voice, "as if she and the knife merged into one thing. You can't imagine—" Betty was wide-eyed as he stared at his empty hand. "—the unbearable finality of it, her life, and mine, suspended at the end of my hand. . . ."

. . . and he flew at his father, who was staring stupefied at the blade, which was still dripping with the blood of his wife, Bruce's mother, and he remembered at the last moment to bring the knife up, but the boy was upon him then, leaping, knocking the knife clear, and although the monster wasn't yet unleashed, wasn't yet anything approaching his full strength, the glimmer of its potential was there, and the father looked into the eyes of the son and knew fear as the boy tore at him like a wildcat, and the boy lost track of his mother, saw her stumble in shock and confusion out the front door, and then his father tried to throw him down so he could get at the knife . . . and . . .

"And in that one moment, I took everything that was dear to me . . ."

. . . he sank his teeth—like an animal, like a berserk, rabid dog—into his father's neck, and tasted his father's blood between his teeth, and the father howled and shrieked and the screams of the father blended and overlapped with the howling of sirens . . .

". . . and transformed it into nothing more than a memory. . . ."

• • •

. . . as the MPs swarmed the house, and his father was dragged away and shoved into a car with whirling lights atop it, and Bruce was screaming and pointing in the direction he'd seen his mother stagger off, but no one could understand him because he wasn't speaking, he was grunting and growling inarticulately, like an ape crying out in distress, and someone was trying to hold him steady and he struggled and yanked and shrieked and the rage seized him and his body started to bubble for a moment and someone yelled "He's got a swelling here, it's huge; get some ice packs, stat!" and "We need to sedate him; he's having a seizure!"

"But you can't step back from what you create, can you?" said David Banner, apparently oblivious to the look of fear and revulsion on Betty's face. "No matter how horrifying. My son—he was fated to become . . . what he has now become. No, it's over for him, and for me too."

And he shoved them away with a strength that none would have thought he could possess, and he sprinted into the house, grabbing the dolls as he went, and up, up into his room, and feet were pounding up the stairs after him, and he was about to hide under his bed when there was some sort of explosion, some noise, and the sky lit up, and he ran to the window and looked out, saw something that he couldn't begin to comprehend, something that made it seem as if the world was all new because what was there before had just been wiped clean, clean away, and there was a man in the street in a uniform, and a little girl looking up at him, and he caught a glimpse of his father's face as everyone froze in a tableau that seared itself into his mind and then buried itself deep, but it was back, back to torment him, and the images were swirling every which way, and suddenly his father was old, the connection reestablished, his hair graying, and the girl was grown and it was Betty, and her father was next to her, and they were all looking up at him, and he couldn't stand it, couldn't stand knowing what was coming, couldn't stand the pain, the agony, it was unfair, it was so unfair, why had it happened, why couldn't he have had a normal life, why WHY WHY because it made him want to—makes us want to—makes me want to just . . . just . . .

"That's why I've come to you, to ask you for a last, simple favor," he said, his voice quavering. "Miss Ross, do you think you could persuade your father—as a man, as a father himself—to let me see my son, for one last time, if I turn myself in peacefully? And then he can put me away forever. Could you do that for me?" asked David Banner, and then he started to weep. . . .

. . . just . . . smash him . . . smash his crying face; I can see him; he's right there, in my head . . . my soul. I just . . . hate . . . hate . . . smash . . . destroy him . . . crush . . . squeeze, blood oozing between fingers, crush, mash, destroy, smash everything, smash it all . . .

Betty regarded him uneasily. "Let me make a call," she said. She left the room. He looked after her, a grim smile replacing his tears.

. . . SMASH IT ALLLLL . . .

• • •

Overlooking the immersion cell from the glassed-in lab, one of the technicians, whose name was Wein, called out in genuine excitement as he studied the flashing monitors. "We're getting a lot of neural activity! Incredible. He's generating enormous amounts of . . ."

And Glen Talbot pushed Wein aside and said, "Let me see!" He leaned in, studied the readouts in approval. "Bingo! That must be some jumbo nightmare he's having."

That was when they heard the roar from within the tank, muted but audible, the liquid resonating with the cries from within. The tank, impossibly, bucked in its moorings, and pulsed, and rippled, and at that instant Talbot realized his catastrophic mistake. A fundamental error, something that a third-grade science student would have known about. But he'd missed it, the technicians had missed it, everyone in the damned multibillion facility had missed it.

"Liquid displacement," he whispered. When Banner's body morphed and shifted and grew into the muscled and monstrous form known as the incredible Hulk, it took up space that had previously been occupied by the fluid within the tank. But the liquid was still there, and the violent growth of Banner's body demanded an equally violent displacement of the fluid to somewhere else, like water blasting out of a pool when someone cannonballs into it. However, the tank was filled almost to capacity as it was; with the sudden arrival of the Hulk, there was nowhere for the liquid to go except out . . .

. . . which it did.

Seams buckled and broke and fluid blew out in all directions, and then there was another roar, and a huge green hand worked its way between the seams. Rivets popped, metal twisted and broke, and suddenly the tank cracked open like a piñata. The metal shrieked, the sound blending with the screams of the onlookers, and bent backward, and as the liquid cascaded every which way, the Hulk rose in the middle, wet and dripping and bellowing a roar that could have been made by an angry T rex sinking into a tar pit. The only difference was that the Hulk's life wasn't in danger.

That couldn't, however, be said of the lives of anyone who was watching.

. . . wet . . . dripping . . . where . . . where . . . no matter where . . . smash . . . kill . . .

Wein, who was standing next to Talbot, didn't panic, because he was far too much of a professional for that. It was, however, requiring every ounce of self-control he possessed not to. And if he'd had the slightest inkling of what he was facing, he likely would have soiled himself.

As it was, his voice was rock steady as he asked, "Should I incinerate?"

Talbot had recovered himself after his initial reaction and said with such disdain that one would have thought the incineration query to be the single dumbest question ever voiced, "No! I can't do anything with ashes." He hit the intercom. "All right, put him to sleep."

The Hulk roared and pounded against the walls of the immersion cell as gas flowed from the walls, enveloping him.

The mind of Bruce Banner was buried deep, as deep as the memories of his childhood had been. The rampaging, bestial mind of the Hulk was in full control, but even so there was just enough of Banner's awareness to allow an actual coherent thought to play across the Hulk's mind

   . . . gas . . . hold breath . . .

and without understanding why, but not caring particularly, the Hulk took a quick and deep breath, filling up his lungs an instant before the gas rose to the level of his nostrils.

In the observation lab, Talbot leaned forward, waiting for the Hulk to slump over unconscious. But the Hulk didn't respond as expected. Instead he flailed at it as if it were just a nasty irritant, and in his flailing, his arm crashed through the wall.

"Oh, my God," Talbot whispered, thinking that—with one arm through the wall—it was only a matter of moments before the rest of the Hulk followed.

The Hulk burst into the adjacent hallway, and some of the personnel ran screaming while others, armed soldiers, yanked out their weapons and prepared to fire. Their intentions quickly became moot, however, for the gas poured out into the hallway. Although it didn't do anything to the Hulk beyond making his eyes water, it did manage to knock everyone else unconscious. The Hulk glanced around in annoyance, then made his way down the hall, not having any destination in mind other than to be elsewhere.

Back in the lab, Talbot swallowed deeply as he saw the swirl of gas in the lab, the large hole, and the complete absence of the Hulk. Keeping his voice steady, he said, "Nonlethals only. I must get a sample of him. Hit him with the foam."

• • •

General Ross sprinted down the hallway as he heard alarms going off everywhere. His aide, Lieber, was half his age, but was still unable to keep up with him as Ross pounded into Command and Control. C and C was a madhouse, with everyone shouting information to one another, their voices all tinged with disbelief.

"Sir!" shouted Lieber, pointing at one of the interior monitors. Ross looked up and saw, in the flickering black-and-white image, a roaring behemoth facing a group of specially trained Atheon security personnel. That wasn't surprising. After Ross had broken up Talbot's little stomp-on-Banner session, Atheon had exerted its mysterious influence and gotten the entire wing from Sectors X through Z, Levels One through Seven, isolated so that only Atheon personnel were allowed there. Ross had been furious over the decision, raging that it was a calamitous mistake, but he hadn't been able to get anyone to listen. This was one of those rare occasions where he hated being proven right.

"Jesus," Ross breathed, and in the next breath said, "Get me Talbot."

The intercom was a mass of crosschatter, and as Lieber tried to punch through it to raise Talbot, Ross watched in amazement. On the monitor, one of two techies stepped forward with a large-barreled gun attached to two tanks on his back. He fired, and a stream of gelatinous liquid covered the creature Ross referred to as the "Angry Man" in sticky foam. The Angry Man was stuck, struggling, the liquid congealing around him. He flicked some of it off, and it landed on one of the men, who was instantly frozen in it.

"Sir!" shouted Lieber. "I've got Talbot on channel six!"

Ross snapped the intercom dial over and barked, "Talbot, this is Ross. Talk to me."

"Under control, General," came Talbot's voice. "I'll let you know if we need you."

Ross couldn't believe what he was hearing. That was it, the final straw.

"Unacceptable," Ross said flatly. "Unseat your asses down there immediately. I want a full-court evacuation now. I'm shutting you down. Lieber! Who've we got down there?"

Lieber was ahead of him, turning with a clipboard. "I've already scrambled units Bravo and Laramie, General—Bravo from above, Laramie from below. They can converge on site in thirty seconds."

It was, of course, a breach of protocol for Lieber to have taken that initiative, and Ross could have kissed him for it. "Good thinking! Send them in!"

Shouting into a headset, Lieber shouted, "Bravo, Laramie, you are cleared! Go! Go!"

Ross continued to watch on the monitor, and couldn't help but feel some degree of awe. The Angry Man was still struggling against the liquid, and damned if he wasn't fighting it off. Some of the old warrior instincts surged in Ross. Now *here* was a hell of an opponent!

Then he quickly shoved aside the thought. This wasn't a sporting event. Good men were going into combat against science unleashed. It was like sending troops to run to a ground zero to try to catch a descending atomic missile with their teeth.

"Talbot, we're coming in! Acknowledge! Lieber, ETA?"

"Fifteen seconds, General!"

The intercom was still silent. "Talbot, I said acknowledge!"

And suddenly Lieber shouted, "General! They're locking down!"

"*What* did you say?"

"Lock down," snapped Glen Talbot. At that moment,
watching the Hulk struggling against the hardening foam,
he didn't know how much power the creature possessed.
He didn't know what it would take to stop him. He didn't
know how many men he might lose. But there was one
thing he knew beyond question: There was no way in hell
he was going to defer this thing to Thunderbolt Ross so
that he could turn around and make Talbot look like a
fool.

Wein looked at Talbot incredulously. "But didn't you
just hear the general?"

Talbot was in absolutely no mood to screw around. He
pulled a sidearm and aimed it straight at Wein's face. "I
said lock down."

Wein gulped and activated the lock down mechanisms.
Talbot's gaze flicked from the readouts—waiting for the
signal lights to come on—to the monitors themselves,
where he could see the doors sliding into place. He nodded in approval and saw the "engaged" lights snap on, in-
dicating that the doors were locked in place.

"I'll show you whose ass is unseated," he snarled. "Get
a security squad up here. I'm taking them and dissecting
that green son of a bitch myself." When Wein didn't respond immediately, he cocked the hammer of his pistol
and snarled, "Do it!"

Wein did it.

• • •

The squad leader of Bravo company would have had just enough time to slide under the door before it locked down, but he would have been cut off from the rest of his troops. Wisely, he skidded to a halt just as the door thudded into place. From just beyond the door, he could hear the angry roars of what sounded like a rampaging lion, or perhaps a rhino. It was hard to tell what kind of creature was loose, but it was making all manner of noise. Whatever it was, it was big.

He shouted into his headset, "C and C this is 04. Doors are down."

Up in C and C, also known as C2, Ross spat out the name "Talbot!" as if it was a profanity. Then he said into the microphone, "Oh four, this is C2 attempting override. Stand by one," which meant that he should stay on station until further communication. Ross glanced at the screen.

The Angry Man was still struggling with the foam, and it was slowing him down, but it wasn't stopping him from advancing on the Atheon security guards, waving his arms and bellowing like something from a Godzilla film. The guards were in full retreat. *Amateurs*, Ross thought grimly as he went on to the radiophone.

Despite the crisis that was before him, Ross's voice was calm and even. Indeed, he was in his element. Struggling with mountains of paperwork, trying to finesse politicos and play nice with corporate goons, these were all things that grated on him, things that he hated. Give him an enemy to fight, troops to maneuver, strategies to implement, and he was a happy man.

"Break, break," he snapped, his voice cutting across all bands. "All units this is C2. I say, spear point; repeat, spear point. Location: Sector Zulu, Level Four, Frame 256. Subject is Banner, Bruce. Interior ThreatCon is

Charlie. I repeat, Charlie. All Laramie units, respond. Secure, neutralize, and report status, over." He held back Bravo, hoping he wouldn't need them, fearing he would.

By pure happenstance, the great green berserker who had once been Bruce Banner turned, faced a camera, and roared like an extinct monster from prehistory sent forward through time.

"This could be interesting," muttered Ross.

what man hath wrought

Talbot moved with a contingent of Atheon security, some of them armed. They approached the area where the Hulk was pinned by the foam and paused as they heard him struggling around the corner.

"Let's get a sample of him," said Talbot. They took the corner and faced the Hulk. The creature took no notice of them, preoccupied as he was with trying to shake loose the substance that was holding him. It was hardening more and more, making it that much more difficult for the Hulk to maneuver or move at all. Most of him was covered up, but there was a small area left clear near the base of his neck.

Talbot approached cautiously, murmuring, "Now, let's take this nice and easy." He brought up a handheld laser drill and punched it into the Hulk's neck. The Hulk recoiled, screaming. His undiluted fury caused Talbot and the others to take several steps back, and then—even though his skin was tearing off in huge chunks—the infuriated man-monster began to rip free from the foam.

Once one piece came loose, others did as well, and suddenly Talbot realized that the Hulk was within seconds of completely freeing himself. Odds were that the first one he'd go for would be the guy with the handheld laser drill.

"Pull back," he ordered, and he didn't have to say it twice. The men retreated around the corner, the last bits of the foam went flying, and the Hulk thundered after them. He shook the walls and floor with each footstep.

Even as he retreated, Talbot heard large door locks beginning to disengage, the loud *ka-klak* of the metal releases echoing up and down the hallways. That damned Ross had found a way to override the lock down commands. Within seconds the doors would be rising and standard army troops would come flying in like locusts. Talbot would never hear the end of it, never.

Unless he stopped the monster first.

If he couldn't get samples from the living monster, he'd do what he could once the Hulk was dead. He just hoped that it wouldn't revert back to Bruce Banner before he could obtain the mutated tissue he needed.

One of the Atheon guards dashed past him, and Talbot grabbed the rifle right out of his hands. He knew it was packing APM2 .30-06-caliber armor-piercing bullets. Nothing short of Type IV body armor would repel one of those, and if there was one thing he could say definitively about the Hulk, it was that he wasn't wearing body armor. As for the guard, he seemed all too eager to give it up. It was just one less thing to slow him down.

Talbot spun to face the Hulk, standing his ground. Despite the fact that the monster towered over him, Talbot only saw him as the pathetic, whining scientist who he'd so easily brutalized earlier. Monster and man eyed each other for a moment, and Talbot thought it might be his imagination, but the Hulk seemed to recognize him as more than just an enemy.

. . . hurt . . . hurt us . . . me . . . hurt us . . . hurt him . . . more . . . hurt him MORE . . .

Talbot gasped and stepped back as the Hulk lurched toward him . . . and *grew*. As if reaching well more than eight feet in height hadn't been enough, the Hulk's mass increased even more, and seconds later he was filling up the entire corridor. He was half again as tall, and just as wide, so huge that he'd actually managed to wedge himself in there. He looked around in frustration, grunted, and flexed his muscles until the walls of the corridor started to creak to accommodate him.

Talbot, temporarily transfixed, watched in awe. He heard the pounding boots of the approaching troops, and all he could think was that it was damned considerate of the Hulk to have made himself an even bigger target than he was before.

"So long, big boy," said Talbot, and he unleashed a hail of powerful automatic fire. The Hulk didn't stagger because he was wedged into place, but his face contorted in pain as the bullets made contact, and for a heartbeat Talbot thought he had won.

It turned out to be one of the last heartbeats Glen Talbot experienced, because the air was then filled with the sound of metallic pinging as the bullets bounced off the Hulk. Having nowhere else to go, they ricocheted around, and a good number of them riddled Talbot. He crumpled to the ground, clutching at his chest. Feeling something soft and disgusting, he tried to shove it back in, whatever it was. And then he went into shock, and he died.

The remaining troops, witnessing it all, turned tail and ran for it.

Ross witnessed it as well.

He saw Talbot struck, and time slowed down. As Talbot fell, Thunderbolt Ross saw a young, eager-beaver officer who was determined to go places and set the world on fire. He saw the up-and-comer he'd made a personal project of because he knew that this was a young man who was going places. And he saw a young man consumed by money and cynicism and power.

In his way, Talbot had been just as corrupted by power as anyone carrying the name of Banner; he just did a better job of covering it up.

All this went through Ross's mind, and then he saw Talbot hit the floor and flop around like a dying seal. At which point the trained military mind of Thaddeus "Thunderbolt" Ross wrote off Talbot, case closed, time to move on. Because with all the evil and deceit that Glen Talbot had accomplished, he had at least managed one positive thing: He had let Ross know with his dying act that the Hulk was a creature against whom conventional weapons simply weren't going to work. And he had a troop of eager young men who were anxious to go monster hunting, charging into battle, all of whom were going to die the instant they opened fire.

"Pull them back," Ross said woodenly, ignoring the fact that he was standing in front of a microphone. "Lieber, pull them back."

"All Laramie units, this is C2," Lieber promptly said into the comm unit. "Pull back. Do not engage subject Bruce Banner; repeat, do not engage."

Run run they run smash ones who run smash them smash smash . . .

Colonel McKean of the Sixth Laramie unit led the retreat as, per orders, the men fell back. They hadn't yet seen what it was they were supposed to attack, but they heard the roars reverberating down the corridors, and McKean had to think they had just dodged a serious bullet. He would never know how literally correct he was.

They dropped back past the metal barricade doors, the ones that C and C had worked so hard to open, and the instant they were clear, the doors slammed shut again. McKean quickly touched base with the other Laramie units as well as with Bravo, getting a ground-level assessment of the situation. Then, confirming his findings with C and C, he said briskly into his microphone headset, "C two, this is Laramie 06, Laramie units pulling back. Subject inside Sector Yolk, Level Four."

The voice of Thunderbolt Ross came in on his headset, issuing orders to call, taking the designation "Laramie 01," to establish that he was at the top of the chain of command. Any command with 01 in it, whether he himself was saying it or it was being relayed as such, was understood to be coming straight from the top. "Concentrate containment on Sector X-ray, Level Three, Frame 185, out."

McKean immediately reaffirmed and rebroadcast the orders to any other Laramie units on line. "Break . . . break . . . all Laramie units, this is Laramie 01, concentrate containment on Sector X-ray, Level Three, Frame 185, out."

"Six, roger," Ross's voice confirmed, "Laramie 01, activate all fail-safe mechanisms. He goes anywhere near Two Foxtrot we know what we have to do. He could make an awful scary mess down there." That was, of course, an understatement. Foxtrot missiles were stored in the underground facility, and armed with nuclear warheads. If the monster started ripping into those, the unleashed radiation alone could kill everyone in the place the moment it hit the air ducts—and that wasn't even considering the possibility of a nuclear detonation.

McKean heard the order, but despite the fact that it originated from 01, it wasn't his primary concern. What worried him was the massive door he was facing that appeared, against all possible rational expectations, to be buckling from the pounding of . . . massive fists. "C two, six, roger that, sir," McKean confirmed, his eyes riveted on the spectacle of the bending door. "But be advised he's not going down there. He appears to be coming right at us, over."

"Six, C and C, roger," shot back Ross, as more troops poured into the main hall. "Prepare active denial and stand by."

. . . grab tear rip destroy destroy so much pain hurts hurt them hurt them all smash them all . . . SMASH THEM ALL . . .

And suddenly the door blocking the main hall from the monster within was torn to shreds, and the Hulk smashed his way in. In the future, when those who survived the altercation would speak of it, their descriptions of the size of the being attacking them would vary from account to account, situation to situation. Ironically, they would all be correct. The Hulk's size fluctuated depending upon his mood and the degree of opposition he encountered.

Immediately the men scattered, no one wanting to be the first one to take on this inhuman threat, all of them sensing that they were hopelessly out of their league. McKean fell back as well, but not in a panicked retreat. He simply took a few steps and watched warily as the Hulk raised his arms over his head and unleashed a bellow of rage and hatred. As this happened, Ross's voice was heard over the comm unit. "Oh one, C and C, initiate strobes, over!"

"Break, break!" shouted McKean, and he prayed that his men would be able to hear him over the bellows of the outraged behemoth. "All units, goggles down; light up the strobes, over."

Each of the troops put huge goggles on. Each pair was equipped with electric shutters timed in syncopation with a massive strobe light array that had been wheeled into the main hall. The strobe was switched on. Instantly disoriented, the Hulk threw his hands up to his eyes. Through their goggles, the soldiers saw the Hulk in flickering white light, stumbling back toward the entrance tunnel. It looked for all the world as if they were watching an old-style movie serial starring the Hulk.

. . . lights . . . hurt . . . hurt eyes . . . hurt . . . make stop . . .

A team ran up and shot nets, which spread instantaneously in front of the Hulk.

. . . stop . . . can't stop . . .

He jumped, grabbed the edge of one of the nets and flung it back at the men. They scattered, desperate to get out of the way, and he grabbed up random pieces of equipment and hurled them at the troops.

"C two, four, he's still on the move, over!" one of the soldiers reported.

"Four, roger that, C and C . . . break, break . . . six," said Ross.

• • •

. . . make light stop!

The Hulk jumped and pounded the ceiling. Huge support beams crumbled and fell across the length of the hall; one destroyed the strobe array. The Hulk landed, hit the floor, still disoriented, then pushed into the entry tunnel.

Ross, watching from C and C, saw it all, even as he received a report from one of the Laramie units. "C two, 04, he's moving topside, out."

"Break, break, all units, flashpoint, authorized weapons release, any means necessary," said Ross. "C and C, out . . ."

The monitor on which Ross was watching the skirmish came alive with flash fire as the soldiers blasted the Angry Man's departing form with everything they had in their arsenal. Ross desperately hoped that the circumstances, which he already thought were inevitable, wouldn't, in fact, come to pass.

Then, from high above, he heard the sound of earth crumbling, a pause, and then a rumbling of the ground, similar to the sound of an earthquake but more focused.

He knew. Even as confirmation came from the surface through on-site witnesses, he knew what had happened. His heart sank, and he glanced once more at the dead body of Glen Talbot, lying splayed and bloody in the hallway. His mood black, he thought, *Talbot, you arrogant ass*, even as he announced, "Javelin 6, this is C2," said Ross. "He has breached. Move on Sector Five, X-ray."

The Hulk had dug through the ground, broken the surface, and leaped away. He was gone, and there was a better-than-even chance that nothing was going to be able to stop him.

• • •

Free . . . free . . . free . . . place . . . peace . . .

The Hulk landed in the deserted, quiet neighborhood. His first instinct—and it was purely instinct on which he was operating, not reason—was to look around and see if more men with the sticks that spit hurtful pellets were hiding somewhere around. But there was no one around; his flared nostrils told him that.

One of the houses caught his attention. He had no comprehension that he had once resided there. He had very little understanding of the world in terms of how it related to him, or he to it, beyond pain and anger and a desire to crush anyone or anything that he saw as a threat. All he knew was that he felt drawn to it on a fundamental level that he couldn't understand.

Pulled by a power greater than his own—the power of a shattered memory—he approached the house and peered in through one of the windows, studying the dusty interior. The sound of vehicles rose, but it was difficult to know whether they were real or originating from some fragment of memory. A ghostly glimpse of the past swept through him, and there was glittering from within. A small green spruce tree was festooned with decorations. He saw a small boy, and the boy looked vaguely familiar but was also extremely irritating, and the Hulk wanted to just come right through the wall and crush the young boy in his oversize hands. He wanted to do it because he sensed that if that happened, he would be free of the annoying voice of reason which kept trying to intrude on his activities.

Then the wind howled as if it were trying to warn him of something, and abruptly the whole place erupted in flames as missile fire was let loose on the neighborhood.

The Hulk, still trying to sort fact from fiction, was caught unawares, and wound up being blasted back by the force of the explosions. He landed hard in the dunes, sending up a plume of sand.

As he got up, a group of LAVs—fast-moving desert attack vehicles—closed in on him. He was disoriented for a moment, but only for a moment. Then he jumped in front of one of them and grabbed the short tow chain attached to its bumper. The car jerked to a stop. The driver leaped clear, but there was a machine gun perched on the back, and a gunner seated right behind it. The gunner swung the weapon around, aimed it at the Hulk . . .

And suddenly the gunner was in the air. For the Hulk, with a grunt, had yanked on the chain and sent the vehicle whipping around like the hammer in a track-and-field event. He swung the vehicle through the air and the machine gunner, desperately trying to aim, wound up firing in all directions. Soldiers and vehicles scattered to get out of the way, and then the Hulk released his grip on the chain and sent the vehicle and the gunner both flying. The gunner was still firing.

Finally the machine gunner tumbled out, falling clear, which turned out to be his good fortune. For the vehicle's course caused it to land on one of the Abrams tanks that was quickly approaching. The tank had begun blasting away with huge amounts of firepower, but the flung jeep landed atop it, immobilizing it.

A second tank rolled past, trying to target the fast-moving green figure, but it had no luck, blowing up real estate all around the Hulk without once managing to hit him. The Hulk made it to the tank unscathed and lifted the gun turret, twisting off the entire top of the vehicle. Hoisting the turret clear, he smashed it repeatedly into the ground, reducing it to a mass of bent and twisted metal as he continued to roar and howl defiance. The tank tried to back up, but the Hulk—having grown bored with venting his rage on the turret—grabbed the rest of the tank and upended it, much in the way a child would shake loose the prizes from a box of cereal. This caused the soldiers inside to tumble out. They watched in astonishment and horror as the Hulk lifted the tank completely over his head, and needed no further incentive to bolt and run. They had side arms in their holsters, but they didn't even bother to go for them. Somehow there seemed to be very little point.

Ground troops had been moving in behind the tanks, but when they saw the uncontrollable monster flinging a tank around like a shoe box, they needed no further incentive to fall back before they became the target of his ire.

The triumphant bellow of the Hulk followed them across the dunes.

At the command center, Thunderbolt Ross had a satellite phone pressed against his ear. The retreating sergeant had just filled him in via comm link on the details of the encounter, and Ross had paled slightly but told the sergeant that he'd made the right call, pulling the troops back. No need for men to die needlessly, and obviously a straight up face-to-face with the creature was going to be suicide unless there were a lot more men involved than Ross had available to him.

Now he said into the phone, "Be advised this is T-bolt at Desert Lab. Requesting a flash override for POTUS and the national security adviser." POTUS, of course, was the abbreviation for "president of the United States."

"Ohio," said the Satcomm operator.

"Sandusky," said Ross, giving the proper code word response. "I repeat, Sandusky. Authenticate Alpha Whiskey Sierra Five Five Zero Three."

"I copy Alpha Whiskey Sierra Five Five Zero Three, wait one," said the Satcomm operator.

"Roger," said Ross, "standing by,"

The pause then, even though it lasted only a matter of seconds, seemed to last forever. Finally the Satcomm operator's voice came back and said, "This is a secure line. Go ahead, please."

"Mr. President, I have some bad news," said Ross. He had a mental picture of the president on the other end in a briefing room, surrounded by cabinet members and advisers. Then he heard, over the phone, someone in the distance shout, "Fore!" and realized the president was on a golf course. *Your tax dollars at work*, he thought grimly.

"Let's have it, General," came the president's voice.

The national security adviser was also on the line. Ross had met her once; she was a brisk, no-nonsense woman. Ross hadn't liked her, but he'd respected her thoroughness and quick grasp of situations. She displayed that trait now, saying, "I have briefed the president on Angry Man. I assume that's what this is about."

"It is, ma'am," Ross said. "I'm requesting National Command Authority override. Angry Man is unsecure, and I need everything we have at my disposal to stop his movement."

"General, are you expecting civilian casualties?" asked the national security adviser.

"Not if I can help it," Ross replied grimly.

"Consider it done," said the president. "Keep us posted. Oh, and General—"

"Yes, Mr. President?"

There was a pause, and then the commander-in-chief said, "Need I remind you . . . it *is* an election year."

The message was clear: Having voters killed by an out-of-control government project would be an exceedingly Bad Idea.

"Yes, sir. T-bolt out," said Ross.

He cut the signal, and Lieber brought him over a field phone. He had so many means of communication available to him, it was becoming ridiculous. He grabbed it without even bothering to ask who was on the other end.

"C and C, go," he snapped.

"C and C, UH-60 on the tarmac," said a voice on the radio.

"Portland, roger," said Ross, "Break, break. Boulder, heading topside, hold fire, we'll rendezvous at six six nine."

"Boulder, roger, Portland. Say the word, we'll drop the RC on him," said the voice.

. . . free . . . free . . . heart pumping, strength pounding, can't be stopped, can't be stopped . . .

Like a force of nature, the Hulk tore through the desert, leaping high, landing, the earth trembling beneath his gargantuan bare feet, and then leaping again. His strength was unfettered, and for once his boundless rage was mixed with pure, primal joy as he reveled in his strength and the lack of restraints.

He didn't even notice the Black Hawk helicopter that was pacing him. It didn't, however, pace him for long. Unknowing of any attempts to rein him in and, likewise, uncaring, the Hulk built up speed, faster and faster, until he was a virtual blur to the human eye. The Black Hawk tried to keep up, but even though it was able to cruise at 150 miles per hour, it started to fall behind.

And then it became clear that the Hulk's short leaps up to that point had simply been a means of building up speed. With one graceful movement that would have been envied—and feared—by any Olympic long-distance jumper, the Hulk vaulted two miles in one thrust of his impossibly powerful legs. And another two, and another, without slowing. Within moments he was gone over the horizon.

And Ross, aboard the Black Hawk, watched him go. "My God," he whispered under his breath.

For what seemed like the hundredth time that day, he couldn't believe what he was seeing. But even as the Angry Man vanished from view, he was already searching the radio bands, seeking to pick up some radio track of four Comanche helicopters that he knew were supposed to be en route. Within moments he heard cross talk between the choppers and their local airbase.

"Goodman departure, Banshee 0-1, flight of four, airborne, requesting vector and contact."

"Banshee flight, vector 2-6-0. Climb and maintain five thousand. Traffic no factor. Contact is T-bolt on Fox Mike 3-5-6-4. He's an Army Oscar 8 in a Black Hawk at about two to five miles on that heading."

"Goodman. Banshee 0-1 rogers all. 2-6-0 at five grand. Contact T-bolt on Fox Mike 3-5-6-4."

From long practice, Ross was able to make out what they were saying, but the transmission was filled with the crackle and static. The Comanches weren't quite within range yet. The Black Hawk angled toward them on an intercept vector, and Ross wondered just how much damage the Angry Man was inflicting as he waited to hook up with the choppers that he prayed would be able to stop the creature.

. . . leap . . . leap . . . fly . . . so strong . . . strongest there is . . .

The Hulk threw his arms wide, the wind blowing past him as he hurtled through the air, his eyes closed, the vast plains of the desert calling to him. Thoughts of the house were already long gone. Here, exulting in his power, the vistas of the Southwest landscape calling to him, he felt truly at home.

The desert flew past Ross as he snapped into the radio, the transmission having cleared up as he converged with the Comanches, "DBC, be advised subject is moving very fast out there. Terrain doesn't appear to be an obstacle. Launch fixed wing."

"Roger that, T-bolt."

"T-bolt, this is Banshee 0-1, flight of four, coming up on your five o'clock. We are rolling with rockets. Say your target and intentions."

Ross took in a deep breath and exhaled it slowly. "Banshee 0-1, T-bolt. Tracking on key 4-4-3. Mission is to stop this guy. Period."

"T-bolt, Banshee 0-1 understands you want us to attack the, uh, target," said Banshee 0-1. He sounded dubious, even amused. This was a trained combat pilot who was accustomed to assaulting convoys or military targets that were prepared to fire back at him. All he was being told was that he was taking on one exceedingly strong individual. Obviously he couldn't quite comprehend the challenge that awaited him. He might not even be taking it seriously. Ross could only hope the guy got with the program before it was too late.

"Roger, Banshee," Ross said, literally keeping his fingers crossed. "You are cleared hot. Good hunting."

. . . peace . . . peace . . . heart . . . slowing . . . calm . . .
The landscape was that of steep cliffs and rock formations. Hulk leaped to the top of a formation and looked out over the rocky expanse. There was a moment of eerie silence. His breathing grew regular, his heartbeat slowed. Had he been left to his own devices, there was every possibility that Bruce Banner would have reemerged in short order. There was, after all, no threat.

Conditions didn't remain that way.

. . . not leave alone . . . smash . . . SMASH . . .
The Hulk was daunted by the vehicles' arrival for perhaps all of a second, and then he swiftly reached out and grabbed one of the rotors of the closest chopper. The metal slammed into his hand, bent and twisted, and the chopper swung in toward him, its tail whipping around right at him. It collided with him and the Hulk and the chopper tumbled down the side of the cliff. The pilot inside the chopper had no choice but to hang on for the tumble down, shouting a desperate status report all the way.

They continued to roll down the cliff, the metal shrieking and bending in the Hulk's savage grip. They hit bottom together, and it was nothing short of miraculous that the chopper didn't explode. The pilot was still breathing but otherwise unmoving, blood covering his face as he simply hung there in the cockpit, suspended by his seat straps.

The Hulk, meantime, forgot about the chopper as soon as it was stilled, since it no longer presented a threat. The other choppers dashed about, regrouped, as the Hulk picked himself up and began climbing.

He didn't make himself an easy target. The Hulk dashed around various embankments, cliffs, and ravines, moving like a gamma-irradiated Tarzan, practically daring the choppers to keep up.

"Banshee 0-1, rog. Break, break. Banshees, this is 01. Combat stack. Follow me. Watch my run. Upping the ante. Next pass will be Zuni's ripple fire combat spread," said Banshee 0-1.

Ross was desperate to get to the scene. He felt as if his chopper were moving with the speed of molten lead, despite its miles-devouring pace. It was also obvious to Ross that, having actually seen the target involved, the chopper pilots were suddenly aware of the challenge awaiting them. They even seemed anxious to take it on. That attitude concerned him; they had enough problems to worry about without someone deciding to hotdog it.

"Cleared for rockets," Ross told him. "I do not want him any further west." His concern was understandable. Right now they were playing touch and go with a rampaging monster in the middle of nowhere. A battle in a populated area such as Los Angeles or San Francisco could cost hundreds, even thousands of lives. And that would be from direct combat scenarios alone and did not count the deaths caused by panicked citizens fleeing for their lives.

"—ding him with the Hellfires!" came Banshee 0-1's voice.

"DBC, T-bolt," said Ross. "Give me an ETA on that fixed wing."

"T-bolt, Cheyenne control has comms with Fast Eagle and High Bird, wait one, over," said DBC.

"DBC, request you patch us to T-bolt, over," said Cheyenne control.

But Ross had heard them. All the channels from immediate airbases were already crosslinked. "Cheyenne control, this is T-bolt. What do you got?" asked Ross.

"T-Bolt, Cheyenne control, roger. Our C-130 has visuals now, and three fast movers are turning on the ramp. Estimate your position in two minutes, over," said Cheyenne control.

. . . leave alone . . . smash if not . . . leave ME ALONE . . .

The Hulk clambered up a canyon wall as the Comanches blasted away on his tail. The Hulk got to the top of the ledge, stood atop a large outcropping, and turned to face the nearest Comanche just as it fired off a missile. It struck beside the Hulk, blowing off the entire outcropping, and sending the Hulk and the ledge tumbling down the canyon wall, a drop that ought to have been enough to dispose of any living thing.

The Hulk hit bottom, brushed himself off, and started back up the cliffside, looking extremely put out.

"T-bolt, sorry," said Banshee 0-1, and the pilot sounded absolutely stunned. It came as a sharp contrast to the jovial confidence he'd displayed when first entering the fray. "No joy here. We are bingo fuel at this point."

Ross sagged in his seat, but kept his voice steady. "Banshee 0-1, understood. Clear for home and I'd make it on the double. We're going to remove some air from the vicinity. Break, break. Fifty-two, proceed with the drop. I'm moving back."

And that was when he saw the Angry Man, the target he and the others had been pursuing so fruitlessly for what seemed like forever. The green behemoth didn't even deign to notice him. He just continued his leaps, higher and higher, farther and farther, bouncing over Ross's Black Hawk without so much as slowing down.

"What's his course? No, don't tell me. I know," Ross said, his voice cold and controlled and not showing his frustration. Ross was a veteran combat man. He didn't like to lose under any circumstance, and with the stakes as high as these were, he simply couldn't afford to. But even he had to acknowledge the devastating truth: "He's headed straight for San Francisco."

The mood was somber at the base at Joint Tactical Force West. Somber, that is, for everyone who wasn't the father of a monster. David Banner, on the other hand, seemed in a rather jovial mood, all things considered.

MPs were leading him into the base as Betty stood at the main entrance, watching him being taken away. He stopped for a moment and turned, ignoring his escorts who were tugging at him, urging him to move. He held up his manacled hands as if he were a boxer raising his arms in triumph. Apparently it was supposed to be a gesture of farewell, but she couldn't help but think that there was an element of disdain in it.

As he was led away, Betty's cell phone went off. She pulled it out and said, "Yes?"

"Betty," came her father's voice, and she instantly knew something was wrong. Not only that, somehow she knew what it was even before her father voiced it. "He . . . it . . . got out."

The world seemed to sway around her. Her father's use of the pronoun "it" spoke volumes. This wasn't a case of Bruce Banner having cannily mounted an escape. Something had caused him to transform into the Hulk. She could take a guess: Talbot. *When I get my hands on him, he's a dead man*, she thought grimly, oblivious to the irony.

"He's making his way, probably, to you," Ross informed her. "Get to base—"

"I'm already there. And his father—he's turned himself in," said Betty.

"His father! Jesus!" The news seemed to catch Ross off guard but he adapted quickly to the situation. "Just . . . I'll order up a security detail. Just stay there." He broke the connection without further niceties.

And Betty looked at the sky over the Golden Gate Bridge. It was cloudless, peaceful. She had the sick feeling things weren't going to stay that way.

his anger unbound

As Thunderbolt Ross tracked the Hulk's progress, the hunted moved quickly over the Sierra Nevada, uncaring of the three hunters—specifically three Raptor F-22 jets—that were hard on his tail. The planes were having a hell of a time trying to target him. They were used to aiming at much larger things, such as other planes. A single moving individual, even one who was twelve feet tall, wasn't exactly in their comfort zone.

"Dash two rolling in hot lock and Fox Three. Breaking off left," said the F-22 pilot.

"Check fire, check fire," said Ross. "The area's too populated now. At this point we've got to try to get him out to sea, and terminate him there, over."

Moments later, he was on the line with the mayor of San Francisco. Ross could hear emergency vehicles being deployed in the background, and the distinctive "Hut! Hut! Hut!" of SWAT teams barreling toward transport trucks. The mayor's voice was calm, but in that forced way that indicated his equanimity wasn't being maintained without effort. "General, I'm bringing out the welcome committee for whatever it is you're sending me," he said.

"Thank you, Mr. Mayor. I'm hoping our stay will be a brief one," said Ross.

"We're a tolerant city, General, but I have to say I'm hoping your stay will be even shorter than brief. But if you need us, we're here for you."

"Thank you, sir," replied Ross.

. . . Betty . . . planes . . . stupid planes . . .

The Hulk was getting tired. The constant pursuit was starting to wear him down, not physically, but mentally. The longer Bruce Banner was incarnated as the rampaging green monster, the more his primitive brain was required to dwell on the situation to try to make sense of it. He felt as if he should be moving toward something, but didn't know what that might be aside from Betty on the most primitive level. He knew he had to keep moving away from something, as well, that something being those who would hurt him, destroy him. He wanted to stop, to tear them apart, to punish them for harassing him and hurting him and not leaving him alone. But all of it involved far too much thinking. Above all else, the Hulk was a creature of rage, and rage was a very difficult emotion to sustain, even for him.

And worst of all, he could sense Banner lurking in there. Banner, that damned hypocrite, who wanted the Hulk to just go far, far away, but at the same time secretly reveled in his power. But the secret wasn't safe from the Hulk; he knew it, oh yes he did. He didn't completely comprehend it, but he knew it.

The Hulk landed on the Marin headlands, cast a look over his shoulder, and the damned jets buzzed him. He raised his arms over his head, howled defiance, and leaped again. The jump carried him all the way to the Golden Gate Bridge, where he landed atop one of the arches.

The air vehicles were coming in at him like mosquitoes or gnats. Four airplanes, and a helicopter. The Hulk didn't see them for what they were, wasn't capable of thinking, "Oh, look, F-22s and a Black Hawk." All he knew was that they were pursuing him and wanted to hurt him, and he wanted to hurt them back. The rage, which had been subsiding, roared fully to the fore once again, and when one of the planes came a little too close, the Hulk didn't hesitate.

Timing the jump perfectly, he leaped toward the plane and landed atop it. The plane swooped just below the bridge, the Hulk clinging to it, and his back scraped the bottom of the bridge, creasing it, as they passed under.

Then, suddenly, the plane went vertical and flew straight up.

The strategy, developed on the fly, in every sense of the word, by Thunderbolt Ross, was devastatingly simple: Take the Hulk on a ride to the top of the world, and see what some thin air did for him.

The Hulk clung to the plane as it rose up through the clouds. Frost began to cover him, hanging from his hair, his eyebrows. The world started to fade around him. Close to losing consciousness, he stared into the eyes of the pilot through the cockpit's windshield. The pilot flinched, concerned that the Hulk would abruptly recover and try to tear the wings off his plane. But he needn't have worried, for the Hulk closed his eyes completely, and as the plane tilted back—having gone as high as it could safely go—the monster slid off.

He tumbled end over end, and images once again began

to cascade through his mind, and Banner was in front of a mirror shaving, and he was watching himself and listening to the slow scraping of the razor, and seeing other eyes looking back at him from inside the mirror, different eyes, just as he had been the other day, except that time had just been an almost intellectual exercise, except this time the eyes watched him, narrowed, and they were green and filled with hatred, and Banner stopped and leaned closer into the mirror, studying, when suddenly the glass flew apart and the Hulk's hand reached out and took him by the neck, smashing his face back into the mirror and Banner, bloodied but unbowed, stared back into the Hulk's furious face now, the two of them nose-to-nose, and they regarded each other like two old friends and two old enemies, all interconnected, and slowly Banner raised his hand, gently untwined the Hulk's fingers from around his neck, and the Hulk was calm, so calm, and peace beckoned to him, but just as he seemed to calm, his fingers formed a fist, and with a quick blow to the face he snapped Banner's neck back, broken it. He had triumphed, he had disposed of Banner, for he was the strongest one there was . . .

The Hulk crashed into the bay, sending up a geyser of water that could be seen for miles. He swiftly dropped to the floor of the bay and was lodged in the muddy bottom, half-conscious.

"Bring it round again!" Ross shouted as the Black Hawk flew down over the bay. He studied the huge perturbations in the water where the Hulk had gone down, and then he waited. He had to be sure that the Hulk was gone, that the strategy had worked. Although, even if it had, Ross felt no real sense of triumph. More and more, he was beginning to see Bruce Banner as the victim in all this. He had asked for none of it. He was no ruthless terrorist who had plotted and planned. If he did die, he was simply a casualty of war. God knew there had been enough of them over the course of military conflict, but one didn't rejoice in their fate. One simply accepted it as part of man's conflict against man. . . .

At which point the Angry Man broke the water.

"I don't believe it," Ross said yet again.

The Black Hawk was armed with two M60D machine guns, and the gunners used them now to open fire. Considering all the monster had survived, Ross had a feeling that it was a hollow gesture, but he had to do something. Bullets splattered in the water, and Ross was sure that a number of them had to have hit the Angry Man.

But all the Angry Man did was glance up disdainfully at the helicopter, and then he took a deep breath and went under again.

Ross remembered the Hulk's ability to survive on a single breath from the encounter with the gas. The situation wasn't promising, and Ross was beginning to realize that this wasn't simply a case of man against man. This was man against a force of nature . . . and unfortunately, in such conflicts, man always came up on the losing end.

It also meant that Ross might have some hard decisions to make. There was always the possibility that Banner was going to head away from the city. On the other hand, he might make a beeline right toward it.

And if, in his rage, he did choose a direct assault, he might not just stampede around in open view. Ross knew there were underwater drains that emptied into the bay not far from the city's edge; the Angry Man, if he spotted them, might make his way in through one of those. If that was the case, he could cause a kind of structural havoc not seen since the World Series earthquake back in 1989.

Ross leaned into his radio unit, and when he spoke, it wasn't without effort. "Legends Dash one, two, three, four, prepare to go weapons hot. Subject Banner may be heading toward city. You are authorized to engage. I will give you vectors shortly."

"Uh, roger, T-bolt," said the pilot designated Legend Dash two. His voice was somewhat cautious, as if he knew Ross was aware of what was about to be said, but felt he needed to say it anyway. "Be advised we are hanging serious weapons here. This stuff is gonna cause a lot of damage if we start shooting into downtown San Francisco."

"You are cleared to fire on the target, Legend," said Ross. "Let me worry about collateral damage." And he knew it was indeed his worry; he'd likely be drummed out of the military for it. He had no illusions on that score. American citizens like their military maneuvers nice and tidy and devoid of casualties . . . particularly civilian casualties, and most particularly American civilians. In addition to signing the death warrants of the citizens, he was signing the death warrant of his own career, as well. He was looking at court-martial, loss of rank, possibly even jail time. Because the howl would come for somebody's head, and as the president had pointed out, it was an election year. Ross just never suspected he was going to be the one who got elected.

"T-bolt, Legend Dash one, roger. All units are weapons hot," said the F-22 pilot.

Ross's face was grim. It then occurred to him that there

was one weapon he had not yet employed, and although it killed him to admit it, it was possibly the only one that might prevent widespread damage.

"Take us to Tactical Base West," Ross abruptly ordered.

The pilot glanced back at Ross to confirm what he'd just heard. Ross nodded without repeating it and, with a small shrug, the pilot did as he was ordered.

A cable car rang its bell and moved toward Market Street. No one on the car, or anywhere nearby, expected this to be anything other than an ordinary day, despite the odd military maneuvers some of them had spotted occurring near the Golden Gate Bridge. There had been rumors flying around of some sort of monster traipsing around atop the bridge, but the general thought was that it was some kind of hoax that had probably originated on the Internet, as so many things seemed to these days.

Nobody saw the small crack in the street that followed the cable car's path, almost as if the cable car was leaving it in its wake. And then other cracks began to radiate outward, widening, becoming bigger, heaving upward.

Pedestrians started to notice and jump out of the way, and naturally the first thing that occurred to them was earthquake, except there seem to be no rumbling or shifting beneath their feet. Cracks were just starting to appear everywhere, for no discernible reason.

Water mains began to break. At each fire hydrant the caps flew off and water blasted out in all directions, soaking anyone standing nearby and making it even harder for passersby to stay on their feet as the sidewalks became slick. Cars were blasted as well, sent careering into one another, either from the direct impact of the spray or else from trying to get clear of the geysers that seemed to have unexpectedly turned up everywhere.

San Francisco was officially under siege. It was just that no one realized it yet.

found again

Betty Ross sprinted toward the tarmac as her father's Black Hawk settled down. The side door slid open and she saw his face as he gestured for her to clamber aboard.

She had been more stunned than she'd thought possible when the call had come in that he was picking her up. It couldn't have been an easy decision for her dad to make. Obviously he felt that whatever input she might have to make regarding Bruce was of such importance that it necessitated her being brought into the conflict. On the other hand, normally his overwhelming impulse was to keep her safe. He had proven that time and again whether by assigning guards to her or ordering her off Desert Base. So bringing her in now was completely against his nature, which indicated to Betty just how desperate he must be.

She clambered aboard and the chopper pilot barely waited for the door to slam behind her before he took off. Without having to be told, Betty slapped a pair of earphones on her head so she could speak to her father, since the pounding noise within the Black Hawk made communication without such a device almost impossible.

"Dad," she said with a brisk inclination of her head.

For just a moment, a look of helplessness flickered

across his face, to be replaced just as quickly by grim frustration. "Betty, I don't know what choice I have," Ross said. "I have to destroy him."

She shook her head vigorously. "You can't. Enraging him only makes him stronger. And you'll destroy San Francisco in the process."

He nodded grimly, and she realized she wasn't telling him anything he didn't already know. That was really the reason she was here: because the situation seemed hopeless, and he didn't know where else to turn. He was like a macho redneck, lost on the interstate, sucking it up and stopping to ask directions. It would have been kind of sweet in a way, if the stakes hadn't been so high.

"There's only one way to stop him: Give him some breathing room," said Betty.

Ross pondered that, and she knew exactly what he was thinking: He could give the Hulk breathing room, sure, but how much breathing room was the Hulk going to give San Francisco?

. . . wet . . . stupid, more water, more water, hate more water, can't smash water hate stupid, dark, dark, smells . . .

With each step through the storm drains, the Hulk pushed up with his elbows. He wasn't doing it to wreak havoc on San Francisco, although that's what was occurring. He was just doing it to make more room for himself.

Finally he came to a juncture point and looked up in surprise when he saw daylight filtering through a manhole cover. He clambered upward, not pulling himself up on the ladder, but rather simply pushing himself toward the surface with the power of his hands braced against either side of the vertical tunnel.

He poked his head through the manhole cover and squinted against the light of day. With a low growl he climbed out of the sewer, reeking, and surveyed his surroundings. He was standing at a steep intersection, with steps leading down to it from the hill above.

At least fifty people on the sidewalks or crossing the street froze when they saw the monster emerge from the sewers. It was like a moment on the African veld, when a herd of antelope are momentarily paralyzed upon seeing a lion rise up, fierce and terrible, from the high grass. For long seconds, nobody moved. Both parties—the people of San Francisco and the Hulk—looked equally surprised to see each other.

And then the Hulk let out a roar that shook windows and rattled doors within a three-block radius. The bellow snapped the spell, and as one the people tore away from him in all directions. This proved to be a major inconvenience for the combined forces of the military and the SFPD, all of whom were struggling toward the scene like salmon swimming upstream. All the shouts of "One side!" and "This is a police matter!" went unheeded as people seemed far more interested in distancing themselves from the scene than obeying orders.

Several soldiers glanced at one another and, operating with a single thought, unleashed a short burst of automatic fire into the air. They weren't worried about upsetting people; there was already panic in the streets. The unexpected burst of noise did, however, cause the sea of bodies to part, and the cops and soldiers were able to plow their way through.

Several SWAT trucks barreled forward, converging from all directions, and the drivers of those vehicles didn't give a damn about anything that might be in the way. They entered the terror-filled area and barely slowed, leaving it to the pedestrians to move. This the pedestrians did, albeit with effort and much hurling of profanity

. . . kill them smash them smash them all . . .

while meanwhile the skies overhead came alive with a fleet of helicopters, bristling with armament. The F-22s were speeding toward the scene. They were intended as a last resort, to be used only if the ground forces were annihilated by the Angry Man. But when the hundreds of National Guardsmen and soldiers and policemen arrived on the scene, and the SWAT teams took up stations on buildings overlooking the Hulk's position, all ready to unleash whatever firepower they were packing, the Hulk didn't appear at all intimidated. The F-22s roared past overhead and he tilted back his head and howled his challenge. A Black Hawk helicopter arced past as well, looking for a place to set down.

When a terrorist attack brought down skyscrapers in the midst of the greatest city in the world, many commented that witnessing it was like watching a big-budget action movie come to life—minus the comfort of knowing it was all pretend. For everyone on the scene the day the Hulk came to San Francisco, it was like witnessing a monster movie come to life. And again the citizenry lacked the comfort of knowing that at the end, the lights would come up and everything would be normal. Staring into the face of such unparalleled rage, every person there knew beyond question that the very concept of "normality" had undergone a stunning and permanent change.

Nobody was nearer than two hundred feet, so that a gigantic circle radiated out with the Hulk at the center. He bellowed defiantly, shook his fists once again, as if daring someone to get within range. No one was suicidal enough to take him up on it.

He roared once more, and it resounded off the streets and the buildings. Then there was the sound of several hundred hammers being cocked and rounds being chambered, and one other sound which caught the Hulk's attention.

A simple, steady *klik-klak* of a woman's high-heeled shoes.

It was so completely out of place in the moment that the Hulk couldn't help but notice it. He growled, but it sounded more like a question than any sort of threatening noise. Somewhere in the distance, the voice of Thunderbolt Ross was heard coming from a blaring radio, ordering, "All units, hold your fire," but the Hulk paid it no mind.

His mind was filled with thoughts of destruction, but her scent penetrated the haze of anger, and the images and thoughts and sensations associated with her came into direct conflict with the drive to destroy.

. . . smash . . . want to . . . want . . .

. . . Betty . . . ?

One careful step at a time, making no sudden moves, Betty Ross approached him. She knew every person watching was convinced that the moment she drew within range, the creature would pound her into paste, and it seemed unlikely that all the firepower in the world would be able to act fast enough to prevent it. But if she was aware of the mortal danger she was putting herself in—and she most definitely had to be—she didn't let it show at all. She kept her chin up, her gaze level.

And to the shock of everyone—with the possible exception of Betty herself—the Hulk dropped to his knees and let out a cry of pain and shame. He sounded like a mortified child caught at being naughty.

She came closer still, came within arm's length, and the Hulk, a creature who could have broken her with one twist of a huge paw, winced, flinched back. But she came to him, touched him, caressed his face, and made gentle "shushing" noises, as if she were reassuring a terrified infant, telling it that everything was going to be all right.

. . . Betty . . . oh, God . . . Betty . . .

The Hulk's body began to contract. Fluids emerged from every pore as the monster shrank before the eyes of the onlookers, and there were gasps, followed by a stunned silence, as the Hulk dissolved into the form of a slim and utterly harmless human being. Only the noise of the choppers and circling planes shattered the stillness of the morning.

Bruce Banner looked at Betty with an exhausted half smile. "You found me," he said.

Betty took a quick glance around. "You weren't that hard to find," she said, seeing morbid amusement in the moment.

"Yes," said Bruce, "I was." And Betty knew that he was referring to something else completely, and she began to cry.

"Hey," Bruce continued softly, and now he was the one who was comforting her. "I'm just grateful we got the chance . . . to say good-bye."

And they clung to each other then, two people surrounded by the physical wreckage left in the wake of the Hulk, a symbol of the emotional wreckage of the couple themselves.

• • •

Several hundred miles away, Monica Krenzler watched CNN's footage of an as-yet-unidentified, dark-haired man clinging to a young woman, sobbing piteously in the midst of the real-life horror show his life had become. Monica's tears as she watched were more copious than his.

In his cell at the Joint Tactical Force West brig, David Banner sat upright on his cot and smiled.

"Soon," he whispered. "Very, very soon."

Soon he knew they would come for him. Soon he knew that he would be brought to see his son. Soon he would be invincible.

"Can I get a pizza in here?" he called to the guard. No answer was forthcoming. He reminded himself to kill the guard as soon as he was the greatest power on earth.

sins of the father

In a grudging, almost perverse way, Bruce Banner had to admire the ingenuity of the scientists at the base. They'd come up with a rather clever way of keeping him immobilized, having rigged up the entire thing in an otherwise empty airplane hangar.

Essentially, he was positioned on a large platform between two huge electromagnetic arrays. The entire area was illuminated by immense klieg lights, making it that much easier to see Bruce—not that he was doing much of anything interesting. He just sat on a cot, staring at one of the arrays with vague curiosity.

He had every reason to be interested. The arrays were large enough and powerful enough that, although they likely wouldn't have much effect on the Hulk other than to annoy him further, they would be able to incinerate Bruce Banner in a matter of seconds. He would be the most powerful pile of ashes in California.

It didn't matter to Bruce. None of it did. He had examined the situation, turned it over and over in his mind. With all that, he hadn't come to a conclusion that was substantially any different from what he'd already intuited back in San Francisco. He'd clambered back to reality and found Betty, like a drowning man surfacing and gasping in lungsful of air. But even in that moment of joy and salvation, he had known instantly that it was going to be temporary.

He was, quite simply, too dangerous to live.

Betty Ross had come to much the same conclusion as Bruce. The only difference was she was far more unwilling to accept it.

She was at the far end of the hangar, watching him on monitors that had been rigged up near a communications truck. Thunderbolt Ross was addressing her and several other scientists and high-ranking officers who she didn't recognize.

"Here's the deal," said Ross. "He stays on the base here until we get final word from C Three on how to dispose of him. The slightest hint he's putting on weight, or he starts curling his lip a little too meanly, or he starts looking like an avocado, we turn up the juice and he's incinerated immediately." He hadn't been looking right at Betty as he spoke, but now he did. His expression softened slightly, but only slightly. This wasn't a situation where he was going to try to sugarcoat it for her. "Betty, you'd better prepare yourself for the orders we're going to get."

"We've established a two-hundred-yard perimeter, sir," said a colonel whose nametag identified him as Thomas. "If we deploy the electromagnetic array, there should be no collateral damage."

"It'll be a hell of a show, though," said Ross. Betty shuddered when he said that, and he looked as if he immediately regretted having made the comment. But he'd said it, and, frankly, he was probably right. The electromagnets would unleash a light display that would look like the Big Bang, except the intention would be to destroy, rather than create.

Betty looked around at the soldiers who were stationed at the controls. They looked to be on hair triggers, tense and waiting for the slightest sign that the lethal device should be activated. Hell, they were so keyed up that if Bruce chose that moment to sneeze, they'd probably fry him, and get a medal and commendation into the bargain.

God, what had she done? Because of her, Bruce was now helpless. But what other options had been open to her? Do nothing and let him destroy San Francisco? *Well, if he'd leveled it, no more worrying about climbing those damned hills.* She wanted to laugh and cry at the thought, and managed to keep herself from doing either through an impressive display of self-control.

Then she heard a personnel transport truck pull up, and she knew, even before the doors were opened, just who it was that was in there. Guards jumped down and opened the back, and David Banner—in chains—was led out of the vehicle, escorted by the troops. He passed Betty and Ross, making eye contact but saying nothing. His escorts pointed him toward the open end of the hangar. Betty watched him approach the hangar, and she didn't know whether she wanted to kill him or . . .

No. On second thought, she did know.

Bruce Banner, half-blinded by the lights, sat up, and saw the figure of a man approaching him in a slow, shambling manner. Nevertheless, he recognized his father almost instantly. Slowly David Banner traversed the length of the hangar, stepping right up and in between the electromagnets. It was a not-so-subtle message to his son, Bruce realized. If Bruce began to transform into the

Hulk, his father would share his fate. Perhaps David thought this was generous, or a show of goodwill on his part. To Bruce it simply qualified as just desserts.

He stood before his son and hung his head.

"I should have killed you," Bruce whispered with ill-concealed venom.

"As I should have killed you," his father acknowledged.

"I wish you had," replied Bruce. He sank down onto the cot, his head in his hands. "I saw her last night. In my mind's eye. I saw her face. Brown hair, brown eyes. She smiled at me, she leaned down and kissed my cheek. I can almost remember a smell, like desert flowers—"

"Her favorite perfume," said the father.

"My mother. I don't even know her name," said Bruce, starting to cry.

At the other end of the hangar, Betty and her father watched on the monitors. The sound was low, distorted, but they could just make out the conversation. And Betty had to admit something to herself: As messed up as her relationship with Thunderbolt Ross might have been, he was Father of the Year compared to the nut Bruce had gotten stuck with.

David Banner didn't seem bothered at all by his son's sobs. "That's good. Crying will do you good." He walked toward his son and reached out with manacled hands.

Betty couldn't help but be appalled. To see this man suddenly trying to act solicitous after the things he'd said, the things he'd done. She was relieved to see Bruce pull back from him.

"No, please don't touch me," Bruce said, recoiling. "Maybe, once, you were my father. But you're not now. You never will be."

"Is that so?" asked David. His eyes narrowed. All pretense of affection and compassion were evaporating. "Well, I have news for you. I didn't come here to see you. I came for my son."

Betty was confused when she heard that, and Bruce was obviously no less so.

David Banner continued, "My *real* son . . . the one inside you. You are merely a superficial shell," and his voice started to get louder, "a husk of flimsy consciousness surrounding him, ready to be torn off at a moment's notice."

"Think whatever you like," Bruce said tiredly. "I don't care. Just go now."

And then the father seemed to look right into the camera, sneering at Betty, before leaning in toward Bruce and murmuring so softly that no one monitoring the conversation could hear him. That was Betty's first warning that something truly disastrous was going to happen.

Bruce tried to back away, but his father gripped his legs and held him in place. "But Bruce," he whispered, "I have found a cure—for me." His tone grew more menacing. "You see, my cells, too, can transform. Absorb enormous amounts of energy, but unlike yours, they're unstable. Bruce, I need your strength," he said with growing urgency. "I gave you life, now you must give it back to me—only a million times more radiant, more powerful."

"Stop," said Bruce, trying to pull away.

"Think of it," David said, and he made a gesture that took in the entirety of the hangar. "All those men out there, in their uniforms, barking and swallowing orders, imposing their petty rule over the globe. Think of all the harm they've done, to you, to me—and know we can make them and their flags and their anthems and governments disappear in a flash. You . . . *in me.*"

Bruce was aware that his continued existence hinged on keeping absolutely calm, but at that instant he didn't care.

"I'd rather die," he said.

"And indeed you shall," his father assured him, sounding as if he were trying to be accommodating. "And be reborn a hero of the kind that walked the earth long before the pale religions of civilization infected humanity's soul."

All the possibilities of the moment went through Bruce's trained, analytical mind as he looked deep into the eyes of his demented parent. And he suddenly was certain that whatever his father was talking about, it wasn't just the ravings of a lunatic. He definitely had some sort of plan, and although there was no questioning that he was—as Bruce's adopted mother used to say—crazy as a soup sandwich, there was also no questioning his brilliance. Bruce was positive that his father had a plan, and the ability to pull it off. And it involved Bruce Banner.

Knowing he was triggering his own destruction, but determined to head off whatever the hell his father was up to, Bruce leaped to his feet and screamed, "Go!"

The shout was directed to those who held his life in their hands. He wanted them to go ahead, to annihilate him right then and there.

Enough already.

Betty, he thought bleakly, and he wasn't sure if it was his mind thinking that or another's, but then he heard the electromagnets powering up and knew it should take no more than a few seconds. He thought he heard Betty cry out in dismay, but she was very, very far away, and it hadn't been much of a life, but damn, it had been interesting. . . .

And David Banner, thinking that he'd been the subject of the strangled "Go!" snarled, "Stop your bawling, you weak little speck of human debris. I'll go. Just watch me go!"

With that, displaying a strength that he shouldn't have possessed, he grabbed one of the thick electrical cables lying on the floor and tore it apart. The live wires sputtered, and then he took them into his mouth, a perversion of a newborn being suckled by its mother. Overhead, the klieg lights in the hangar began to sputter.

"No!" howled Bruce, and he jumped toward his father but was bounced back by the current. If he'd seen his own reflection as he hit the floor, he would have seen a definite hint of green in his eyes.

"What the hell!" shouted Ross, watching the confrontation between the two Banners spiral out of control. Betty, sensing something was wrong beyond the catastrophes they already had to deal with, tried to stop the soldier from slamming the switch home.

But it was too late as the soldier at the controls, already extremely jumpy, yanked down on the switch. The electromagnetic arrays came to life and a burst of enormous energy surged from them. But instead of radiating out, their energy flowed directly into the outstretched arms of David Banner . . .

. . . and kept on flowing.

The lights on the island, then on the bridges, and then throughout the entire Bay Area, went out.

Bruce watched in horror as his father, his body coursing

with electrical energy, crackled and broke open his shackles. The arrays imploded in a flash. David flung out his arms, sending up an electromagnetic field that made the entire hangar sizzle.

The monitors went dark. Even the headlights and the ignition systems of the vehicles sputtered out.

"Hit them again," shouted Thunderbolt Ross.

"We can't, sir!" one of the soldiers said desperately, manipulating controls that had gone dead. "There's no power, some kind of counterelectromagnetic field—"

"Then move in there with everything you've got," said Ross. "Fire at will."

It won't do any good, thought Betty, who was becoming rather tired of being right all the time.

The father, laughing, looked over at where Bruce had been thrown—and was met by a huge green fist which lifted him, in a lightning flash, into the air, through the roof of the hangar, and across the bay. The Hulk, with a roar, leaped after him

. . . *smash* . . . *killer* . . . *murder* . . . *smash him, yes, SMASH HIM* . . .

and for the first time the minds of the Hulk and Bruce Banner were not split, were not pulling against one another, but instead were acting as one vast engine of destruction, aimed straight at their mutual father.

He collided in midair with his father and the impact carried them miles into the night as a firestorm of electricity crackled around them. They landed by the edge of a distant mountain lake, staggered back, and faced each other. The slightly waning moon stared down at them.

David Banner stood almost as tall as the Hulk, the electricity now drained from his body, laughing. "You see, nothing can stop me, son. I absorb it all, and give it back."

The Hulk roared at his father, a sound so loud and unique that it registered on one of the monitors at Ross's command center.

"They're painted," said a technician. "Snider Lake."

"Call up the task force," Ross ordered.

Unaware of who or what was coming for him, and uncaring as well, the Hulk pounded David Banner with both fists. But not only did it not seem to bother him, but with each blow Banner took he seemed to grow bigger, greener, absorbing the Hulk's energy, his cellular structure. The Hulk stepped back, regarded him with horrified confusion as the father stood. They were the same height.

Once more Banner's mind informed the Hulk as they thought, *What the fu—?*

"Go on, son," David Banner said defiantly. "The more you fight me, the more of you I become."

The Hulk was more confused now, and kept his distance—ready to strike but holding back. Then he crouched down and, scooping up an enormous boulder, lifted it and crashed it down on David. Instantly it caused his father to transform into stone, which would have been daunting . . . for anyone who was incapable of shattering stone. But that definitely wasn't the Hulk's problem, as he pounded away, again and again, his rage growing and his strength escalating. With a final blow, he reduced his father to a pile of dust and rock fragments. They fell on the Hulk, and he pushed them off in what he thought was the end of the problem.

But in doing so, he transferred energy back to his father that David Banner was able to reshape his body so that he once more mirrored the physical makeup and endurance of the Hulk.

. . . killer . . . murderer . . . smash, kill, tear, rend limb from limb, kill . . .

In a white-hot fury, the Hulk lashed out once again with his fists. The two of them, locked in a struggle, made their way to the lake's edge, wildly pounding away at each other. With each blow, the air around them seemed to grow cold, vacant. Even the water began to turn opaque and icy. The two of them seemed almost to merge as the lake's water began to freeze around them.

Having their subjects targeted via long-range signals bounced off satellites, Ross and Betty stood at the monitors back at the hangar. Betty's mind was racing, trying to come up with some means of stepping in without getting herself or Bruce or both of them killed. Nothing was occuring to her.

"Strange," said Colonel Thomas at one of the monitors, zooming in on one of the satellite images. "We're reading a phenomenal drop in temperature there but a simultaneous radiological activity."

Ross looked blankly at his daughter. "The ambient energy," said Betty matter-of-factly. "They're absorbing it all. That's where the additional mass comes from. They're literally converting energy into matter."

"Can they convert it back?"

"If they can," Betty said softly, "we're all dead."

Fighter jets flew overhead, passing by the two enormous figures, locked in a death grip, upon a lake that was now completely frozen. Sparks of energy, neural charges, spiked through the frozen water.

And as the Hulk struggled in that frozen grip, the mind and thoughts of Bruce Banner struggled against the Hulk's, seeking something, grabbing at something, and there were *Thousands of images, bits of memory and desire, suddenly coalesced into a moment of absolute calm and clarity in the Hulk's frozen eyes, and he knew right where to look, right when to look; it was right there, right there, Christmas, David Banner sat on the floor playing with his son, fighting, except it was in play, each of them holding a stuffed toy, one of those two toys, and Bruce said, "This one can fly, he's faster," and David replied, "But mine will eat yours right up!" and the way he said it caused momentary panic in Bruce, and his little features tightened, and he said, "No! He won't, mine is flying away," and David smiled and said, "Yes, you're flying away!" and he threw the doll down and it was*

right

there.

Right where it had always been, the knowledge he needed, the obligation upon him, the way to beat him, the way to defeat himself, right there in the pointlessness of the dolls battling and giving up and flying away, and when he spoke it was to his father or to himself, it didn't matter. It was all the same as he wondered if he'd ever even had a father, or just another incarnation of himself, and his voice was utterly calm as he said, "I know how you plan on winning, Father," and his father said, "Do you know?" and Bruce told him, "By harnessing my rage," and there was the approving laughter of a father who was finally proud of his son for making an intuitive leap, and he said, "Yes, I will take it from you," and Bruce replied, "But you won't—because I will take it from myself," and the father, genuinely interested, asked, "And how will you do that?" to which Bruce answered, *"By forgiving you. Take him. He's yours."*

And the ice was cracking beneath their feet as David Banner rose up from the melting ice, lifted the Hulk's fist, and held it to his stomach. The Hulk struggled, but he was bewildered and unfocused, as if he didn't know what to do with his rage—or no longer possessed it at all.

"Come to me, my son," said David Banner.

The Hulk seemed to dissolve, but Bruce Banner could be glimpsed briefly inside the falling shape as it dropped into the lake. His father, victorious, towered above the mountains. He saw on the horizon a fleet of puny Stealth fighters and jets making their way toward him, and he laughed and laughed, and his laughter resounded like thunder.

Then he paused, and looked down at his stomach. Swirling energy radiated into his whole body making it bigger, bigger. He thrashed about, looking for his son or the Hulk, and began to scowl.

"You!" he shouted to no one. "The reaction—you tricked me! Take it back! It's not stopping!"

Nor was it. It spun out of control, the different energies colliding, his body absorbing everything, the moonlight, the air, the wind, and when there was nothing else, his body—seeking new energy sources—found the largest one around: itself. His body literally began to devour itself, the effect flowing from the middle and surging outward, and as the father clutched at himself and screamed and howled, a voice sounded in his head, and it might have been his own, but it sounded like his son's. And the words—the parting words from his offspring—burned into his fevered consciousness.

. . . things fall apart . . . the center cannot hold . . .

David Banner stumbled to the top of the mountain, and this time he didn't notice the fighters swiftly approaching from behind.

And in the far, far distance, Thunderbolt Ross looked at his daughter as he gave the final order. "Gentlemen, release."

The thermonuclear missile took off from one of the planes, heading straight for the father who continued to grow and distend in an agony of energy. Something warned him at the last moment, and he turned and saw it coming. For a half-second a grin split his face as he anticipated more energy to absorb, but then he realized, *Too much! Too much!*

. . . the center cannot hold. Best wishes from this rough beast . . .

The missile struck him and his center shredded and blew apart, unable to contain it, as a massive explosion— an explosion evocative of that which had haunted Bruce and Betty's dreams for as long as they could remember— engulfed the sky.

On the monitors, they watched the explosion grow larger and larger, and Thunderbolt Ross, grim, lowered his head and put his face in his hands.

And bridging the barrier of years and resentment, Betty reached across and put a hand on his. "It's okay," she whispered as, on the monitor, the planes pulled back and away and the winds rose to the heavens. "It's okay."

the cross of red

It was several months later that Betty Ross, studying twisted strands of DNA under the lens of a microscope, answered the ringing phone that was to her immediate left. These days she never positioned herself far from a telephone. She never knew who might finally call . . . or when . . . presuming he could . . .

So lost in thought was she that it took a few moments for it to penetrate that her father's voice was saying repeatedly, "Betty, is that you?"

She sighed. "Hi, Dad."

"I'm glad I caught you," said Ross.

She looked at the materials she was deep in the middle of researching, and smiled to herself. Catching her was never a problem; she was in the lab practically all the time. She didn't have much of a personal life; then again, at this particular point in time, she wasn't all that interested in pursuing one. Her father, of course, knew all that. Nevertheless, they had this little ritual they pursued every time he called, and she went along with it. "I'm glad you called," she replied, and she genuinely was.

"Betty—" He hesitated, which was unusual for him. He was usually the king of coming straight to the point. "You and I, we both know, of course, that Banner, well, he couldn't have survived that, that explosion and all . . ."

She'd been slouching a bit, but now she straightened. "Dad, what's up?"

"You know, the usual loonies," said Ross with a sigh, "thinking they've spotted big green guys."

"They have," she replied, relaxing slightly. "On the side of their frozen bean packages."

"I know this goes without saying," her father began, and she hated that phrase, because naturally if something went without saying, it wouldn't be necessary to say it. Ross continued, "But if, and I say *if*, by any chance he should try to contact you, try to get in touch, you'd tell me now, wouldn't you?"

She actually laughed at that. Once upon a time, what she was about to say would have annoyed the hell out of her. Now she just found it funny, having surrendered to the Big Brother absurdity of her life. "No, I wouldn't. You know as well as I do, I wouldn't have to. My phones are bugged, my house is under surveillance, my computers are tapped. So contacting me is the last thing I'd ever want Bruce to do, because—" Betty hesitated, her voice choking slightly. Suddenly this had become a good deal harder than she thought. "—because I love him; I always will. And I pray to God every night and every morning that he never tries to see me or talk to me again for the rest of my life."

There was a long pause, and her father, whom she had thought for so long didn't give a damn about her, said, with utter sincerity, "I'm so sorry, Betty. I am so sorry."

"I know you are, Dad. I know," Betty said.

And as she looked out the window, the phone still

against her ear, she looked out at a couple of trees in the parking lot, swaying in the wind.

She didn't believe he was dead. Not for a moment. As corny as it sounded, she would have felt it if he'd died. Then she turned and looked at the framed photo she'd taken from his office, the one of them up in the woods, at the cabin. She hoped, wherever he was, there were trees. Tall, strong . . . and plenty of green.

He'd probably relate to that.

In the jungle clearing palm trees thrashed around in a stiff wind that lashed against a makeshift canvas covering the shelter. Three white-clad Red Cross workers tended to a few rural families; kids, their parents, grandparents. One of the Red Cross workers was a man wearing longish hair and a beard. The other two were fairly new to the job and a bit tentative in their actions, but the man with the hair and beard moved with an ease that underscored his confidence.

He examined an eight-year-old boy being held lovingly by his father. The child looked feverish, glassy-eyed and slack-limbed. The worker looked at the boy's father and pulled a pill bottle out of his kit.

"You need to give him this three times a day, for ten days, okay?" the Red Cross worker told him in flawless Spanish.

"Gracias," said the father. "Thank you."

The worker turned to the boy and said with mock severity, "You listen to your father when he tells you to take this medicine, okay?" The boy bobbed his head and said he would. Then he exchanged glowing smiles with his father, secure in the knowledge that all was right with the world, and that all would be right with them. The bearded man looked from one to the other and sighed in a manner that might have been seen as wistful, or envious, or just a bit sad.

Then he heard a gasp from another Red Cross worker, a pretty young local girl named Anita. He glanced in her direction and his brow furrowed. He saw what she did: a group of heavily armed men coming out of the jungle. A look of concern crossed her face. The bearded man saw her gesture to the next child on line and smile reassuringly. But it was a very forced smile, and the bearded man knew it, just as he knew that this had the potential to develop into a situation.

The armed men came into the tent, driving the locals out. They began rifling through the supplies.

Without hesitation, the bearded man approached the fellow who was clearly in charge of this little paramilitary organization. It was always easy to tell who was in charge, for some reason. Speaking quietly but firmly, he said, "We need these medicines for the people who live here."

The soldier glowered down at him, towering over him by at least a head. "Who are you to say what is needed, foreigner?" he said disdainfully. "These people are helping our enemies. And maybe so are you." With the implicit threat that the bearded man wouldn't want to be considered an enemy, the intruder grabbed the medicine kit and snarled, "*We* need these too. They are now the property of the government." And just to show what a big, tough guy he was, the paramilitary soldier pushed a child into the rain and raised his AK-47. His men stood up and gathered around menacingly.

They expected him to back down. Why wouldn't they? He looked like nothing.

He felt a distant thudding in his head. And he did nothing to restrain it. "You shouldn't have done that," said the bearded Red Cross worker. "Now say you're sorry and get out of here."

The paramilitaries raised their eyebrows and chortled. "What?" said one.

The pounding increased, growing in strength and intensity. He wondered how no one else could hear it. Then again all that mattered was that *he* heard it.

He closed his eyes, took a deep breath. "You're making me angry," said the Red Cross worker, and the men were laughing, and then they heard a growl from his throat that sounded like nothing human as his eyes snapped open, glowing a deep shade of green as the voice within his head intoned,

. . . *smash* . . .

And the last words he spoke before the screaming began were, "You wouldn't like me when I'm angry."